Murder, Magic, AND WHAT WE Wore

Also by Kelly Jones

Unusual Chickens for the Exceptional Poultry Farmer

Murder, Magic,
AND WHAT WE
Wore

KELLY JONES

ALFRED A. KNOPF

New York

Text copyright © 2017 by Kelly Jones
Jacket art copyright © 2017 by Sarah Watts

All rights reserved. Published in the United States by Alfred A. Knopf,
an imprint of Random House Children's Books,
a division of Penguin Random House LLC, New York.

Knopf, Borzoi Books, and the colophon
are registered trademarks of Penguin Random House LLC.

Visit us on the Web! randomhouseteens.com

Educators and librarians, for a variety of teaching tools, visit us at
RHTeachersLibrarians.com

Library of Congress Cataloging-in-Publication Data is available upon request.
ISBN 978-0-553-53520-4 (trade) — ISBN 978-0-553-53521-1 (lib. bdg.) —
ISBN 978-0-553-53522-8 (ebook)

The text of this book is set in 12-point Horley Old Style.

Printed in the United States of America
September 2017
10 9 8 7 6 5 4 3 2 1

First Edition

Random House Children's Books
supports the First Amendment and celebrates the right to read.

For everyone who has escaped into a book

Chapter One

IN WHICH MISS ANNIS WHITWORTH IS CONFRONTED WITH TERRIBLE NEWS AND TWO HANDKERCHIEFS

When sorrows come, they come not single spies
but in battalions. —*HAMLET*, by William Shakespeare

We were at home when my father's solicitor arrived. The morning was overcome by a soggy rain, and even Aunt Cassia did not choose to drag the flounced hem of her indigo walking dress in the unspeakable ooze that washed over London's cobblestone streets. Cassia was sitting at her walnut desk writing letters to educated ladies she knows all over the Continent (one of her favorite activities), while I lay on the chaise in front of a cozy fire, reading the gossip columns. "Lady Castlewright insists that Hortensia Thomas must have the siren talent," I reported.

Cassia looked up from her letter and blinked. "Miss Thomas? Who couldn't decide whether she preferred lemonade or tea last time she called? I shouldn't have thought her voice could convince anyone to do much of anything."

I shrugged. "Perhaps it's a talent that improves with training?

Lady Castlewright insists that if Miss Thomas had not sung 'Have You Seen the Bright Lily Grow?,' her son would never have tried to kiss Miss Middleton on the balcony after the musicale. But Miss Middleton's mother demands to know why only Mr. Castlewright was affected, and why Miss Thomas's performance of 'Flow My Tears' caused not a single tear." I frowned. "It is a great pity—Miss Middleton finally obtains a suitable gown, only to face such a scene! I'd better call on her later, or she'll never wear it again, and all those alterations I made will be nothing but a waste of time."

Cassia snorted. "I've never in my life heard of siren magic affecting only one member of an audience, and, I can assure you, improper gentlemen will behave improperly regardless of what one is wearing. Lady Castlewright ought—"

But I never heard what Cassia felt Lady Castlewright ought to do, for just then Jenkins announced Mr. Harrington, my father's man of business. Cassia put down her pen at once, without even blotting the page, and I sat up straight and set the gossip column aside.

"Thank you, Jenkins. Would you be so kind as to ask Mrs. Parker to send up a pot of tea?" Cassia said, eyeing our visitor's tired face and wet boots.

Jenkins bowed. "I have already taken the liberty of doing so, madam."

Cassia nodded. "I think a plate of sandwiches too, if you would?"

Jenkins bowed and left at once, and Cassia closed the door to the sitting room. After a heartbeat, maybe two, she dropped to her knees, peered through the keyhole, then stuffed her handkerchief in it. (Cassia has always insisted on the value of a clean handkerchief, but I had never seen this particular use for one.) Then she rose smoothly to her feet and nodded to Mr. Harrington as though nothing had happened. (Honestly, I do think Cassia is becoming rather eccentric, even for a lady intellectual.)

I'd pictured my father's man of business as white-haired and ancient, but Mr. Harrington could not have been much older than I was, even if he was dressed like a man twice his age. Was it to convince his clients to trust him to manage their money? I wondered. His coat fit properly and his boots were no muddier than could be helped on such a day, but he might have worn some other colors than unremarkable brown, more brown, and tan, especially since his hair and his eyes were also brown. But he smiled at me as Cassia made the introductions, and it was a nice smile, if sad.

"I hear the Lakes are beautiful at this time of year," he said to Cassia.

What an odd thing to say. Had he stopped by the alehouse before calling on us? He did not sound inebriated, though.

Before I could ask what he meant, Cassia nodded and said, "Indeed, very good hunting, they say."

I stared. Cassia had gone quite pale, and Mr. Harrington hadn't come so far for small talk.

Cassia gripped the back of her chair with both hands. "Tell us. Quickly."

Mr. Harrington's face fell, and he looked so very tired. "Allow me to express my sincere condolences on the death of your brother."

I stared at Cassia's white face, trying to understand the words. It was not until her eyes filled with tears that I believed him. My father was dead.

The delicate fretwork of the chair snapped under Cassia's

grip. She stared down at it for a moment, her face blank. Slowly she released the chair, one finger at a time, and a piece of gilt wood fell to the floor.

Then she grabbed her penknife and stabbed it through the letter she was writing and into the beautiful carved wood of her desk. The knife quivered there for a moment, then fell, knocking her inkwell over into a black pool that dripped onto her skirt as the tears ran down her face.

I stumbled to my feet, grabbed my handkerchief, and handed it to Cassia, but she just crumpled it in her fist, squeezing so hard her knuckles went as white as her face.

"When?" Cassia asked, her voice choked.

How I wished she'd sounded surprised—but she didn't. My stomach bunched and twisted like the handkerchief in her hand.

He sighed. "The night before last. He was traveling alone from Paris to Calais when his carriage overturned. He had an injury to the head, and his neck was broken; he did not suffer."

I looked at him sharply. "But there was no moon that night. Why would he travel such rural roads without even the moon to light his way?"

Mr. Harrington looked down at his boots. "He was to meet me in Calais the next day, to sign some business documents before he embarked on his next journey. He'd sent his trunk to Hamburg that morning—I'll arrange for its return—but I've brought the personal things he had with him." He held out a leather document case.

Calais was just across the Channel from Dover. Had my father even considered visiting us before leaving for Hamburg? I wanted to ask, but when I opened my mouth, my words couldn't squeeze around the ache in my throat. My father was dead.

Cassia scrubbed her face with my handkerchief and held out her hand for the case. "Have you brought his will?"

Mr. Harrington handed her a paper from the sheaf he held.

She read it, frowned, and bit her lip. "I see."

"I'm so sorry," he said softly. "It will take me some time to collect his overseas accounts. Do you have family to visit?"

Cassia did not answer.

I swallowed hard. "The rest of my father's family is dead. My mother's family was French; she believed them dead in the war, and we have never heard otherwise. I suppose there's no one left but us. Why, are we destitute now?"

I'd meant it as a joke, but Mr. Harrington did not smile. "Your father lived off his military half-pay, from when he was in service before you were born. That died with him, I'm afraid."

"That is what paid this house's lease, our household expenses, the servants' wages . . . ," Cassia trailed off.

There was a noise like a gasp in the hallway, and then, quickly, a tap at the door, and Cassia sighed.

Slowly she got to her feet. She put her shoulders back and pressed her lips together until they stopped trembling.

"I will make every effort to secure Mr. Whitworth's overseas accounts as quickly as possible," Mr. Harrington said as she went to the door.

Mrs. Parker's eyes were wide as she set down the tea tray.

"Mrs. Parker, please ask the servants to gather in the dining room in half an hour," Cassia said, her voice calm, though her eyes were red, and ink still dripped from her skirt. "I shall have an announcement to make as soon as we've finished here."

Mrs. Parker bobbed her head and left, closing the door softly behind her.

"Do have a sandwich," Cassia said, handing Mr. Harrington the plate. "You must have traveled all night." She poured him a cup of tea, her hand perfectly steady, not spilling a drop. "For you, Annis?"

I shook my head.

There was a commotion in the corridor, and a loud tapping on the door. Cassia was there in an instant, opening it.

"Pardon me, but there seems to have been an accident involving Mr. Harrington's coach—"

Mr. Harrington was up and out the door before Jenkins finished speaking, with Cassia right behind, pausing only long enough to hand me the document case and to tell me to stay where I was.

For once, I did not argue. I felt trembly, distant, not ready to cry, not ready to speak. I hadn't seen my father for months—he had been traveling for most of my life, for weeks, even years, at a time. And now he was gone forever. I ran my finger over the damp leather of my father's document case. Then I untied the cord and opened it.

He had so little with him when he died. A couple of cravats, carefully rolled so as not to set creases (my father had a simple but elegant way of tying his neckcloths that was always admired when he came to London), a few sheets of paper that looked boringly businessy, his cravat pin, his signet ring. There were two of the handkerchiefs I'd embroidered for him for his birthday—so they had reached him after all. An unsigned note confirming that passage had been booked for him from Calais to Dover. I paused. So he had meant to call on us. Then why had he sent his trunk ahead to Hamburg?

I felt around in the corners of the case, but there was nothing else. Where was the silver pocket watch with my mother's portrait inside? He couldn't have been robbed by highwaymen, not with the rest of his valuables intact. But he was never without it. It was the only picture of my mother we had.

When I was two years old, my mother fell ill of a wasting fever while my father was traveling. Cassia had come at once. Her parents thought it improper for a girl of her age, but she'd come anyway to help my father's housekeeper all through my mother's illness and after her death. When my father was delayed yet again, she decided to stay on to care for me. Now I could no longer remember my mother's face, nor a time before Cassia had come.

I placed the note next to the business papers I'd set aside. The hand was the same. Surely Mr. Harrington had drafted the papers? But why say he was to meet my father in Calais, after he'd booked his passage to Dover? I frowned. Mr. Harrington had lied about my father's destination. Why? Who could it matter to now, when he was dead?

I picked up the handkerchiefs, remembering the time I'd spent embroidering my father's initials, wondering where he was, hoping he was safe.

The door opened, and I jumped, but it was only Cassia. "It was nothing," she said, hurrying across the room. "A lamplighter blundered into Mr. Harrington's hackney cab and singed it a bit, and he and the driver got into a scuffle. Since Mr. Harrington had traveled all night to deliver his news, I suggested he go get some rest." It made perfect sense, but her voice sounded strange.

She glanced at the handkerchiefs in my hand, and wrapped me up in a hug.

"Aunt Cassia, something is very wrong," I whispered.

She squeezed me tighter, but didn't answer. Then she took

a deep breath. "Annis, I am afraid things must change from this point forward. Can I trust you to make the best of things, whatever happens next?"

I took a deep breath too, and nodded.

She let me go. "I must go speak to the servants before the rumors grow out of hand. Then I must sort out how we can pay the debts and bequests your father left—and pay our shop accounts too, I suppose, before everyone in London learns of our troubles. Will you cancel our engagements and procure our mourning clothes? You will need to choose frugally, for once."

"Of course," I said. I might not know whether or not to trust Mr. Harrington, but I knew what we must wear, and how best to obtain it. "Will we hold a funeral here?"

She shook her head. "Mr. Harrington told me he was buried in Calais. And, I think, this is not the right time for that kind of attention or expense. Our friends would notice the change in our table, and would wonder what's to become of us."

She was right, I supposed, but I hated the thought of my father disappearing from the minds of everyone in London without a trace. I glanced up at her, ready to argue, and saw the tears welling up in my aunt's eyes again as she tucked my father's things back into the document case.

I hugged her once more and hurried from the room, the handkerchiefs still clutched tight in my hand.

Chapter Two

A MESSAGE IS DISCOVERED,
AND EXTREMELY HORRIBLE GARMENTS ARRIVE

Fetch me the handkerchief: my mind misgives.
—*OTHELLO*, by William Shakespeare

I rang the bell for Danvers while I considered how long it would take to buy black fabric, design mourning gowns, and have them made by my usual modiste. I sighed. Too long. And too expensive besides. We would have to buy those shapeless black gowns ready-made for unexpected mourners. But it didn't matter. I must finish this task as quickly as possible, and tell Cassia about Mr. Harrington's lie. Despite her rare display of emotion, Cassia clearly had not been surprised that my father, a healthy man of thirty-eight whom all of London adored, was dead.

Nor was I, for I'd feared this day ever since I'd worked out that my father was a spy.

Over the years, I'd begged my father to take us with him on his travels, but he never had, not for so much as a country visit. And it took ages for me to piece together why. So many bitter years of wondering why my father preferred to spend his time abroad visiting strangers, rather than in London getting to know me. I pondered why his travel plans were always changing—and how he always seemed to be in the areas the wives of military officers were suddenly discussing as well. Everywhere he went, battles broke out, assassinations occurred, and ships were captured. And yet he never talked of politics and wars and all the other things gentlemen talked about. He smiled and discussed fashions on the Continent, though his eyes were often sad. He was a puzzle, my father, and I was determined to solve him.

Every time he arrived home, he left early the next morning, always heading off in the same direction. Finally, one day, I wrapped myself up tight in the huge gray wool shawl that Cassia keeps in the back of her wardrobe but never wears, and followed him—all the way to the War Office. I watched as he nodded to the horse guard and walked inside. He had left the military years before—in an official capacity.

There was only one explanation: my father was a spy for England.

I wondered if I should tell him that I knew—if that might somehow keep him here, away from danger. But I was old enough to understand that my father had made his choice, even if I wished he hadn't.

I thought of telling Cassia. But then . . . she had never told me. Did she assume I'd long since figured it out, the way I now assumed she had? That any sensible person accustomed to using her brain must work it out eventually? Was it one of those things that wasn't polite to mention, like when Mrs. Jefferson drank seven glasses of rum punch, stood on a chair, and sang a (very loud) song about how she wished she were an opera dancer and then was ill in a potted fern? Every time I thought I really must say something, Cassia changed the subject.

So I held my tongue and embroidered handkerchiefs for him. Cassia said one must always have spares, no matter the circumstances, and one could never have too many, and there was no telling how useful they could be. Handkerchiefs would fit in his luggage; they were something he could take with him everywhere. And with every stitch I made, as silly as it might be, I wished he would stay safe. But now two of his handkerchiefs were here, and he was gone. All my wishing hadn't worked.

It took quite a long while for Danvers to appear, long enough that I had time to note Cassia's measurements as well as mine, and our preferences in sleeve length, bodice style, material, and neckline (not that they would matter, for gowns that had been sewn for anyone at all to wear!), as well as write our apologies for Lady Tittlevrim's soirée that evening, and the salon at the Misses Baillie's home the evening after. When Danvers arrived at last, her eyes were red.

"Danvers, I need you to go out at once and purchase two mourning gowns, one for Miss Whitworth and one for myself. No, I don't need to choose—they'll have to be those awful Piccadilly ones, for we must have them at once, and I suppose they're all equally horrid. I do hope I can retrim our bonnets myself, for theirs are certain to be too dreadful to wear."

Danvers immediately burst into tears, and I sighed. She was terribly good with hair, but fancied herself in the midst of a tragedy even at the best of times. "Oh, miss—I am so—that you should be driven from your home by this—this frightful sorrow!"

I felt my face immediately settle into the impenetrable mask

Cassia had insisted I practice before I could attend the afternoon teas hosted by sharp-tongued matrons. "Nonsense, Danvers; no one is driving me from my home."

"But—Miss Whitworth said you'll be leaving. The house is to be let to someone else—and what am I to do now?" she sobbed.

I felt my heart clench tight. Leave? But I had always lived here! "First, you will send a footman to deliver these notes. Next, you'll purchase the gowns I requested." I hesitated. What if she had heard wrong? But no; Cassia would have been certain that everyone understood her perfectly. She'd told me to be ready for life to change. I just hadn't imagined this drastic a change. "Then, you'll go to Lady Jersey's house, where you'll ask the housekeeper if she's heard who is leasing that lovely house with all the gilt near the park—you know they've been getting it ready for the new tenants. If they're coming to London for the season, they'll need a proper lady's maid. Everything will be fine, you'll see."

Danvers gulped, blew her nose on her handkerchief, and nodded. "Thank you, miss."

I gave her the measurements and sent her on her way. Then I looked around the cozy room, trying to imagine how I could live anywhere else.

My eye fell on my father's handkerchiefs once more, and I picked one up and held it to my face, trying to catch the smell of his snuff, his boot oil, the pomade he sometimes used when he had to attend a ball. But every bit of him was gone; it was only cloth.

Then I frowned, examining it more closely. Someone had darned the corner—had there been a hole? No, it wasn't darned, it was embroidered, an odd, spidery, lumpy embroidery, white thread on the white linen, barely perceptible, all around the border, starting and stopping on either side of the monogram I'd done.

I picked up the other one, and the embroidery was the same— only, it wasn't exactly the same, after all.

Crossing to the window, I held them up in the dim afternoon sun, trying to get a better look. I placed one on top of the other to compare them, and stopped. With the handkerchiefs together like this, and held up to the light, a message appeared.

RAIN LEAVING FIELD.
REROUTE CORBEAU AWAY FROM S.H.
CPTN. J.F. MURDERED.

It made no sense to me. Well, aside from the weather, though why one would bother to embroider something as transitory as the weather was a mystery.

I sat down at my dressing table to think. Whether or not the message made any sense to me, it was important, if a captain had been murdered. Was the message so important it had cost my father his life too? Whatever it meant, I was determined it would not be wasted.

I folded the handkerchiefs carefully and tucked them into my bandbox. I needed to visit the War Office and deliver them to someone who would understand. Cassia wouldn't approve, but I could never entrust such a critical errand to the second footman. I didn't trust Mr. Harrington. So I would do it myself.

I was startled out of my plotting by a tap at the door. "Bring them in at once," I called, rising to face my latest misfortune.

But it was not Danvers. A maid I didn't recognize brought in the paper-wrapped package.

"The gowns you requested, miss," she said, bobbing a curtsy and handing me the parcel. "Miss Danvers sent them back with the footman, and continued with her errands."

It was true that I had told Danvers what to do next, but I had thought she'd at least help me sort out what I was to wear before securing her own future. Apparently, today's tears were less about poor Miss Annis and more about poor Danvers. "Very well; please send one of the other maids to assist me. I'll be going out."

"They've all gone out, miss. Miss Whitworth said they might." She didn't look up from her worn boots.

I examined her. She wore an old brown dress that had been mended neatly several times, and her blond hair was braided back and tucked under her cap. At least she knew something about hair.

Still, I didn't recognize her. "Why haven't I seen you before?" I asked her.

"I hired on yesterday, miss," she said softly. Then she straightened her spine and met my eyes. "Mrs. Cohen sent me, and Mrs. Parker agreed to take me on."

I suppressed a sigh. Mrs. Cohen, one of Cassia's friends, ran a program for maids who found themselves without positions due to various difficult circumstances. It was a pity that this one was to find herself sent back so soon. But then again, it did make her the perfect companion for my errand. Even if she understood what was happening, whom could she tell?

"Very well—what was your name?" I asked briskly, opening the package and shaking out the gowns.

"Millicent O'Leary, miss," she said. An Irish maid, then; no wonder she'd faced hard times in London.

I shuddered at the horror in my hands: a veritable tent of

scratchy black bombazine. "Fetch my workbasket from the sitting room at once, if you please, Millie. We shall have our work cut out for us, I see."

For who would listen to a person who could not even dress herself properly? Surely not the spies in the War Office.

Chapter Three

IN WHICH A TALENT IS REVEALED

Her godmother only just touched her with her wand,
and, at the same instant, her clothes turned into cloth
of gold and silver, all beset with jewels.
—"CINDERELLA; OR, THE LITTLE GLASS SLIPPER,"
by the Frenchman Charles Perrault

Clearly, this would take more work than I'd thought. I dispatched the maid to the cheapest ribbon shop I could think of for more supplies. Then I tried on the horrible gown.

It was exactly as I'd feared: itchy, shapeless, with a chokingly high lace collar that my mirror told me was uneven, and a hem that swept the floor and then some. It simply would not do.

So I removed the gown, picked up my scissors, and cut off the collar, deciding that anything would be an improvement. The resulting bodice was plainer, but far more serviceable; I sighed in relief. I'd made small alterations to dresses before, of course, but nothing quite so drastic. Still, Cassia had pounded into my head that, during moments of crisis, it was critical to choose a course of action and throw oneself into it, getting something done at least, rather than whimpering in a corner.

In for a penny, in for a pound: off came the horrible ruffle dragging the bottom of the gown. After I'd evened up the cuts a bit, and then evened them up a little more, I tossed all the discarded bits into a heap on the floor, threaded my needle (I had to make do with indigo, as I'd no black at all—it is a horrid color on me!), and began to hem the bottom at a more reasonable length. (Or at least I hoped it would be more reasonable—it is surprisingly difficult to put a pin where you want the bottom of a dress to be while wearing it yourself.)

As I've often found, hemming went quickly, and I could hardly see the stitches when I'd finished. I allowed myself a small smile, noting that, with that huge lace collar gone, the fabric wasn't really so terrible after all. Honestly, it was a crime that shops should sell such dreadful gowns, when a nice one was so easily accomplished! I began to finish the new neckline, turning under the edge in such a way that the whole thing felt more polished and elegant.

By the time Millie returned, I'd sliced off the drooping cuffs as well, using half as much lace to finish them off, making them far less prone to falling in teacups. I'd donned the final result and was tilting the cheval glass to better see my reflection, trying to examine the effect of the hem. "There you are!" I said, taking her parcel. Quickly I opened it, chose a wide black satin ribbon, and tied it where the waist ought to be (not that this gown had one). "Would you tilt the mirror down—yes, there! I suppose it will have to do."

Millie's eyes were wide. "Do you need Miss Whitworth to come up so you can glamour hers too, before you visit the agency, miss?"

I blinked. "Whatever do you mean?"

"Your aunt was making arrangements to visit the employment agency for ladies in distressed circumstances." She bit her lip. "I didn't mean to listen, miss. Only, I thought you'd want to know."

I sat down on the bed rather quickly. Cassia was seeking employment? But she couldn't leave me alone—which meant . . . that I was to seek employment too? I considered Miss Davies, the youngest of five ladies, who had knocked out a front tooth in a carriage accident and had to become a governess when no one would marry her. She'd once confided that she'd saved for a new pair of gloves, only to have them chewed up by her youngest charge. I shuddered. "When?"

"Tomorrow morning, miss."

I took a deep breath. There was still a little time. I had already chosen my course of action, so I must forge ahead.

"Shall I fetch Miss Whitworth, miss? Or can you glamour her gown without her in it?"

I blinked at her. "Don't be ridiculous. I can't sew glamours; only glamour modistes have that talent, not ladies."

She shrugged. "Well, most ladies don't need to sew their own dresses, miss, so how would they know if they could? And who would they tell? They'd have no reason to set up shop."

I shook my head. "Millie, I don't know what the other maids may have said, but I have no magic, and I certainly can't sew glamours."

She kept her eyes lowered as she nodded, but she didn't budge. "Yes, miss. No one said anything, miss. But you see, the only person I've ever seen who could change a gown so quickly—so that even the fabric is different!—was a glamour modiste."

"It's wondrous indeed what a few stitches can do. But that's all this gown needed." I stood up and went to the dressing table.

"It's brocade now," she said, so quietly I wasn't sure she'd spoken.

I glanced down at the gown I was wearing. It was silk brocade, not bombazine. Which was not possible. Unless . . .

I sank down into the chair at my dressing table. "Please tell me everything you know about glamours, Millie."

Her eyes widened. "Only what everyone knows, miss. They're magic dresses. Those who can sew them are rare; I've only ever seen one true glamour with my own eyes, until now. In Dublin, when I hired on with a lady who was coming here, she bought one from a modiste. Walked in with one gown, and out with another, looking ten years younger and happier than she ever had in her life—that's what her lady's maid said, anyway." She pressed her lips together. "I don't mean to gossip, miss. It was just so—so magic. I saw her wearing it, and it was true." She sighed. "But then she ran off with a military gentleman, and I lost my place, and never saw that glamour again."

I considered this. I had always thought my alterations were minor, a simple stitch here or there to make my gowns a bit more flattering. True, I seemed to have more skill than many, but that didn't mean I had a magic talent. "I saw a ballet once about the cinder girl who sewed a glamour for the ball out of rags. When she did it, persons waving scarves appeared and surrounded her, and when they vanished, she was wearing a white silk ball gown instead of a pile of black rags, and a new diamond necklace and tiara. Did the maid in Dublin say anything about persons with scarves?"

Millie shook her head. "Perhaps that was merely to show the audience that magic was happening while the actress changed costumes, miss. I imagine a true glamour artist wouldn't be working as an actress, would she?"

Undoubtedly, she was right, or we'd be seeing persons with scarves all over London anytime a spice baker made a cake or a gardener used a green thumb. Still, this felt terribly mundane in comparison. Could it really be possible to use a magic talent, without feeling any magic at all? Had I really . . . ?

"Will that be all, miss?" Millie asked.

I shook myself. "Please bring me Miss Whitworth's black bonnet with the cream ribbon—it really is a pity; I did like that ribbon—and the gray one with the silk cherries."

Millie bobbed a curtsy.

As soon as I heard the door close behind her, I rose to my feet.

I needed to visit the War Office and alert them to my father's message. And now I had an additional reason to call.

If Cassia intended for me to find employment, then very well, I would do so. I'd become a spy, like my father. Surely they could use a glamour artist.

I must simply sew something that would impress the War Office, in under ten minutes.

∽◐)(◑∾

A glamour, people said, could make a person unrecognizable—could make them disappear, even. A glamour could show the cinder girl's noble heart and inner beauty (and, apparently, cause people to ignore the kinds of smudges one gets when one has been sitting on the hearth all day sewing).

But there was no reason a glamour had to be a gown.

I opened my wardrobe and pulled out my largest shawl, hesitating just a little. My father had brought it from India, the mustards and reds blending with tangerine and cream in whirling patterns he called paisley. I had so little to remind me of him.

Still, it had to be done. Taking a deep breath, I threaded my needle and drew it through the shawl. I thought of darkest black, of secrets, of all the things spies valued: shadows, silence, trust.

Nothing happened, aside from an ugly looping thread in the middle of my favorite shawl.

Oh, I wanted to set it aside and have a good whimper then. But, if I failed, I would have to hire myself out as a governess, and only appear before dinner to show off horrible young people who were menaces to fine gloves, and all my friends would feel sorry for me and whisper behind my back about how dreadful I looked. Cassia would hire herself out as a lady's companion and be doomed to wear ugly lace caps for the rest of her days, and never get to attend lectures about how finding a silver mine half-way across the world would make muslin cost twice as much.

No, I would not have it. My father had devoted his life to his country, and so would I. And with that, I began to sew as fast I could, stitches that would impress upon the War Office that I was not to be ignored, that I could hide myself in plain sight, and they had better believe me.

And behind each stitch, a wave of darkness filled up the patterns of my beautiful shawl, turning them solid black.

Chapter Four

A VISIT TO THE WAR OFFICE

First gain the victory and then make
the best use of it you can. —Admiral Horatio Lord Nelson

∞)(∞

After a minute more, my beautiful shawl was entirely black. Not allowing my lip to tremble, I knotted the thread and snipped the end free as Millie tapped on the door and slipped inside, setting the bonnets on my bed.

I picked up the black bonnet and took a few stitches through the cream ribbon, remembering the sad face of young Mrs. Dillon after her husband was killed. The ribbon turned as dark and purple as her gloves. I tied off the thread, sighing.

When I looked up, Millie's eyes were wide. I smiled. She was plain to the point of forgetting, and her dress was much mended. Still, spies must be used to all manner of costumes in their lines of work—if they bothered to notice a maid at all. "I must make a call, and since Danvers is busy, I'll need you to accompany me." Then, before I could lose my nerve, I tied on the bonnet, snatched up my bandbox, folded up the shawl and tucked it inside, threw open the door, and marched out.

I recognized no one as we walked. Though the rain had ceased, the afternoon was dark and cold, and the London social season had not properly begun yet. Taking advantage of the quiet, I began to plan out what I would say when we reached my destination.

If only my father had told me he was a spy! If only Cassia had ever discussed his true occupation with me, and explained the proper etiquette. Did such men call themselves spies, or practitioners of espionage, or some other, more genteel term? Did one address a spy as "Sir," or were there ranks involved? And what did one discuss before one got to business? Remembering Mr. Harrington's strange greeting earlier, I decided that if all else failed, I should rely upon the weather.

I believe I planned quite an effective speech as I bore down on the entrance; unfortunately, whatever I'd meant to say flew out of my head when the mounted guard appeared. Still, I pulled my shoulders up straight and announced that I had business inside.

He took a long look at me. I'd managed to keep my dress fairly clean, and I knew there was nothing amiss with my hair or my bonnet. From his expression, it appeared they did not have many young ladies of quality visiting. But that was just as well; they'd have all the more need of my skills.

"May I proceed?" I called up, with my best imitation of Aunt Cassia being annoyed.

He hesitated, then nodded, moving his horse aside. We

had just enough space to squeeze through, but I stalked haughtily through the gates anyway. I am a person who can make do, after all.

The maid tugged at my sleeve, eyes wide, but I ignored her. Perhaps I was a little nervous that if I paused long enough to reconsider, I might not see the thing through. It was an imposing building, with a lot of important people inside, and my best imitation had not even managed to impress the horse, let alone the gentleman riding it. I hurried up to the guards at the doors. "Miss Whitworth, here on business," I said, and wondered if I should send up a card, as one does when visiting for tea.

Apparently not. The doors opened, and I walked inside, where the butler gestured to a footman, who guided us to a small, plain room. There, a young man was lounging against a desk, trying to look important (but not doing a very good job of it).

Here, I hesitated, while the young man jumped, then tried to cover his surprise by looking down his nose at me. Should I request an audience with the spies? Or would it ruin my chances to speak of such things?

"Terrible wet weather, wouldn't you say?" he said, eyeing me with a mix of confusion and hostility.

Which only confirmed how suspicious Mr. Harrington's small talk had been. "I hear the Lakes are beautiful at this time of year," I answered. I raised my chin as he continued to stare. "I am Miss Whitworth. I should like to speak with your supervising officer," I added, since I couldn't imagine that this young man would be of any use to me.

The young man lunged toward twenty-odd bell cords, carefully selected one, yanked hard on it, and saluted me, his mouth agape.

Although I had no objection to his change in reaction, it seemed a bit astonishing. I found myself uncertain of the social niceties of salutes, not having received one before. Does one salute back? I tried a noncommittal smile, as one might give an unknown young man when one's dance card was already full. He simply stared at me. If the spies were hiring young men such as this one, they should be delighted to have me.

The door flew open and a harried-looking man in plain dark clothes shot inside, hair all askew. One sleeve appeared empty, so I quickly moved my eyes back to his face. He stopped, examined me, and then looked at the young man. "We shall have to discuss your definition of *emergency*, James." He turned as if to leave.

"Sir, there's a report from Mr. Finch on the situation in Geneva—" James said anxiously.

"Not now, James," the man said, without so much as a glance back.

I was not about to be ignored. "I am Miss Whitworth, come to discuss something of great importance," I announced.

He stopped dead. Then he turned around.

Encouraged, I continued. "You see, my father—"

"I shall return shortly, James," said the man. "Miss, please follow me."

Cassia has very strict instructions about not allowing oneself to be alone with a gentleman, and I did not imagine they would not apply to spies, so I grabbed the maid by the hand and dragged her along with me as we followed the man into the back halls of the War Office.

I saw nothing remarkable. Dusty wood paneling, lined with closed doors. There was a low hum of conversation, but somehow I could never make out the words. Once, a man in a decorated uniform stopped and saluted smartly to the man we followed, who waved him aside and kept walking. (I noted he certainly did not salute back.) At last, he came to an open door and motioned us inside.

I immediately took the only chair present, a plain wooden affair next to the empty desk, forcing him to stand. "Thank you for your time, Mr. . . . ?"

He smiled a little. "You may call me Mr. Smith."

"Very well, Mr. Smith. I've come to let you know I should like to follow in my father's footsteps. You are aware of his work?" I watched him closely.

He gave no shock of surprise, but merely raised an eyebrow. "It would be most unusual for a young lady with no military training to serve as a lieutenant in His Majesty's army."

"It would, indeed. But that was not the work I was referring to."

He shrugged, looking bored. "Thankfully, with the war with France over and Bonaparte imprisoned, there is no longer much need for the dangerous work carried out by lieutenants."

"Napoléon is imprisoned for now, but will he remain so? He escaped from Elba three years ago and raised a new army in no time at all. Do you truly believe that no one in France still wishes to defeat England and put their emperor back on the throne? That no one is worth watching any longer? We've underestimated Bonaparte before—do you wish him to successfully invade England this time?" Did I imagine it, or did he find my fury amusing?

"Saint Helena is one of the most remote islands on earth, between Africa and the Kingdom of Brazil in the South Atlantic Ocean—not that I'd expect a young lady to know anything of geography. But you may rest your mind; Bonaparte will not escape his prison this time."

The island of Saint Helena. *Reroute Corbeau away from S.H.* Then the *Corbeau* must be a ship. . . . "He might escape, if you refuse to listen to a properly educated young lady," I snapped.

"There is no work for you in my department: no children to be educated, nor ladies in need of companionship."

I rose to my feet, the threat of governessing steeling my resolve. "My father was carrying a message when he died." I opened my bandbox and took out the handkerchiefs, carefully unfolding them. I glanced at Millie, but she was examining the keyhole in the door. Was that a flash of motion I saw through it?

No, I decided, surely it was only my nerves. Who would spy on the spies in their lair?

Swiftly I matched up the corners of the handkerchiefs and held them up to the lamp so that Mr. Smith could read the message.

Even in the light of the small desk lamp, the words stood out against the white linen. *Rain leaving field. Reroute Corbeau away from S.H. Cptn. J.F. murdered.*

He glanced at it, still looking bored. "Rest assured, the military men of England can do without your assistance."

I raised my chin. "I sincerely doubt it, if you choose to ignore that message. At least one man has already been murdered!"

Mr. Smith did not look impressed. "We have our own sources. Miss Whitworth, please return to primping for your next ball or whatever it is that young ladies do these days."

I narrowed my eyes. "Though you do not understand the value of a young lady's appearance, I should hope you recognize the talent it takes to disguise one." I pulled the shawl from my bandbox and threw it around my shoulders. "I can sew glamours." According to the novels, having sewn and used a glamour in my time of great need, I should feel shivers run through my body and feel my purpose coalesce into a gleaming brightness. I waited to feel transformed.

I felt nothing, saw nothing.

He didn't even blink. "Miss Whitworth, your father served honorably during his time with the army. Undoubtedly, you are overcome with grief and shock. Perhaps you would like a carriage called to convey you home?"

It must have been tears of anger that welled up in my eyes. I had been so certain. . . . Slowly I pulled off the shawl and stuffed it back into my bandbox, along with the handkerchiefs, swallowing down my disappointment until I could speak. "Mr. Smith, I am aware that society thinks young ladies have not a brain to pass amongst them, and no skills other than playing the pianoforte. I assumed your organization might prove more perceptive, but perhaps it would be less frustrating to educate children than to reason with dull, plodding tortoises such as yourself. Nonetheless, I have a duty to serve my country. I shall be in touch." With that, I pushed past him and threw open the door, relishing the flash of surprise in Mr. Smith's eyes.

I might not know precisely how to respond to a salute, or why my glamour had not worked, but I did at least know how to conduct myself in a large, unfamiliar building. Despite our hurried entrance, I'd memorized each twist and turn of the hallway, just as Cassia insisted I do when we visited large homes. She said one must be able to exit on one's own from any room without assistance, and it was indeed a great relief to me not to have to speak one word to Mr. Smith as I stalked along the corridors. Mr. Smith followed us all the way back to the reception room, but he remained silent as I marched past the now-alert young man and out the door. I did not stop until we were around the corner and out of sight of the guard on horseback.

"That did not go according to plan," I muttered.

The maid had sharp hearing. "Perhaps you ought not to have called him a tortoise, miss?" she said diffidently.

I considered this. "No, it had to be done. I couldn't allow him to send me on my way without making him wonder about something. He might as well wonder if he's acting like a tortoise." I pulled my handkerchief from my sleeve and dabbed at my eyes, then turned toward home.

Suddenly a large man knocked into me, as if inebriated, snatching the handkerchief from my hand, then reaching for my bandbox.

"Thief!" Millie shrieked, and threw herself toward his stomach, elbow out, knocking him away from my hand.

I lunged toward my handkerchief, but he lurched away from us—and then took off running at a speed utterly unlike a drunken man. "Stop! Thief!" I shouted, and went after him.

Well, for about three steps, until Millie grabbed my arm and held me back. "Miss, that's no common thief," she insisted while I tried to pull my arm free. "It's too dangerous to follow."

She was right, of course. Not to mention that he'd already disappeared into the crowded street, all while passersby stared, then quickly looked away, so as not to have our troubles become theirs.

I discovered I was trembling like a girl at her first ball. Annoyed, I straightened my posture and clenched my bandbox tight with both hands. "Why would a naval officer—who's clearly no common thief—steal my handkerchief?"

"You already know why, miss." Millie took a step closer to me,

29

her eyes scanning the area around us. "What makes you think him a naval officer?"

"His boots, of course," I told her.

Millie tipped her head. "He did smell like the sea. But perhaps he stole those boots too?"

I glanced down the street at the growing twilight and shivered, and not because it looked likely to rain again. It could not be a coincidence that I carried a spy's message hidden in handkerchiefs and that someone had stolen a handkerchief right out of my hand—even if it was the wrong one. I'd shown my father's message to no one but Mr. Smith. But if he'd wanted the handkerchiefs, why not simply keep them? No, Mr. Smith lacked a motive for the theft, much as I was in the mood to pin it on him. "Thank you for your quick action, Millie. We'd best hurry home." I set off down the street once more, still clutching my bandbox tightly. I hadn't shown the message to anyone else. But what if my father had? Or Mr. Harrington, before he'd brought my father's things to us?

Or what if the murderer guessed my father would try to send such a message? I grabbed Millie's hand and pulled her faster down the darkening streets.

Chapter Five

MISS ANNIS WRITES TWO LETTERS

All the business of war, and indeed all the
business of life, is to endeavour to find out
what you don't know by what you do.
—Arthur Wellesley, First Duke of Wellington

*B*y the time we reached home, I was jumping from every shadow, equally exhausted, terrified, and annoyed at myself for being so. It was not as though this were an uncommon day for a spy, I reminded myself sternly. But I'd never been so glad to rush through the mahogany front door of my safe, familiar home.

Cassia was putting on her cloak in the foyer as we came in. She looked as tired as I felt, and didn't even ask where I'd been. She stepped forward, catching my hands in hers and giving them a squeeze. "Annis, I've made arrangements for us to visit an employment agency tomorrow morning." She looked away. "I've examined the sums up and down, backward and forward, but there's simply nothing else to be done."

I blinked, as though somehow that could make my ears understand her words. I opened my mouth to ask what she was talking about, but no sound forced its way past the sudden lump in my throat.

Pulling me close, she gave me a hug. "We'll talk more later," she whispered. "Be brave." Then she hurried out the door, leaving me staring after her.

Mrs. Parker bustled into the foyer. "That Miss Danvers has given her notice, packed her things, and left, miss."

I nodded and thanked her, hardly knowing what I said. What did it matter now, when I was to become a servant myself? I'd never need anyone to do my hair again.

Millie took my arm and led me up to my room. Slowly I sank down onto my bed, still clutching my bandbox, as Millie built up the fire and lit the candles (which Danvers never would have stooped to handle herself). "Shall I ask Mrs. Parker for a supper tray?" she said.

I looked at her blankly until my stomach let out a loud growl of agreement. "I would appreciate that. Thank you."

She gave me a tiny, sympathetic smile. "Things'll look up once you've eaten something, miss."

I set the bandbox down on my bed and sighed as she left. I felt chilled and weary, grayer than gray in my mind and my heart. And it was clear that our troubles were worse than I had imagined.

I had failed to convince the War Office to hire me as a spy, and had instead gained the attention of a mysterious thief. I bit my lip, wishing my handkerchief had not been monogrammed. He would know by now that it was not what he was looking for, and he would soon learn who I was.

If we were to visit the employment agency in the morning, that meant someone in London would hire us. Most likely someone I knew. There was the dowager Duchess of Harksbury, who suffered from sudden collapses and required her companions to learn an unnatural procedure of lung deflation for reviving her. And Lady Ravenscroft was searching for a governess for her children, but everyone said they were quite wild.

More to the point, neither employer could protect me from the mystery surrounding my father's death, nor from whoever might come after me.

If only I had other, better options!

Well. There was one obvious option—marriage.

Sitting down at my dressing table and taking a sheet of notepaper, I picked up my pen and dipped it into the inkwell.

My dear Mr. Mareton,

If you have enjoyed the pleasure of my company these past many evenings as much as you claimed to, and if you spoke the truth when you said you owed me a great debt indeed for making you aware that Mr. Fitzwilliams intended to attend Almack's in exactly the same coat as you had just purchased, I must beg of you to call upon me just after sunrise tomorrow morning. I realize you are unused to such early hours, so remain awake all night if you must, but please do not delay.

Respectfully,
Miss Annis Whitworth

Carefully I blotted the letter, then folded and sealed it with a wafer. Pushing the curtain aside, I stared out into the dark shadows of the street, until I felt sure no one was lurking about to harm our household. Then I rang the bell.

John, the third footman, was instructed to take my note at once to Mr. Mareton's residence and to request an immediate reply. Off he went as Millie slipped back in with a tray of tea and sandwiches. I stuffed a sandwich in my mouth before my stomach could even think of rebelling.

Millie was quite correct; things did seem a bit better once I'd devoured a few sandwiches. Mr. Mareton had a truly regrettable primrose-yellow waistcoat. However, if there were a terrible accident involving it and a glass of claret or a bottle of ink, surely no one would blame the future Mrs. Mareton. True, I had not seriously considered marrying Mr. Mareton before. But I must live somewhere now, and there was no point in waiting until I'd been dragged off to wear lace caps and chewed-up gloves before seeking a suitable match. Mr. Mareton was an excellent dancer, lived in London year-round, was wealthy enough to support Cassia as well as myself, and could protect me and my handkerchiefs from thieves. Despite the waistcoat, he would have to do.

That done, I turned back to the day's work. If my father's message was important—and it must be, as men did not steal one's handkerchiefs every day—and if the War Office did not choose to understand that, what choice did I have but to sort it out myself?

I tapped the nib of my pen on the rim of the inkwell, sending tiny splotches of ink onto the blotter. Who would be in France now? And who might have seen my father? Oh, but of course— why hadn't I thought of her at once?

My dear Mrs. Lightburne,

How funny it is, to write to you as a real married lady! I hope that Paris is as wonderful as we thought it would be, and that you are enjoying life with your new Colonel immensely. Alas, London is dreary, and, as you may have heard, my father was killed in a carriage accident, and we shall be living the quiet life until our mourning is done.

Do write to me and tell me of all the lovely parties you've been to, and whom you've met—the other officers' wives, I imagine, and there must be some other English travelers, now that the war is over? Tell me what you wore, and all the gossip, even the weather, else I shall perish of boredom! And, if anyone happens to mention my father, would you write at once and tell me everything they say? I find myself now wishing I'd known him better, when of course it's too late. I should be very grateful for any gossip of how he spent his last days—I would prefer to think of him in some crowded Paris ballroom than traveling alone to his death.

My best wishes to the Colonel, and I do hope you are seeking out the finest modistes in the city!

Your dear friend,
Miss Annis Whitworth

PS It's a silly thing, but do you happen to know to whom "Cptn. J.F." might refer? One of Aunt Cassia's friends wrote to her about a scandal in Paris involving a ship's captain—with a murder, even!—and used only the initials, and of course she thinks I'm too young to hear any more. It does keep niggling at me! Is it anyone we know? And if you know the details, surely you will tell me!!

PPS Do try to remember that you really must not wear any yellow whatsoever, even if it is the Colonel's favorite. I assure you, it will not be any longer, once he sees it on you!

I blotted the letter, folded it, sealed it with a wafer, and sent it off as well, then sat down once more to stuff myself with sandwiches and wait for Mr. Mareton's reply, wondering all the while how to tell Cassia about my plans.

Chapter Six

EMPLOYMENT; OR, A TEST

How much more respectable is the woman who earns
her own bread by fulfilling any duty,
than the most accomplished beauty!
—*A Vindication of the Rights of Woman*,
by Mary Wollstonecraft (far too scandalous for Cassia to allow me to read,
but far too important for her to miss any opportunity to quote at me)

I do not know how late Cassia was out that night, nor which
of her friends she'd preferred to discuss our futures with, rather
than telling me. I know only that when Millie shook me awake
just before dawn, as I'd requested, I was still wearing my black
dress and clutching my bandbox. Millie tried smoothing out
the wrinkles with a damp clothes brush, and I tried sewing
them out in some sort of glamour against wrinkles, but neither succeeded. It did not matter; it was all I had, so I put it
back on anyway. Feeling like a crumpled, discarded governess only made me more determined to find some other way
forward.

I hurried to locate the third footman. "Where is the reply
from Mr. Mareton?"

"No reply yet, miss; his butler tells me the gentleman is away for a few days of sport with his friends. I left your message; he'll get it next week, soon as he's back."

I blinked, silently wishing Mr. Mareton and his waistcoat at the bottom of the ocean. How dare he go off now, ignoring my plans for him! "Go back at once and fetch my note, if you please. I don't wish him to have it after all."

The third footman opened his mouth, caught the look I gave him, and shut it. "Of course, miss."

Now, in the early-morning light, under the third footman's pitying gaze, I was beginning to wonder if I really wanted to spend the rest of my life convincing Mr. Mareton not to wear horrid waistcoats anyway. Marriage to a pleasant enough gentleman was the easiest option, no doubt, but I was too irritated to try again today. Very well; I'd find my own way through our troubles.

I stormed back up to my room to think.

I could see why Mr. Smith thought gentlemen would make better spies, since they were forever doing just as they pleased, with no notice or reason, without anyone thinking anything of it.

The light shining through my window grew stronger as I paced the floor. What now? Mr. Smith didn't listen, Mr. Mareton had left town—who was left? I picked up my bandbox and took out the handkerchiefs, holding them up to the light once more. I must show Cassia.

But as I hurried down to the sitting room, Jenkins announced a Miss Spencer, to see Cassia.

I stuffed the handkerchiefs into my pocket as Cassia turned toward me.

"Ah, Miss Spencer, this is my niece, Miss Annis Whitworth,"

Cassia said. "Annis, my friend Miss Spencer is here to take us to the employment agency. Truly, we cannot thank you enough."

Miss Spencer smiled. "It's no trouble—I have the use of a carriage while I am in London, and if we cannot have the luncheon we'd planned, at least we may visit a bit while we travel. But what a good thing you've introduced me, Miss Whitworth, or I should have thought you sisters! A pleasure to meet you at last, Miss Annis; I've heard so much about you." She looked to be about Cassia's age, and the quiet elegance of her gray dress suited her.

"A pleasure to meet you as well," I said hurriedly, without taking my seat. "Aunt Cassia, before we go I really must alter your gown. It will take only a few moments. . . ."

Cassia looked as though she had not slept a wink, and her dowdy black gown was frightful to behold, for I hadn't yet had time to alter it, nor to explain what I'd learned I could do. But that could wait; my father's message could not.

Cassia caught my hand and squeezed it. "After our appointment, Annis."

I frowned. "I must tell you—"

There was a slight cough from the door, and I saw that the third footman had returned.

I tugged on Cassia's hand. "Please?" I said. "I only need a moment. . . ."

But she shook her head.

I lifted my chin, ignoring the prickle of tears. "I'll get my bonnet, then." Half running from the room, I snatched my note from the footman, and hurried up to my room to burn it.

Watching the flames consume my letter did not calm my thoughts. I was out of time. Ought I to try the War Office once more? But who would listen to me? Not that silly young man who could hardly manage his bellpulls. Not Mr. Smith, who did not believe me. No, I must catch Cassia alone and somehow force her to listen.

"There you are at last," Cassia said, opening the front door as I returned. She hurried down our steps toward an elegant carriage and climbed inside before I could stop her.

I could see Miss Spencer in the carriage, waiting.

Suddenly I realized that this was truly happening—we were off to seek employment. I swallowed. "You may as well come along, Millie; I suppose you may need new employment now too."

Cassia looked down at me from the carriage, her eyes kind. She reached out to wipe a smudge from my cheek. "I am sorry, Annis. If only there were another way."

"There must be!" I said, climbing into the carriage. Millie followed.

"There is not," Cassia said, and directed the driver to the nearest employment agency. The carriage began to move.

"My dear aunt, you have always taught me that a lady can accomplish whatever she sets her mind to."

"True, in theory—but it is much easier to accomplish if the lady in question remains a lady in the eyes of society. That is why we must seek respectable employment. In theory, we could become actresses, or highwaymen—er, highwaywomen— but there would be no path to return to our former lives. You know as well as I do that all our friends' doors would be barred to us."

I considered this. "I believe one would need to be proficient with firearms to become a highwaywoman."

"Quite true." Cassia nodded. "And I do not have time to teach you today."

"But that does not mean that I will be able to breeze into Al-mack's for a waltz in a month or two as Lady So-and-So's govern-ess," I went on, thinking of what my friends would say—let alone those who were not my friends. There would simply be no way to look fashionable in a horrid drab gown, even once I was out of mourning, and absolutely everyone would know I was a govern-ess. "You cannot wish to spend the rest of your days wiping noses and reviewing the most basic of sums!"

Cassia raised her eyebrows. "My dear Annis, if I had my way, I'd be off to see the Parthenon. But hard work did not kill me when I cared for you after your mother died, and I should vastly prefer genteel employment now to a debtors' prison. Wouldn't you?"

I shuddered, wishing I had not seen that particularly dread-ful play with the heroine who dropped dead of hard labor just as her suitor found her at last. "We must try all available alternatives before we agree to either such disaster."

Cassia ignored me. I recognized her iron will settling about the situation. Once Cassia made up her mind, it would take one of those new steam locomotives to drag her in a different direc-tion.

I could feel the panic flowing through me. At any moment, the lace cap would descend onto my head, and all would be lost.

But Miss Spencer, of all people, threw me a rope. "May I ask what other alternatives you've considered, Miss Annis? Since a highwaywoman would require skills you do not yet possess?"

I considered her. She was beautifully dressed, in a fine light-gray wool, though now that I gave it my full attention, I found the gray too boring to truly suit her artfully dressed red hair. She seemed most intelligent. She smiled under my gaze, and I decided these were desperate times, and I must trust someone. "Certainly, it is a rather unusual alternative," I said. "But I am determined to seek employment of a most secret nature, as a—"

"Lady's companion," Cassia said firmly.

I shook my head. "Certainly not. I shall never wear a lace cap, nor let any old lady set me to embroidering handkerchiefs for her nephews! No, what I really mean to be is a—"

"But you know ladies can't be dressmakers, miss." Millie's quiet voice somehow cut across my words. "It's profitable work, but not respectable."

Cassia blinked twice. "You are absolutely correct, Millicent. It is the most unsuitable plan you have ever entertained, Annis."

This seemed rather unfair, as I had never planned to be a dressmaker. Why on earth had Millie suggested it?

Surprisingly, Miss Spencer picked up my imagined cause. "My dear Miss Whitworth, both you and I know that, although not ideal for a young lady of quality, there are far worse things than dressmaking."

"Perhaps," Cassia allowed. "But to go into trade! All her friends would be lost to her. She would never again—"

"Allow me to remind you that I myself run a patisserie and tea salon," Miss Spencer chided Cassia gently. "Am I not still your friend?"

My aunt had the grace to blush. "Your pardon, Miss Spencer."

I studied Miss Spencer more closely. She spoke like a lady; I would have never guessed her to be in trade. She was out in London on business, had the loan of a carriage, and did not appear cowed in the least. I could not imagine Mr. Smith calling her a silly girl. I was not certain what owning a patisserie involved, aside from lots of the finest pastries, but how could that be worse than debtors' prison? It was shocking, to be sure, but I could not deny it certainly looked better than being a governess. "Remind me, dearest aunt: why should I not be a dressmaker? Half the young ladies of London already ask my advice on their new gowns."

"Because your reputation will be ruined; you have no business sense at all, and no money to invest in such an endeavor," she snapped. "Honestly, Annis! We must have income at once, if we're to pay our bills—we certainly can't be shelling out on such wild dreams!"

"But Mr. Harrington is collecting the money from my father's overseas accounts, so we will have a few resources soon enough. You must admit I know exactly what would look best on someone, and how to explain to them what they should be wearing," I said. "And your excellent business sense would see us through."

"It is not as though you must begin in London," Miss Spencer said thoughtfully. "I live in Flittingsworth, a small town between London and Dover, near The Downs, as does Mr. Harrington. There are plenty of ladies who must buy new gowns in the country, and far less competition, you know. There is an empty shop near mine that would be perfect; you'd need only enough space to store the fabric your customers bring you, and to sew the gowns, of course."

I did not relish the thought of moving to the country. What could one possibly wear, and who would appreciate it? But, if Mr. Harrington lived there, I'd be well placed to keep an eye on him. I did not yet understand why he had lied about my father's travels. Was he a spy as well? Was he working for or against my father?

Something caught my eye on the street outside, and I searched the crowd, but if the man who'd stolen my handkerchief was there, he had vanished. Still, my heart continued to pound. Perhaps it would be best to leave London for a while.

"It is ridiculous," Cassia said firmly.

She couldn't think it ridiculous if I had not just skill, but magical talent. I took a deep breath, and caught her hand in mine. "I can sew glamours."

If the carriage had not been stopped, I would never have heard Cassia's quiet gasp as she snatched her hand back. I straightened my spine and tried to look mysterious. It was not every day that I managed to surprise my aunt.

Miss Spencer's eyes were wide. "How interesting! I've heard of no working glamour modistes within a day's ride of London, not for years now. And Millicent is correct, dressmaking can be profitable even without a talent, though it is not deemed respectable."

I looked down at my lap. Was I truly ready to leave my old life behind forever? My friends would not be as understanding as Cassia's eccentrics.

My eyes fell on the corner of my newly glamoured shawl, barely peeking out of my bandbox.

Ignoring Cassia, I considered Miss Spencer again. "What if I became a dressmaker in disguise? I could hardly ruin my reputation if no one knew who I was."

She tipped her head and examined me. "Hmm . . . With a powerful glamour . . . I suppose it could be possible." She clapped her hands in sudden delight. "I know! Add a wig and an accent, and you could pose as a widowed French dressmaker—a modiste. Ladies would trust her taste more readily than someone of your age, and no one would ask any questions, for no one wants to risk tales of war tragedies, no matter how bad your French." She nodded at Cassia. "I believe I read a novel once where something very like that happened. It worked perfectly."

Cassia shook her head. "Your pardon, Miss Spencer, but we cannot live in a novel. Annis, however much you might wish that some imagined magic will save you, you've never shown any signs of that talent before."

I remembered the disappointment in the War Office, and hesitated. But the shawl had not always been black; I had some magic, certainly. Just because I was not sure how to work every aspect of it did not mean I could not sew glamours.

Millie touched my hand and gave me a tiny nod. She had seen what I could do.

I met Cassia's eyes. "I can sew glamours."

She stared at me for a long moment. "These facts remain: we must have money at once to pay our creditors, and you are a young lady of quality, with no money to invest, no shop, no customers, and a reputation to protect. No doubt your new employer will appreciate your talent, and perhaps even pay you more for it."

For a minute or so, the slow turn of the carriage wheels on the cobbles was all I could hear, the gentle lurching combined with the pounding of my heart and the sloshing of my stomach. She would not budge. My eyes fell on Miss Spencer, who was looking at Cassia in some surprise. Miss Spencer believed I could do it. My plan truly was possible, then. I must only prove it to my aunt.

I glanced out the carriage window and chose my next move.

"No. I will prove to you here and now that I have the talent, and I will not waste it on such a dreary life. Find me—if you can—and we will do it your way. Fail, and we will do it mine."

And with that, I threw open the carriage door, leapt down into the street, and ran inside the British Museum.

Chapter Seven

IN WHICH MISS ANNIS PROVES HER POINT

A large income is the best recipe
for happiness I ever heard of.
—*Mansfield Park*, by "a Lady"
(though Cassia assures me it was written by Jane Austen)
(not half so thrilling as *Frankenstein*, of course!)

Thankfully, the museum was as packed as I had hoped. I slipped through the crowd quickly, and ducked down a back stairwell. Trying to catch my breath, I pulled my sewing kit from my bandbox and threaded the needle, irritated at how my fingers trembled. Why shouldn't I work a glamour? I had done it only the day before, even if I could not remember exactly how I'd managed it, and even if it hadn't worked precisely as I'd planned. I shoved the needle through the black brocade of my skirt and pulled the thread along with it, filling my mind with the image of a faceless lady in a nondescript dress, too plain to look at for more than a second. I tugged the thread through again, willing the fabric to change under my needle into dark gray.

It did no such thing.

The door opened. I admit a gasp slipped out before I could

stop it. The museum guard looked down the stairs at me, surprised. Then he nodded awkwardly and shut the door again.

He thought I was mending my skirt, I realized. But he'd remember if Cassia asked him anything about me. I thought of her dragging me off to the employment office, and knew I must make this work. I yanked the needle through again, and startled as a wash of gray flooded the fabric. I took another stitch, and another, muttering "Hide me from Cassia" to myself. If the guard returned, he'd think me escaped from Bedlam, but I didn't care anymore. I felt not so much as a shiver of magic, but I sewed on anyway. I stitched until the length of thread was used up.

Quickly I tied off the knot. Then I pulled the shawl from my bandbox and threw it about my shoulders. What did I care if that glamour had failed to impress horrid Mr. Smith? There was magic in it somewhere. It was just that I had never thought I'd be testing my newly found magic against the sheer force of my aunt Cassia, intent on finding me.

I took a deep breath. Then I walked up the stairs, opened the door, and let the crowd carry me deep into the galleries.

The crowd was thickest at the beginning of the illusions, so I stopped there as well, moving ever so slowly, watching Mrs. Wong's painted orange cat try to reach past its frame toward Mr. Varhola's watercolored goldfish pond as the fish swam around the gilt oval. There was no cry of discovery. I moved on to the couple in the rowboat, her fingers trailing delicately drawn droplets of palest blue across the paper surface as her companion bent and stretched the painted oars, over and over. I wished I could lose myself in the beauty of these tiny painted movements, wished I could come back another day to see if the sun had moved across the painted sky, or the lady's gloves had fallen in the river. But I would be leaving London.

Forcing myself to walk slowly, I stepped toward the apple tree in the old farmyard, watching it pass through season after season. Then my ears caught a familiar voice, and I froze, too frightened to move, through three cycles of blossom, leaf bud, fruit, falling leaves, and delicately drifting snow. *Breathe in; hold it,* I reminded myself. *Breathe out ever so slowly. Do not let your face give you away, no matter what they do. Do not let your eyes find them, even if you hear your name.* Every trick Cassia had taught me as I entered society, I used now for my own purpose.

Finally, I looked up. Cassia and Miss Spencer had moved through the gallery and were almost at the exit. Even from here, I could see Cassia's crinkled brow, but her eyes slid right past me. Millie, on the other hand, was staring straight at me.

I looked away immediately. What now? How long should I wait? And a very tiny voice inside me muttered that Cassia was not likely to be patient with me after today's events. What if she simply left the museum to continue with her plan, leaving me behind? What would I do then?

There was a cough at my elbow.

I jumped. It was Millie.

"Your aunt's outside, crying her eyes out," she said matter-of-factly. "She says if you'll come back, she'll do her best to help with your heedless, foolish plan."

I nodded. It was as good a concession as I was ever likely to get from Cassia. "How did you know it was me?"

She hesitated. "Earlier, on your errand, when you put on that shawl, you looked like a different lady—and you look like that same lady now."

I stared at her. So it had worked then too. Why hadn't Mr. Smith been impressed by my magic? "What do I look like?"

"Plainer," she said. "A bit older. Not so noticeable. It's hard to look right at you. . . . But your boots are the same as Miss Annis's, and your bonnet."

I nodded thoughtfully. Millie was proving to be a useful addition to our new household.

Millie was correct in all things. Cassia was wringing her handkerchief outside the museum, and did not stop crying until I removed my shawl and let Millie brush out my skirt, somehow changing it back to black in the process. I was extremely relieved when Miss Spencer managed to shepherd us all back into the carriage. "Gunter's, please," she told the driver.

I smiled. Miss Spencer was a shopkeeper, yet she was taking us to Gunter's for ices. Being a shopkeeper rose several notches in my estimation.

Once at Gunter's, I ordered my favorite lemon ice.

Cassia stopped her sniffling at once. "Apple will do just as well, Annis," she said firmly.

Apple is the cheapest on the menu; we've had this argument so many times I've memorized it. "But apple tastes of nothing. Lemon is lovely."

"Four lime ices, please, and my usual table," said Miss Spencer, slapping a handful of coins down.

Neither I nor Cassia would be so rude as to stare, of course, but I caught Cassia sneaking a look at Miss Spencer just as I did myself. We were led past Mrs. Stephenson and her granddaughters, and on to a lovely table in a sitting room, with no nearby neighbors. Lime ices were not on the menu, so far as I knew. And I had never seen even my progressive aunt buy an ice for a maid.

But they seated us all, and brought four lime ices immediately, and they were perhaps a tiny bit lovelier even than the lemon.

I could see the wheels beginning to turn in my aunt's mind as the ice restored her equilibrium. Before she could come up with yet another objection, I turned to Miss Spencer. "As a business-woman, what would you recommend we do next?"

Miss Spencer pursed her lips thoughtfully, spooning out the last drop of her ice. "Even with a small shop, you'll have some unavoidable expenses. You'll need a budget."

"Budgets require money, and we have none," Cassia said.

I opened my mouth to argue, but Miss Spencer beat me to it. "What if Miss Annis sold her jewelry?"

Cassia's eyes went wide. "She's far too young for such a task."

But Miss Spencer shook her head. "This is Miss Annis's venture. I'm certain Millicent will assist her." She smiled at Millie, who smiled back. (Millie was a much daintier eater than I'd expected, with perfect table manners. I would have to learn how she made her eyes so inscrutable.)

I thought about this. I didn't much like the idea of selling my things, but Miss Spencer was clearly correct. "I'll do it," I said.

Then I waited for Cassia to say *She'll do no such thing*. But she didn't.

"Not her mother's jewelry," Cassia said.

Miss Spencer paused thoughtfully, then nodded. "Perhaps something else from the household, then."

Everyone looked at me. A tiny flicker of worry went through me—that someone would see me and spread the gossip that I was penniless, or that I would do it all wrong and Cassia would say I had ruined our chances. Then again, if I believed I could make this all happen, I could hardly say I couldn't even manage the first step of my grand new scheme. Selling jewels was better than being a governess. "I shall sell my grandmother's jewels," I announced.

Cassia froze, and then broke into a grin. "How fitting. Certainly, sell the lot of them." At Miss Spencer's raised eyebrow, she added, "My mother cut me off without a penny when I left to set up house for my brother and take care of his young daughter. The last words I heard from her were that I was heedless, reckless, and doomed to failure and ruin. When she died, she left her jewelry to Annis, not me. She couldn't bear to be wrong."

I nodded (not that I'd ever met her). "Also, she had no taste."

"That fault was more my father's than hers," Cassia conceded. "If only he'd let her choose her own trinkets! But get as much as you can for them—you'll need all they're worth, and more, to make this ridiculous scheme work."

Chapter Eight

AN UNEXPECTED KINDNESS

I prefer liberty to chains of diamonds.
—Lady Mary Wortley Montagu

*S*oon we were headed home, where it was agreed that I would sell Grandmother's jewels while Cassia did businesslike things with Miss Spencer.

Miss Spencer would generously extend her London stay to assist (she claimed that our preparations would be far more entertaining than her usual shopkeeper's duties, though I began to doubt it).

I set my glamoured shawl aside and chose a warmer one (I saw no need to be fashionable above warm when one could so easily be both, with only a little planning and taste). Then Millie objected to my fashionable reticule. I did learn a lot of useful information about cutpurses as she repacked everything into my shabby old reticule, with its much sturdier handle. But, after instructing me that I ought not to let anyone I didn't know near it,

Millie solved this by carrying it herself, as she didn't really trust me to do it properly. She appeared to have taken Miss Spencer's confidence in her abilities utterly to heart.

Once outside, Millie paused and looked at me. "Are you certain you want to do this, miss?"

I swallowed. Should I admit that I had no notion of how to go about selling my jewelry? No. If I was going to start a whole new life, I'd simply have to learn by doing. "Of course I am. Lead on."

She straightened. "Then this way to Mr. Goldstein's establishment, miss." And she led me down Charing Cross Road to a tiny shop.

I stiffened my spine, put Cassia's no-nonsense look onto my face, and turned the knob of the door to the jeweler's.

Inside, silver lined the shelves on each wall, everything from teapots to candelabras, all shining in the lamplight, even if some were a bit battered.

The proprietor was a middle-aged man wearing a small black velvet cap. He rose to greet us, nodded at Millie, and gave me a considering look, then nodded at me too. Millie was already hurrying inside with my reticule, so I inspected his boots: decidedly not in the naval style. Ignoring the man's expression, I followed her in.

The man (Mr. Goldstein, presumably) waved at a chair for me, then seated himself back at his desk. "How may I be of service?" he asked.

The tray on the desk held a very fine, if modest, sapphire necklace, and a selection of earbobs I couldn't help but admire. What a pity he should have such excellent taste!

"You seek a jet brooch perhaps, or a personal memento?" He opened a drawer and brought out a small selection of mourning jewelry. "The artists I work with can create something unique for your loss. . . ."

Millie held out the reticule to me and I took it, shaking my head. "I find myself in need of funds, and so I've come to you with my grandmother's jewels, to beg you to help me."

"Hmph," he said, and set the mourning jewelry aside. "Show me."

I brought out my parcel and unwrapped the cloth, laying the topaz necklace on the desk before him.

He shuddered. "Alas, miss, I find there is little demand for such pieces these days."

I couldn't blame him for speaking the truth; who would seek out clumsily cut, mismatched topazes, combined with a miniature of the previous owner's dog? But the gold setting was well enough. I opened my eyes wide. "Oh, but I always receive such compliments whenever I wear it!"

He flinched as I pushed it toward him. "Ah, but the fashion is for matching earbobs, and you can see this would be, er, difficult to match. . . ."

Triumphantly I unwrapped the matching earbobs, tiny portraits of the spaniel swaying as I thrust them forward. It looked extremely elderly, but perhaps that was the artist's fault. At least they were not illusions. "Yes, precisely! Oh, I can hardly bear to part with them—I have never seen their like elsewhere." (Millie had instructed me to say exactly this, in order to gain a sympathetic edge to my bargaining—something she clearly knew quite a lot about.)

"Perhaps something else would grieve you less?" he asked.

I looked at Millie, who was biting her lip. She gave me no sign as to what I should do, so I improvised. "Well, there are the garnets, but they are far less unique. . . ."

He brightened as I unwrapped the garnets, but quickly lost his smile when I laid out the necklace on the desk. The garnets themselves were unexceptionable, but the mass of hairwork they'd been set in defied the boundaries of artistry and good taste. I don't know whose hair had been used—it looked like half a village's, with strands from many members—but it had not held up well over time, and the sproinging strands gave an unpleasant fuzz over the whole that obscured the pattern. "I have the matching earbobs, of course," I said, remembering how even Cassia—who frequently set out for balls with ink smudges on her nose—had stated she would never be caught dead wearing such a thing.

He shot a glance at it, and recoiled. I felt quite in sympathy. "You know, it would be no work at all to cut that up and reset the stones," I said consolingly.

Was it my imagination, or did he look a bit more interested?

But Millie felt things ought not to be left to chance. "Oh, miss, not your grandmother's necklace!" she cried, dabbing at her eyes with her handkerchief. "It's just too terrible! You, having to sell your things, with your father barely in the grave! But it's only for a short time—what with all those rich gentlemen hovering around, wanting to marry you!"

Here Mr. Goldstein gave me a rather dubious look, and I can't say I disagreed with his assessment of my appearance, for I had not had much time at all to dress, and black will never be my color. "Oh, but, Millie, you know there are hardly—"

"Left all alone in the world, with only your aunt and your faithful maid!" she cried, and blew her nose in a resounding trumpet to finish.

Unfortunately, that part was true. I bit my lip and looked away. "Please hush, Millie; I'm trying to conduct business," I said, through the thickening lump in my throat.

The jeweler looked at me, then glanced at Millie, and then at the lunch parcel he'd pushed aside, which I saw had been tied with a bit of red ribbon. "Might as well show me the lot," he said, sighing.

"Oh, how good you are!" Millie burst out as I began unwrapping the remaining jewels.

He smiled kindly at her. I could see he was making an effort not to shudder at each new horror.

At last, they were all displayed on the desk in their dubious glory. Now that the suggestion had been made, I could see Mr. Goldstein inspecting the settings to see what could be dismantled, and I reminded him the bracelet of strangely shaped golden mushrooms could be melted down completely.

He muttered to himself as he turned each piece over. Finally, he looked up. "Fifty pounds," he stated.

This seemed well enough for jewels I'd certainly never wear; I wouldn't have paid half so much for them. But Millie gave a shriek. "She could not possibly agree to so little!" she said, glaring at the jeweler. "And her with her father only just buried, and—"

"Very well," Mr. Goldstein said hurriedly. "Seventy-five, then."

Again, I would have been only too happy to agree, but I looked to Millie first, and she went into an impassioned discussion of the value and rarity of topazes of such color and beauty, and how garnets were all that could be seen at Almack's, until he held up his hand.

"One hundred, and that's final," the man said. Millie opened her mouth again, but this time I held up my hand, and she held her tongue, though she looked a bit skeptical. I rose to my feet, picked up a large silver teapot with a slightly dented spout from a crowded shelf, and put it on the desk. "One hundred, and this teapot," I said firmly.

Mr. Goldstein's eyebrows rose, and he looked at me more carefully. I have no idea what he saw. But he nodded slowly, took out a key, and unlocked a drawer in his desk, in which I got a glimpse of quite a lot of money. He counted out one hundred pounds, and gave me a stern look. "Pay her well," he told me as Millie tucked it all away in the reticule. Then he shooed us out into the street.

Millie carried the reticule, thieves being what they were, she said, while I carried the teapot. Neither of us mentioned the man with the naval boots, but I was careful not to take out a single handkerchief as we walked homeward.

"Millie, you were a wonder—I cannot imagine how you convinced him to pay so much for such hideous jewels!" I said at last.

"Oh, he'll sell the topazes for perhaps forty pounds—fifty if he can find a half-blind collector of miniatures—twenty for the garnets, once they've been cut up, ten pounds for the gold to be melted, and another ten pounds or so for the rest, I'd say," Millie told me.

I stared at her. "But—he'll lose at least ten pounds on the deal, perhaps even more!"

Millie nodded. "That wasn't real business, miss. That was kindness."

"Perhaps." Or, perhaps Millie didn't know the true value of the jewelry.

"I'll bet he has a daughter, who packed his lunch for him—didn't you see that pretty ribbon?" She shrugged. "He would know what it's like to have few options to earn his way, none good. Why shouldn't he have sympathy for your situation?"

"I suppose he might." I looked away.

Millie stopped walking and waited until I turned to meet her gaze. "When I needed funds once, I went to sell the last thing I had. He gave me money for food, but he wouldn't take my mother's locket. He told me he'd lost everything too, once. He was kind to me, and to you too."

How awkward, to be instructed by one's maid, to be the object of a stranger's sympathy! It reminded me of my very first ball, standing uncertainly in front of a crowd of tittering ladies in that horrid, horrid gown, wondering what had gone wrong.

Then I recalled something I had not thought of in months: the Countess Lieven herself had found me in the retiring room at that very same ball, trying to hide.

"Will you retreat?" she'd asked me. "Or will you come forward and learn how to fight?"

I'd had no idea what she'd meant back then, no notion that it was possible to salvage such an evening. I'd stared at her, openmouthed, unable even to answer, and once she'd left, I'd sat in a corner and cried.

But I was not the same naive girl now. And, although Millie was no Countess Lieven, she knew the ways of the world in which I found myself, and had led me safely through my first battle.

"Thank you," I told her. "I'd have failed utterly without you."

She shrugged, but I caught a tiny smile before it fled her face. "Best be on our way. They'll be wondering what's become of us."

Chapter Nine

IN WHICH MADAME MARTINE ENTERS FLITTINGSWORTH

England is a nation of shopkeepers.
—Napoléon Bonaparte

*T*wo nights and two mornings later, I awoke very, very early in a small, plain, chilly room in a tiny cottage in a village I'd never so much as visited before.

Everything had felt like such a blur: that first shock, seeing Cassia in tears, and then the spinning world of spies and hand-kerchief thievery, not to mention employment, glamours, seamstresses. . . . Now that it was quiet, I realized I couldn't remember the sound of my father's voice, and I felt a choking, twisting emptiness.

I trusted Miss Spencer's belief that it would be easier to open a shop in a less cutthroat environment than London (particularly while managing my disguise and double life). I had no wish to encounter my old acquaintances' pity at my new circumstances, any more than I wished to check every dark street corner for suspicious naval boots.

Still, I could not help wishing that something familiar had been left to me.

I picked up the gossip column I'd brought from home. Turning the sheet to the early dawn light, I began to read, feeling as though I were peering through glass into another world, an aquarium or some such thing, beautiful and strange and impossible to touch.

Ladies, guard your daughters, for the newly promoted Cptn. W.J.'s Aguilucho has sailed into The Downs. He is said to wear a well-fitted coat indeed, and to have a ready smile for a well-heeled young miss, and has been seen in drawing rooms near Chatham.

Meanwhile, at Lady T.'s soirée, Mr. E.M. was seen dancing three times with Miss M.W. (lovely as always in watermelon jacquard), to the obvious jealousy of Miss K.T., who danced with him only twice. . . .

I crumpled the gossip column and threw it on the floor. No wonder Marianne Wentrich had not written, nor Kitty Tittlevrim, nor Mr. Mareton! Clearly, they were missing me terribly. I sniffed. I ought to have let Marianne buy that tangerine silk she'd wanted. It would have looked atrocious on her.

I sat up in bed, twitched the curtain aside, and stared out at the dark hedgerows and muddy fields. Spiderwebs dripped from bare tree branches, and somewhere a bird chirped once, then stopped. I didn't blame it a bit, for what was there to sing about?

Cassia had rented a cottage and a tiny shop with the greatest possible speed—which meant that we were now living in Flittingsworth, the home of Miss Spencer and her patisserie, since she'd known of the very places already. (She'd also teased Cassia about how impressed her solicitor had been with Cassia's accounting methods, causing Cassia to blush, to my great glee. I did like Miss Spencer.)

Meanwhile, Millie and I had devised a plan for my disguise. When the shop was open, I would be Madame Martine, a widowed French modiste, who (rumor had it) could sew glamours. Millie had gone to nearby Puddlesmith to purchase the pieces of my costume (and spread the aforementioned rumors). Millie would split her days between two employers, as was not uncommon, helping Madame Martine during shop hours, and the Misses Whitworth the rest of the time; she needed no disguise, for no one would think anything of it. Once again, I found myself relieved Mrs. Cohen had sent her, for I certainly could not imagine Danvers stooping to handle porridge and chamber pots, as well as hair.

Best of all, this would give me time out from under my aunt's watchful eye, to figure out what ought to be done about my father's message, and to do it.

I hopped down from the bed, wincing as my bare feet hit the cold stone of the cottage floor. Where had I put my slippers? And how had Cassia found a cottage that did not even have a fireplace in my bedroom? Quickly I pulled on my stockings, slid my feet into my slippers, and wrapped myself in my warmest dressing gown.

Cassia was not only awake but fully dressed, already silently arranging her books in the sitting room. I rolled my eyes at the piles everywhere, but was secretly glad to see the same yellow-patterned cloth on the same small wooden table from our old morning room.

On it sat the battered silver teapot from Mr. Goldstein's shop, and I smiled. Just as I'd suspected (for Lady Tittlevrim had one just like it, only with a cracked spout), it was an antique heat-amplifying pot, from before the war, when all those with metal magic were pressed into other service. I crossed to the table now and gripped the handle, watching with pleasure as it took a bit of my body's warmth and heated the tea within, a small puff of steam swishing out of the spout. I poured the tea in my favorite cup and sat down in my usual chair.

The door to the kitchen opened, and Millie brought in a plate of sliced plum cake with butter.

"I see the teapot I bargained for will come in handy," I said, grinning as I reached for the cake. Cassia had had no patience with what she called my "silly luxuries" when I'd brought it home.

"I suppose so," Cassia said, coming to join me. (But I noticed she heated the tea before she poured it also, and smiled to my-self.) "Just like the leftover plum cake, which you laughed at me for packing." She raised an eyebrow, looking at my plate.

My mouth was full, so I chose to merely nod in reply. How was I to know we'd be living in a cottage that lacked even an oven, let alone a cook?

"We must begin dressing you, miss," Millie said, her eyes on the small mantel clock.

I swallowed, the plum cake suddenly stale and dry in my throat. "Of course." I followed her back to my bedroom.

Millie laced a down pillow into my new corset, to star-tling effect. The secondhand black gown she'd bought—and I'd altered—was dropped over my head and hooked up. Millie pinned my hair flat, and a rather greasy black wig was fastened over it.

"Jump," Millie ordered, and I jumped up and down as she commanded and shook my head, feeling quite ridiculous, until we were certain nothing would budge. She powdered my face and added white streaks to my wig, then covered it with a small black lace mantilla.

When she held up a mirror, I could hardly recognize myself. I looked far older, with heavy black brows and even a few wrinkles. Smiling, I went out to show Cassia.

But Cassia did not smile much these days. She hardly glanced at my transformation, peppering me instead with every tiny detail she could think of. "Do you have the key to the shop? What about the key to the cottage? Have you packed your scissors? What about your pins? Really, Annis, you must stop admiring yourself and hurry!"

My head was spinning by the time I peeked out the curtains. This would be the trickiest bit, for no one must know that Madame Martine had any connection to the Misses Whitworth.

Millie held out my shawl, and then my cloak. "The mail will be arriving in five minutes, madame," she said, picking up my bandbox as I wrapped the cloak around myself.

"Then let us be off," I said grandly, as a famous and very expensive modiste might. (Cassia had despaired when I'd tried to speak with a French accent, but Miss Spencer had assured her that the best modistes only pretended to be French, and had no better accents than mine, while one who actually was French pretended to be Spanish to avoid a Troubled Past.) "Au revoir, Miss Whitworth." And I swept out into the lane without waiting to hear Cassia's reply.

There were no lights in the windows of the cottages near the inn, so no one saw us arrive in the carriage yard, what with all the bustle and hurry of changing horses, and travelers complaining that they'd miss their meal. It was as easy as Millie had said it would be to give an impression that we'd just arrived with everyone else. Not that anyone seemed to care where we'd come from.

As I walked from the inn's carriage yard back down the lane, past the smithy, and the greengrocer, the cobbler, and the stationer (who, I was pleased to see, carried ribbons and other important items as well as paper and quills), and stopped in front of Miss Spencer's patisserie, I supposed Flittingsworth would do. It was small enough that Madame Martine would be noticed, particularly as there was no other dressmaker in town, and quiet enough that my disguise would not have to withstand much scrutiny.

In short, it seemed completely, utterly dull.

I drew a deep breath, taking one last look in the window of Miss Spencer's patisserie, with its green-trellised paper and twinkling lumen lights (such a clever, beautiful use of magic!), as though I could breathe in the air of London's Covent Garden one last time.

Then I walked up to my own shop's front door, digging the large iron key out of Madame's bandbox to unlock it. Millie hurried inside to light the lanterns, and I stepped out of the dark, muddy lane and into my new life.

It was just as I'd imagined it: tiny, but perfect, every detail speaking of quality. The walls were covered in a pale-apricot paper with delicate black traceries (which Millie had found for such a bargain on Piccadilly Street that even Cassia had not been able to find fault); the floor was covered in a deep-plum-and-black carpet that had been my mother's, and anyone familiar with our former east drawing room would recognize the desk we'd had sent down, the small gilt chairs, the marble-topped worktable, and any number of other things. The rosewood chiffonier had been in Cassia's bedroom for as long as I could remember, but she'd offered it up to hold the lengths of fabrics my customers would bring in to be made into gowns.

I crossed the room to straighten the folded length of muslin—just waiting for my customers' fabrics to join it—next to the neat stack of all my issues of *La Belle Assemblée,* with slips of paper still marking my favorite designs.

Millie coughed. "Madame, please, you must walk more like this." Slowly she glided across the floor toward the chiffonier, as though her hems were weighted with lead.

I put my hands on my padded hips. "That's just what I did, exactly as we've been practicing."

But Millie shook her head. "When you are Miss Annis, you walk like this." Quickly she tripped across the lovely carpet toward the dress form, light as air. "But when you are dressed as Madame, and do not quite remember her walk . . ." She swooped forward, then up with each step in a most remarkable fashion.

I burst out laughing. "You look exactly like a gas balloon trying to break free of the ground!"

Millie frowned disapprovingly, though I could have sworn the corners of her mouth twitched a bit. "Do practice, madame. I'll just be in the back, putting all those threads and ribbons and pins in order."

I began to slowly pace around the shop as though a book were balanced on my head—at least until Millie disappeared into the tiny back room, when I could not resist trying her balloon-swoop walk.

I was midswoop, still smiling, when suddenly the door flew open.

Chapter Ten

. . . AND RIDS HERSELF OF HER FIRST CUSTOMER

Never interrupt your enemy
when he is making a mistake.
—Napoléon Bonaparte

I stopped swooping at once and gave a curtsy (exactly like Millie had taught me) as a lady dressed head to toe in puce stalked in. (I cannot imagine where she found those puce gloves, for any shopkeeper with sense must have known they'd look ghastly on almost everyone. The puce-trimmed bonnet did her watery-blond hair no favors; I'd never go back to a shop that sold me that. And Cassia says I have no business sense!)

She stopped in front of me and examined the gown I was wearing in a way that was, frankly, quite rude. I caught the footman's eye; he smiled apologetically. But I was a modiste, after all; it was natural for customers to wish to see what I could do. I bit my tongue and held my temper, even when she gave a little sniff, as though not very impressed with my work.

I could not help but assess her right back, only regretting that

I had not Cassia's skill of raising only one eyebrow and not the other. Her gown was newly made, of a design I had not seen, quite modern in the sleeves and the width of the skirt. I would never have chosen it for her, but I would consume Madame Martine's black lace mantilla if she had paid less than fifteen pounds for it. "How may I assist you, madame?"

She paid no attention to the haughty young man who trailed in after her and lounged against the chiffonier, so neither did I (other than to note that his boots resembled the cavalry style rather than the naval, and that he smelled, strongly, of an unpleasant blend of claret and snuff, not of the sea). Snapping her fingers, she reached out a hand, and the drab maid who'd hurried inside after her gave her a piece of paper.

Carelessly she handed it to me.

It was a fashion plate I'd never seen before (a rare thing, indeed) for a pomona-green gown all trimmed in rosettes. It was a daring new style, certain to be eye-catching; a pity it would look absolutely ghastly on her. My heart began to pound. This was a ball gown, not a walking dress, and would go for well beyond fifteen pounds, even without my talent. It was beyond dreadful, but I could find some way to turn this into a gown she would love. I had to.

Something of my astonishment must have shown on my face, for she nodded. "My husband brought it for me from Paris, only yesterday, along with the fabric. No one will have anything like it." The maid pulled out a carefully folded length of eye-wateringly bright canary-yellow satin.

I nodded for her to place it on the table, unwilling to even touch it. "*Très bien*, my lady. Now, if I may suggest, I would narrow the skirt to flatter your figure, and include, oh, perhaps half

the rosettes—or maybe one-third? A nice cream would look él-
égant with your hair—"

"Certainly not," she snapped, her eyes narrowing. "You will
sew this style, exactly as pictured, out of my fabric—and I expect
you to account for every snippet left, for if I find you selling a
similar gown or so much as a scrap of my fabric to anyone else, I
swear I will ruin your business."

Millie had insisted that nothing should shock Madame, but I
must admit I gaped at the lady's forthright unpleasantness.

She smiled at me. "Now that we understand each other, I
suggest a bit of sport. If you deliver my gown by dawn tomorrow
morning, I shall pay you one and a half times your usual fee. If
you are so much as a minute late, you'll get nothing."

Here, my heart gave up pounding and sank instead to my
boots. "Madame, we are not a ready-made shop."

She glared at me. "As though I would buy a ready-made gown!
Do you have the magic, or don't you, you foolish seamstress?"
Folding her arms, she studied me. "Oh, very well. Two times your
usual rate. I am traveling with Lord Prippingforth to Paris tomorrow morning; best get to work at once."

Something about her words caught my attention. Was it possible Cassia was posing this terrible lady as a test?

Was it possible my talent could simply whip up this gown, exactly as pictured, with no trouble at all? I had never sewn an entire
gown before, but there was no time like the present to try one out.
And if I did not manage to complete it in time, what was the harm
in trying? I'd receive no payment, but it was not as though I had
other customers who would be waiting while I attempted it. Still,
failure would do Madame's reputation no good.

"Madame . . ." Millie stepped out of the back room and

stopped, suddenly stiff as one of the stuffed gazelles in the British Museum, so pale I feared she would faint.

The haughty young man leaned forward, an ugly smile on his face. "Ah, now here's a bit of sport indeed!" Slowly he began to walk toward Millie.

The lady turned from Millie to me, frowning. "So you've hired that wicked, lying girl. If she gave you a reference from me, she wrote it herself, or paid someone else to, for I'd never write her one! A piece of advice: you'll want to turn her out immediately, or you'll regret it, mark my words."

Millie closed her eyes.

I am certain there was no hint of a gas balloon in my stride as I bore down on the lady. "You will apologize to my shopgirl this instant, or our conversation is at an end."

The young man took another step, and I changed course, almost charging toward him; I did not like the look on his face.

"Never in my life have I been so rudely treated . . . ," the lady spluttered.

Very well; this was simply not going to work out. I marched over to the table, picked up the fashion plate and the fabric, and shoved them at Lady Prippingforth's maid, who stared at me openmouthed. Then I strode to the door and threw it open. "Good day, madame; best of luck finding someone who will sew for you."

"How dare you—" Whatever it was she might have called me, it was lost in the crash as I slammed the heavy shop door behind them and turned the lock.

Then I turned to Millie. "What on earth was all that about?"

"Oh, you oughtn't to have done that, madame," Millie said, biting her lip.

"I'm sure Cassia will say all that and more," I said dryly. "But had you met her before? Or has she escaped from Bedlam to go shopping?"

Millie sank down onto a footstool as though her legs could no longer hold her. "That was Lady Prippingforth, madame. I was the scullery maid at her house in London. She dismissed me when . . . when her nephew locked me in a cupboard."

"That was him?" I asked, and she nodded, looking at her boots.

"Tell me," I said, and even without the French accent my voice sounded nothing like my own.

A shudder went through her. "He came to visit his aunt sometimes. All the maids were afraid of him. I was always careful. . . . But he rang for the housemaid to bring him his cocoa, and she was younger than I was, and so afraid, and I thought, with tea about to be served, perhaps he wouldn't bother with me. . . . But he pushed me into his cupboard and locked me in, for later, he said." She raised her head and looked at me defiantly. "The housemaid let me out before he came back, and I told the housekeeper. And when she wouldn't speak up, I told Lady Prippingforth, after tea. She called me a liar and told me to leave."

I could feel the anger rising in my chest. That some horrid gentleman would attack Millie, and then insult her in my shop—how dare he! "Doesn't Lord Prippingforth have any sense? Surely he cannot allow such behavior under his own roof!"

She shrugged. "No one knows, for he is almost always in France; something to do with the war." She looked up, and I was horrified to see she was crying. "It didn't matter. I would never have stayed, not after that."

I pulled out my handkerchief and passed it over. I cleared

my throat, but could not think what to say. All those lectures Cassia had given me, on the misfortunes of young women who were born without the privileges I enjoyed; all those teas with Mrs. Cohen, bent on improving the lots of maids facing unfortunate circumstances—and yet I had never understood. I raised my chin and looked at her. "I will never sew a gown for that woman, so long as I live. And if that horrible nephew so much as looks at you, I will stab his eyes out with my scissors."

Millie looked a bit shocked, but at least she stopped crying. "But your aunt . . . ," she said softly.

"Aunt Cassia will hold him down as I do it, if she doesn't go for him first," I said. I leaned forward, as though I could make her believe me just by willing it. "You are safe with us."

As though in answer to her name, a loud rapping came from the front door. "You've forgotten to unlock the door," my aunt's voice called.

Chapter Eleven

MISS WHITWORTH IS AGHAST, AND ANOTHER LETTER IS WRITTEN

Secrets travel fast in Paris.
—Napoléon Bonaparte

$\mathcal{I}$ put my hands on my (much larger than usual) hips and gave Millie a stern look. "You will leave this to me."

Millie didn't even meet my eyes, just gulped and nodded. That worried me more than her tears had; the maid in the jeweler's shop would never have just let me handle anything.

But I was going to make certain things turned out well for her. I had to.

So I called out, "One moment, *s'il vous plaît*," and went to unlock the door.

I tried to give Cassia a Significant Look as she entered, so she'd know not to say more before I'd had a chance to send Millie back to the cottage, but she'd already swept in and surveyed the shop and both of us before I'd finished wiggling my eyebrows.

"Well?" she snapped. "Will you be open today, or not?"

"Indeed," I said haughtily. Madame Martine was not to be

trifled with, not even by my aunt. "I have already received my first order, declined it, and will open again as soon as you've finished inspecting the place."

Her eyes narrowed. "You've done what?"

It truly is impossible to slip something past my aunt.

The bell tinkled; Millie gasped and shrank back. I froze. Cassia stared at me suspiciously.

"Was that Lady Prippingforth I saw storm past?" Miss Spencer said brightly, closing the door behind her. "Oh, hello, Miss Whitworth! How goes the unpacking?"

Millie slumped back on the footstool. And, at the sight of her tired, terrified face, I—well, I suppose I might have lost my temper.

"Lady Prippingforth came to order a ball gown, to be delivered at dawn tomorrow, which is of course quite impossible. In the process, she insulted Millie beyond bearing. I requested that she apologize, and when she would not, I declined her custom and suggested she and her horrid nephew leave. She obliged." I folded my arms and dared Cassia to say anything.

"Oooh!" Miss Spencer clasped her hands together, her eyes glowing. "You know, I would have paid at least five pounds to see her face when you threw her out."

"I should be happy to do it again. I will send you an invitation as soon as the opportunity arises," I assured her. "She is headed to France tomorrow with her husband, but I assume she'll return far too quickly."

"Oh, she packs for France every time Lord Prippingforth comes home, but he never actually takes her with him," Miss Spencer explained. "Of course, I can hardly blame him; she is quite unbearable."

But Cassia was not attending to the important details. "So

you are telling me that not only have you declined your first order, but you made a spectacle of your first customer?"

And, normally, I would have been properly cowed by her flashing eyes and fiery tone. But today, in Madame Martine's gown, I was not having it. "Are you daring to tell me that I should have used my talent to glorify a woman who allowed her nephew to attack a maid and lock her in a cupboard? Who dismissed her when she dared complain?" I grabbed Millie's limp hand. "I take Millicent O'Leary's word over Lady Prippingforth's. And I will not see her suffer further!"

"In a cupboard?" Cassia asked, frowning at Millie. "As some sort of joke?"

"So he could take his time later," Millie whispered.

Cassia froze. She stared down at Millie, eyes flashing, lips pressed tight together.

Millie looked terrified. "I'm very sorry, madam," she whispered.

"You have nothing whatsoever to apologize for," Cassia spat. She began to pace the very short length of the very small shop, and she did not look at all like a gas balloon. "When I think of how gentlemen—Ha! If one can even call them that!—how they dare treat . . ." She whirled around, and I am ashamed to say that Madame Martine gave a highly undignified squeak at the look in her eye. "I shall look into what can be done about this—this scum of the earth. . . ."

"What is the scum's name, Millie?" I asked.

"Mr. Hustlesmith," she whispered.

"You shall have nothing to fear from Mr. Hustlesmith any longer," Cassia told her. "As for you—we shall discuss your behavior toward your customer later, Annis."

"Of course," I said. Perhaps she'd forget about it by then. I pointed at the packet she was holding. "Did you bring that for me?"

Cassia slapped the packet down on the table. "I believe I need that cup of tea after all," she told Miss Spencer, and they turned and left the shop.

I closed the door behind them. "There, now, that's settled. Didn't I tell you not to worry?"

Millie shut her eyes, her shoulders still sagging.

Perhaps she needed another moment to recover.

⚭)(⚭

The packet was addressed to Miss Annis, in London, but had been forwarded here (by Mr. Harrington's efficiency, no doubt). I recognized my friend Mrs. Lightburne's near-illegible scrawl, and was thankful I'd had years of practice interpreting it.

Inside was a delicate satin reticule in palest rose, beaded in jet, and a letter.

My dear Miss Annis!!!

Paris is gloriously, heavenly wonderful, as is my dear Colonel, as you must of course know!! I cannot imagine why you should want to know about the weather, but it has been lovely ever since I arrived, chilly but clear. I have taken tea with so many kind ladies, in French nonetheless, and only one rather rude lady laughed at me. (I hear I complimented her glass gown rather than her green gown, and I suppose that could strike one as humorous, but they ought not to make the words so similar if they don't wish for that to happen!) All of my dresses are new, for of course my old girlish ones

75

do not suit me now, and there is a shop here with the most amazing watered silk I have ever seen! If you were not in mourning, I should send you some at once, but they have no black.

I am so sorry for your loss, for I am sure you must be grieving, even though you hardly ever saw your father. I did ask, but no one can give me much of an account of his trip, even though everyone saw him around town. Old Mademoiselle Borrel said she heard he had gone off to visit Lord Prippingforth to buy one of his horses, which did not make sense, for what would your father do with a horse in France? Perhaps she got the word wrong, or perhaps I did. But my darling Charles says Lord Prippingforth lost all his money in the war, so perhaps he only meant to be kind? Either way, nothing seems to have come of it, for your father was found dead on the road the next day.

Really, it makes me want to weep. What can he have been thinking, when there was no moon at all? But take heart, for I have happened upon a piece of luck: the one time I saw your father, he complimented my new reticule, and asked me where I had bought it. And you will hardly believe this, but the very next time I was in the shop, buying another for my cousin, the shopkeeper said she'd sold the second to last one to your father, but that he had never picked it up, nor the handkerchief whose color he'd had her match! Well, he can only have meant it for you, so I explained the situation, and as he'd very sensibly paid for it before dying, here it is!

As for your aunt's gossip, I swear I would tell you, only I have not been able to discover what it could be. I could not think of a single Cptn. J.F. who'd been murdered. And when I asked my darling Charles, he insisted the only one he could think of was Captain John Fitzhugh, of the East India Company ship called the Aguilucho, *who was a very boring, earnest sort of man who did nothing more interesting than drowning next to his boat the day before your father died. Which is sad, but hardly a scandal, particularly as everyone says he did not touch a drop of liquor. But you can rest assured that as soon as I ferret out the scandal, I shall write to you at once.*

PS You need not worry about the yellow, for I have a new yellow silk sash that rests nowhere near my face, and the Colonel compliments me every time I wear it, so I do not care what you say.

I shook my head. It was a good thing that Mrs. Lightburne was the sweetest creature imaginable, and that her Colonel had brains enough for the both of them. Well, I was quite pleased that Lord Prippingforth had lost all his money, for his horrid wife and nephew deserved any misery they got, and I was glad my father had not bought his horse. Probably, once he had met the man, he'd quickly seen that he was not worthy of sympathy.

I ran over my father's message once more, burned into my mind from hours of pondering: *Rain leaving field. Reroute Corbeau away from S.H. Cptn. J.F. murdered.*

It was odd that Captain John Fitzhugh had drowned only a day before my father died. Could it have been murder? But there was nothing of an *Aguilucho* in my father's message, only the *Corbeau.* I couldn't shake the feeling that the message was important, but I could not find a way to unravel it.

I touched a fingertip to the reticule and sighed. Rose was not one of my best colors, but it was not as though my father would have noticed what I wore, any more than he would have remembered to retrieve a gift for me—not when duty called.

Inside was a pale-rose handkerchief, unmonogrammed; it matched the reticule perfectly. I examined the lining for secret pockets or crinkling papers, but there was nothing hidden within. For a moment I wondered if perhaps it was all a fiction of Mrs. Lightburne's kind heart, wanting me to have some last memento of my dead father, inventing presents he ought to have given me. But no; if Mrs. Lightburne had chosen it, it would not have been rose; she knew my taste too well.

But none of that mattered when there was work to be done. There was no help for it; I must try harder to gain the War Office's attention. They were bound to have more information than I did, and would know the "Cptn. J.F." in my father's message, and if drowned Captain Fitzhugh had anything to do with my father's work. I would not be so easily dismissed.

I sat down at my desk, took out a piece of notepaper, dipped my pen in the inkwell, and wrote a letter.

To the (Most Likely) Highly Esteemed Mr. Smith,

 Surely it will interest you to know that a modiste of no small Talent and Skill is residing a mere day's drive from London, in the town of Flittingsworth. I am certain you have never seen the like before. Do come at once, and bring proper measurements with all your requests.

Respectfully,
Madame Martine, Glamour Artist

Spies must need disguises. How could they resist such an offer? And if he came to visit, and I could fool him, I could make him see that I would be an extremely valuable addition to his force. And if not, I could at least keep him here until he examined my father's message properly and vowed to avenge his death.

I ignored the wobbling in my stomach, and resolved to focus my efforts on the present. Carefully I blotted the letter, sealed it with a wafer, rose to my feet, and strode over to Millie, holding it out. "I'll need you to slip this in with Cassia's correspondence when you deliver it to the mail coach tomorrow," I said.

She took the letter, but didn't move. "Yes, madame," she whispered.

It made me angry that horrid Mr. Hustlesmith could still terrify her.

I'd never faced an experience like hers. What could I possibly do to help her? The only thing I was truly good at was choosing what people ought to wear, and that was hardly what was needed now.

I studied Millie's worn brown dress. Then again, how could a new dress hurt? I'd always chosen my gowns to give me a little more confidence—what if I could sew that in for Millie as well? Perhaps even a bit of protection, somehow? "Hand me that lilac muslin," I told her. "It's time to begin your shop gown."

Chapter Twelve

ON THE DIFFICULTIES OF MONEY, OR THE LACK THEREOF

It is a truth that man is difficult to know, and that,
if we may not deceive ourselves, we must judge him by
his actions of the moment, and for the moment only.
—Napoléon Bonaparte

*M*illie did at least look up when I began hacking the lilac muslin to pieces with my scissors. I didn't worry much about the cuts, for surely my talent would appear when we most required it. My cause was just, my intentions pure—how could it abandon me now?

"Let me tell you a story," I said. "Once, when I was a young girl in London, I allowed my dear aunt to take me to her modiste for my very first ball gown. Now, never doubt that my aunt is a lady of uncommon intelligence, but never allow her to choose your gown either. The modiste assured us it would suit me perfectly—as though hundreds of pale-peach ruffles could flatter anyone! I heard afterward that Lady Alexandra Stafford had allowed the modiste to choose a gown for her, having no patience with fashion, and that her mother had the good sense to send the horrid thing back. I suppose the modiste simply made it over for me. Anyway, off I went to my first ball, feeling like a slightly dubious cinder girl, and Mr. Ives took one look at me and declared me 'in the mode of lettuce *d'orange*.'"

Millie had no reaction to the horror of this experience. I began basting the skirt together at the sides, leaving the edges ragged and mismatched; my magic would take care of those, after all.

"It means 'orange lettuce,'" I explained. "I spent the remainder of the evening hiding from everyone and trying not to cry. The next day, I learned that three ladies in sensible black gowns had each collided with Mr. Ives. Such a pity they were all carrying glasses of Lady Bethany Chadwick's famous grape punch! They apologized profusely, of course, particularly the Countess Lieven, but after the third incident his daring new primrose silk pantaloons were so covered in purple spots he was forced to return home and change. All of London agreed that he was never quite so *vivant* again." I rose to my feet dramatically. "So you see, Cassia Whitworth is a formidable ally."

There was no hope of matching up the sleeve sides, as I hadn't paid much attention to their shape when I'd cut them, so I simply ran my stitches wherever they happened to meet up.

"What is your favorite color, Millie?" When she did not answer, I glanced up from my sewing.

She was staring at my work in horror.

I refused to allow her nerves to affect me. "Very well, then; we'll leave it lilac for now—it should look lovely on you." How pleased she'd be, when it all came together at last!

"Once I'd recovered, I insisted on asking Cassia's friend Lady Sylvia Schofield for an introduction to her modiste, and visited her at once, determined to never be the laughingstock of a ball again. And, indeed, as soon as I received my first proper dress, I knew I was equal to anything that might come my way." I beamed at her, certain that the confidence I remembered was flowing into her dress now too as I finished basting the second sleeve.

I held the sleeve up to the body of the gown, only to realize I wasn't sure where it should go, or what it attached to. "Millie, do you happen to know how sleeves are attached to bodices?"

Millie stared at me, her eyes wide with something other than wonder, I feared. She held out a hand, and I passed her a sleeve. We turned the sleeves every which way, but they never seemed to fit onto the gown the way Millie's arms fit onto her body. I decided it was time to give my talent a nudge. "Listen here," I told the gown. "You are to be an elegant shop dress for Millicent O'Leary, and no more of this nonsense."

Millie set the sleeve down very carefully on the table. "Does it do what you tell it to, then? How does it work?"

"Sometimes it helps with alterations," I said, a bit irritably. "But it isn't as though I've sewn a dress from scratch before. Perhaps it needs a few hints."

But, an hour later, it still hadn't come together. Far from cheering Millie up, the gown seemed to have depressed her— quite unreasonably, I thought, because it wasn't as though her old gown was very nice either.

"Perhaps I ought to have sewn the gown Lady Prippingforth wanted," I said. "Did you see the ghastly canary-yellow satin her husband sent her? You must agree it would be horrid on her."

Millie nodded. "Lord Prippingforth cannot see colors," she said.

"Truly? Well, you will not catch me informing Lady Prippingforth that it's possible to overdye an unsuitable color with something better! Unless she is color-blind as well?" I said.

Millie shook her head.

"We shall just have to hope someone else sews it for her, and that she wears it at every opportunity," I told her.

From somewhere down the lane, the thud of hoofbeats broke the shop's silence. Millie froze, her face white once more.

I hurried to the window. "It isn't Lady Prippingforth. . . ."

The carriage stopped, the door opened, and Mr. Harrington climbed out, crossed the lane, and knocked on our cottage's door.

"What could Mr. Harrington be doing here?" I asked Millie. She shrugged.

Well, it was not as though we were making any progress on this dress. "Quickly, then; let us close shop and go, in case Cassia needs us." I locked the door and hurried into the back, tucking the large iron key in my bandbox. "Come along, Millie, and help me get out of all this. We must hurry."

Millie helped me out of Madame's gown, corset, and wig, and even managed to get some of the powder off my face and fluff out my hair a bit, though we hadn't managed a basin in the back room yet. We'd decided that, having arrived, Madame would rarely be seen outside her shop, and I would travel back and forth as myself most days, being careful about entrances and exits. So I stepped into my mourning gown and let Millie do me up.

Moments later, Millie opened the back door. She searched the lane, and took a deep breath. Then she darted out, beckoning me to follow.

Looking up and down the lane, I decided that early spring in the country was a matter of mud, bare trees, and more mud. "Is it always like this?" I asked. "I've seen busier streets at two in the morning in London."

"I don't really know, miss," Millie replied, hardly glancing about as she rushed across to the cottage. "I've only lived in cities until now. It's muddier than Dublin, and dirtier than London, I guess." She ran up the path to our cottage door, clutching the bandbox.

I threw back my shoulders and pushed open the door. "Why, hello, Mr. Harrington—what a surprise to find you here!"

"Ah, Annis, I trust you've finished with your sketching?" Cassia asked, rising to her feet, while I stared at her. Sketching? Is that what she told him I'd been doing?

"Mr. Harrington has come to report on his findings," she said.

I stared past her at Mr. Harrington, who blended in with the wood paneling in his nondescript brown suit. Had he learned what had happened to my father? Did he know my father was a spy? Perhaps he was a spy too—but for which side? He smiled at me, a bit sadly, and I felt a lump swell in my throat. Cassia nudged me. "Do hurry, Annis—we're discussing your father's accounts, and you have a right to know what he's found."

His accounts. "Of course," I stammered. "Please allow me a moment to—to freshen up." I fled down the very short hall to my bedroom, with Millie close behind.

Once in my bedroom with the door shut, Millie recovered a bit of her usual composure. She snatched the cloth from beside my basin and scrubbed at my face, erasing all traces of powder. I turned this way and that before the mirror, trying to see if anything could be done about my bedraggled hair. "Millie, what do you think of Mr. Harrington?"

Millie took down my hair and began to brush it out, her face serious. "He reminds me of the gentleman you met in London, Mr. Smith. He has that same way of almost making you forget him, even while you're looking right at him."

"I believe Mr. Smith is the leader of most, if not all, of England's spies."

"Very likely, miss," Millie agreed, setting aside the brush. Her fingers flying, she began to braid my hair once more.

"Do you find it odd that someone with similar, er, spylike characteristics is now in this very cottage?" I asked.

Millie considered this as she picked up the hairpins. "Well, but your father was a spy as well, wasn't he, miss? So it stands to reason he'd need his man of business to be in the know, and I don't imagine you'd be in the know if you weren't part of it all, don't you think?"

As usual, Millie was quite correct. "Should I trust him?" I asked. "Or not?"

Millie poked in the last pin, tipped her head, and studied me. "I think you're ready to find out."

I got to my feet and brushed out my skirts. "Thank you, Millie."

It is difficult to make much of an entrance when one has only a few steps to travel. Really, I don't know how people manage in such small homes. I decided that quiet and grieving would be best, and slipped back into the sitting room, my eyes downcast.

Mr. Harrington got to his feet at once, even before Cassia looked up; he was certainly observant. "Thank you for joining us, Miss Annis."

Cassia's face was tired. "Mr. Harrington was just about to tell us what he's learned of your father's overseas accounts."

He nodded, taking his chair once more as I perched on the velvet tuffet. "I'm afraid the news is unexpected, even rather dire. I came as soon as I'd learned."

I have been told that financial matters are not for ladies' ears, but my aunt is no ordinary lady. There is nothing Cassia likes better than having a go at our accounts, unless perhaps it is her correspondence with educated ladies in remote places on subjects such as the comparative prices of bread, how the new roadworks are progressing, whether Lady So-and-So will actually be allowed to attend the college of mathematics or not, and what to do about it if she isn't.

Mr. Harrington cleared his throat. "I'd expected to be able to collect the remaining funds in Mr. Whitworth's overseas accounts, since, due to his frequent travels, he'd had quite a number of them. Only . . . ," he trailed off, clearing his throat again.

Since Cassia had made it her mission to educate me, I know how to write down all the household expenditures and how to add or subtract them. I know how much things cost. I know that now that my father is dead, there'll be no more money coming in, not unless I earn it myself.

I sank back on the velvet tuffet. Our cottage and single maid cost very little, and yes, I'd successfully sold my grandmother's jewels, but still . . . I'd brought no money in today. None at all. If no money was recovered—if I couldn't earn any—what little we had would run out, no matter how small our expenses.

"Provide us the numbers, please." Cassia's voice was as crisp and clear as if she were requesting another glass of lemonade. Sometimes I think her blood cannot be made of the same materials as mine.

Mr. Harrington began to read from his list.

Paris, France: thought to contain 5,632 francs
STATUS ACCORDING TO THE BANK: withdrawn the day
Mr. Whitworth left

Cairo, Egypt: thought to contain 2,899 gold coins
STATUS ACCORDING TO THE BANK: bank burned down three
months ago; funds deemed unrecoverable

Rome, Italy: thought to contain 1,345 lire
STATUS ACCORDING TO THE BANK: transferred to account in
Paris, but the Paris bank has no record of such a transaction

Barcelona, Spain: thought to contain 1,006 reales
STATUS ACCORDING TO THE BANK: unable to verify at present,
due to unstable political situation

Munich, Germany: thought to contain 983 marks
STATUS ACCORDING TO THE BANK: bank has no record of an
account ever existing under that name

Cassia got to her feet, with the determinedly pleasant face
she used when taking tea with horrid Mrs. Lowe. "I see. Thank
you very much for your diligence, Mr. Harrington. There's nothing further you can do for us, I'm afraid—though please do let us
know if the Barcelona bank provides any update."

I stood as well, full of new desperation. "Mr. Harrington—
surely you must know this could not be—"

"Annis, there is nothing further he can do," Cassia broke in.

I bit my lip. All of these losses at once could not be coincidence. There must be someone he could ask about what had
really happened to my father's money. Unless he was working
against my father, and these losses were his doing?

"Mr. Harrington, you have been a model of courtesy during
this difficult time," Cassia said, glaring at me. "But we cannot
continue to inconvenience you so, particularly when we are not
able to pay you for your services."

"My apologies, Mr. Harrington," I said, bowing my head.

"None needed," he said softly. And when I looked up into

his eyes, they were so warm, so kind, that I wanted to cry. Oh, I wanted to trust him, but how could I?

"Was that all, Mr. Harrington?" said my aunt, all business.

He cleared his throat. "You are planning to remain in Flittingsworth for the present, then?"

"For now," Cassia replied.

"Then perhaps—if it is not objectionable—perhaps I could escort you to Mrs. Spry's ball this Thursday? She is certain to invite you, once she learns you have moved here."

Cassia raised an eyebrow, as only she can do.

"I simply wondered if Miss—if you ladies might enjoy the distraction," he hurried to say. "It is only a country ball—no grand London affair, and no one will be surprised if you attend but do not dance while you are in mourning. I thought perhaps you might like an introduction to your neighbors?" He saw my hesitation, I'm sure of it. "In London, I know it would not be quite the thing to invite a solicitor—but here in the country, it is common enough," he said, a little stiffly.

But that was not why I hesitated. I might not trust Mr. Harrington, but could I afford to miss an opportunity to see more of him, and to try to discover why he'd lied to us about my father's travel plans? "We should love it if you would escort us," I said, smiling at him. "Thank you so much for thinking of it, Mr. Harrington. You've been nothing but kindness."

Cassia gave me a look, but Mr. Harrington did not see, and I knew better than to allow her to ruin my plans.

Mr. Harrington smiled. "It has been my pleasure," he said. "I've had word that your father's trunk has just arrived in Chatham. I'm off to fetch it now, and I hope to deliver it to you by morning."

"Nonsense," Cassia said firmly. "If you're to go now, we shall accompany you."

Mr. Harrington blinked. "It has only just come by sea. . . ."

"Precisely." Cassia nodded. "We shall come with you to fetch it, and then you'll have nothing further to do for us. It is the most efficient way, I am sure."

Interesting. It seemed Cassia did not trust Mr. Harrington either.

Chapter Thirteen

IN WHICH INFORMATION IS SHARED, AND A TRUNK IS DELIVERED

Nothing except a battle lost
can be half as melancholy as a battle won.
—Arthur Wellesley, First Duke of Wellington

*W*hether it was the most efficient way or not, it was Cassia's way, and though I slumped and Mr. Harrington blinked and Millie stared, we were all packed into the carriage before we knew it (for, as Cassia said, it was not so very far, and why waste the limited daylight arguing?).

And, indeed, it was not very far, or at least it did not seem so once I had accidentally fallen asleep.

Chatham had nothing of note but a large dockyard, with boats in various stages of assembly, and docks where boats waited, like carriages lined up at balls. These, Mr. Harrington explained, were not the ships that traveled overseas, as those required deeper water, but small boats that the crew took to reach the shore. I nodded, but saw no reason to pay any real attention.

"I assume you'll want to speak with Jacky yourself, Miss

Whitworth, as Faber Shipping Worldwide retrieved the cargo?" Mr. Harrington asked Cassia.

"Of course," she replied as he hurried to help her down from the carriage.

My eye was caught by a draper's shop, and I wondered how many of us could possibly be needed to supervise the transfer of a single trunk, even if it was my father's. Surely my presence would not be missed. . . .

So I begged Cassia to let me look inside with Millie while she and Mr. Harrington made the arrangements for the trunk. She frowned, reminding me that persons in our situation did not need more gowns, and I nodded. But then she softened and agreed.

It took no more than a moment's survey to see that the shop was full of shoddily made cloth, with really nothing of interest, aside from perhaps a bolt of plain English poplin. But it was a rather drab dove gray, so I put it back for someone else to discover. When would Cassia finish? I peered out the small shop window, but there was no sign of her yet.

"Ah, you'll be looking for that fine young captain, then, a pretty young lady like you," the shopkeeper said, winking at me.

"I beg your pardon?" I said stiffly.

She laughed. "Oh, there's no need to climb on up your high horse, dearie—I was young once too, if you can believe it! There's no harm in a bit of a chat with a handsome gentleman who's recently been promoted, so long as your maid is with you. And the *Aguilucho* is quite a ship for such a young man."

I stared at her. "The *Aguilucho*?" Where had I heard that name before?

The shopkeeper chuckled. "You'll not get far with a

captain without knowing the name of his treasured new ship, dearie! He's only just been made captain, after the old captain drowned."

Of course; Mrs. Lightburne's letter. Captain John Fitzhugh of the *Aguilucho* had drowned. What had the gossip column said about someone's promotion? *Ladies, guard your daughters, for the newly promoted Cptn. W.J.'s Aguilucho has sailed into The Downs. He is said to wear a well-fitted coat indeed, and to have a ready smile for a well-heeled young miss, and has been seen in drawing rooms near Chatham.*

I made my eyes wide and round, the perfect young miss desperate for the sight of a fine young gentleman. "Please, ma'am— what else can you tell me about the captain and his ship?"

Smiling, the shopkeeper leaned forward. "Captain William Johnson is lucky to have that ship, young as he is. He's just back from France, and he'll be sailing on soon, most likely by way of Spain, they say." She lowered her voice to a whisper. "He'll be headed back to his ship any minute now, but if you wait out there on the docks, you might manage to meet him."

"Oh, thank you, ma'am!" I breathed, still wide-eyed. "Come, Millie—we must hurry!"

Once outside, I found a place on the dock where I could see anyone who passed, and settled into a picturesque pose, staring out at the tall ships as though transfixed.

It was not long before a fine young captain in a nicely cut coat came down the dock, stopping to greet me. "A pity you can hardly see the ships themselves, for a finer sight you'll never see than the *Aguilucho* in full sail!"

I blinked. "Oh! Then you must be—are you the new captain?" I was forced to agree with the gossip column—his coat did indeed fit rather well. But, of course, that was not why I'd come to speak with him.

"Aye, miss," he said, smiling. "I've been given command, may the former captain rest in peace."

Carefully I inspected his boots, but they bore no resemblance to the pair worn by that thief in London. Still, something made me cautious. "Were you in France long?"

He laughed. "You are the best-informed of all the young ladies I've met this week! I was there but a day, to take command upon my promotion, but the *Aguilucho* was there longer. We set sail for Spain in the morning, so I must attend to some business, I'm afraid. Enjoy the view!"

He'd know nothing of Captain Fitzhugh, then; how disappointing. "Well, I wish you a very nice sail," I said.

He bowed, and continued down the dock.

"How do you know so much of the *Aguilucho?*" a deep voice said in French, from below the dock.

I walked over to the edge, with Millie close beside me. There was a dark-brown man sitting in a boat tied to the pier; West Indian, perhaps, or African.

I glanced around quickly; there was no one else in sight. "I heard that the former captain—how do you say it—ah, yes! *Il est mort.* He drowned."

He snorted. "Captain Fitzhugh could swim like a fish," he said. "He never drowned, unless someone made him drown."

"*Quelle horreur!*" I said. So Cptn. J.F. was indeed murdered. "Have you told the new captain?"

He shrugged. "Who paid his commission, and made him captain now?" he asked. He shook his head slowly. "Too many mysteries. I have no wish to join the dead captain in the deep."

"Do you serve on the *Aguilucho?*" Millie asked in French. (Cassia would say hers was better than mine. I wondered how she'd learned to speak it.)

"Aye, miss. I am Isaac Baptiste, midshipman these many years."

She who hesitates is lost or, at the very least, loses her chance to ask questions. I made up my mind. "Did you ever meet a Mr. Whitworth, in France?"

His eyes were dark and sharp as he studied me. "And why might you wonder that, miss?"

I swallowed. "He was my father. He died suddenly—just after your captain died."

"Ah." He looked over the nearby boats, and waited until another small boat rowed farther out to sea. "I never met your father. Captain Fitzhugh went to see him, to tell him something I had learned. The next morning, the captain was dead."

"What did you learn?" I whispered.

Mr. Baptiste shook his head. "Two men are dead already. Why will you not be the next?"

I straightened. "Because I can pass along your information to those in a position to do something about it." I was proud that my voice did not quaver. "Besides, who would assume I could possibly know anything of importance?"

He tipped his head and studied me for a long moment.

"I have a right to know why my father died," I said quietly, ignoring the stinging in my eyes. "How can I rest, with no way to avenge him?"

"And you will keep asking questions, until the wrong person hears, if I do not tell you." Mr. Baptiste shook his head. "Very well. Remember this, and tell only those you can trust: there is another East India Company ship, the *Corbeau.*"

I stiffened. *Reroute Corbeau away from S.H.*

"Yes. I have heard of it."

His voice grew softer still. "We were docked in Calais near each other. I rowed into town to attend church one evening, and overheard their first mate, a Mr. Kent, or so he calls himself, across the water. I do not think he saw me." He scowled. "He agreed to pick up a certain passenger from Saint Helena, for a price. A large price."

"Bonaparte," I whispered, a shiver going down my spine. France's emperor had easily escaped from the island of Elba and led his armies into war all over again. Thanks to the Duke of Wellington and the desperate Battle of Waterloo, Napoléon was captured once more and imprisoned on Saint Helena, far from France and England. But if he were to break free again—if a traitor was hired to bring him back to France—what could stop him from invading England? I shuddered. "Who offered him that price?"

Mr. Baptiste shook his head. "I could not see the other man, and I could not make out his words. I do not think I know his voice, but I could not say for certain. But the first mate was speaking French."

I had known that my father's work was important. But I had not thought I would be trying to stop England's greatest enemy in his place. "Could it work?" I asked. "Surely one cannot just row up to Bonaparte's prison and take him out for a sea jaunt?"

"It could be done," Mr. Baptiste said. "The ship must stop for supplies, and Saint Helena is the only East India Company port in those waters. Two sailors go ashore for supplies. One is fed to the fishes; Napoléon wears his clothes and takes his place—it could be done."

I studied him closely. Could I trust him? "But—you are French?"

Curling his lip, Mr. Baptiste spat into the sea. "No. I am

Haitian. Napoléon broke his word to my general, General Louverture, and betrayed him," he said, and his voice was flat and hard. "Napoléon deserves the same death: that of a hole in the ground, alone. But if I cannot give him that, I will keep him from ever leaving that rock." He looked out to sea once more. "As my general said, 'You have cut down only the trunk of the tree of liberty. It will spring up again from the roots, for they are numerous and deep.'"

Throwing out my arms, I cried, "'Thou hast left behind / Powers that will work for thee; air, earth, and skies; / There's not a breathing of the common wind / That will forget thee; thou hast great allies.'"

I saw him cover a smile, and stopped my proclaiming at once. "It seems Wordsworth was quite right about General Louverture's friends, if they are all like you," I said. "Oh, but I am not certain how to say it all in French. . . ."

"I understood, Miss Whitworth," he said in English.

"It is a poem," I explained to Millie. "About Toussaint-Louverture, the Haitian general who was captured by Napoléon. Miss Baillie copied it out and sent it to Cassia after they had an argument about lonely clouds and daffodils not being relevant to economics, nor useful." Then I hesitated. "Mr. Baptiste, may I trust that you are for England in this matter?"

He laughed bitterly. "France, England—they are all the same to me," he said. "But you may trust that I am on the side against Bonaparte, the man with no honor."

I thought of my father, dead from a rumor of freedom for Bonaparte, and nodded. "I suppose that will do. Thank you."

But Mr. Baptiste had turned his face seaward and was listening to the wind now. "It would be better if you were not speaking with me when the captain returns."

"Of course," I said, as though this were all quite an everyday matter. "Good evening, Mr. Baptiste. Millie, let us examine that poplin once more."

By the time Cassia and Mr. Harrington returned, I had been forced to examine several low-quality printed muslins as well, but my mind was full of Bonaparte, moonless nights, and dark waters.

"We really must hurry," Cassia said, eyeing the fading light, as though I were the one who'd kept them waiting. But I bit my tongue and said nothing.

I would hardly have imagined it possible, with my mind buzzing so, but I must have dozed off once more as we traveled home. (I do hope I did not drool on the carriage robe.) Before I knew it, Cassia was shaking me awake as Mr. Harrington and the driver hauled my father's trunk inside.

"That will do nicely," Cassia said. "Thank you very much, Mr. Harrington. I'm sure you must be on your way now." She locked the door behind him, and turned to me. "Annis, you're obviously exhausted. Millie, would you help her to bed?"

I met Cassia's eye squarely. "I will not go to bed just yet. I have a right to his things too." I was proud that my voice hardly quavered.

She dropped her gaze and nodded. "I suppose so." She knelt down in front of the trunk, and opened the latch.

It had been packed in a hurry. But that was not what made me gasp.

"Oh, miss," Millie breathed.

Every stitch of clothing in the trunk had been slashed into shreds, as though with a very sharp knife. Cassia gripped my arm tightly as I sank down beside her. My hands reached out, turning over the fine fabrics. His cravats, in ribbons. The jacket he'd worn when I'd followed him to the War Office, destroyed. Even the handkerchiefs I'd sewn for him, going back to the years when I could hardly sew a straight stitch, slashed and scattered everywhere, with holes ripped through as though besieged by rampaging battle-moths. Slowly I picked up the shredded cloth, setting each handkerchief into a stack on the floor beside the trunk. He'd kept every single one I'd ever sent; even through the slashes I recognized them.

When I reached the last few, with the embroidery I'd wished so hard could keep him safe, I could not help it; I clutched the torn linen, and I wept.

Chapter Fourteen

A NOTE; A HIDING PLACE;
A DECIDED LACK OF INVITATIONS; AND A PLAN

To understand the things that are at our door is the
best preparation for understanding
those that lie beyond.

—Hypatia (that Greek lady mathematician Cassia is always raving
about; she was not clever enough to keep herself alive, I note)

I awoke the next morning with the pale sun streaming in my
window, and sat up with a gasp, jolted awake from a dream full of
dark waters filled with ships. I clutched my pillow until my heart
slowed once more.

Should I tell Cassia what I'd learned? But what could she
do about it? Better to use my own connections, tenuous though
they were. I slid my stocking feet into the slippers next to my bed,
wrapped myself in my dressing gown, and went to my dressing
table. Hurriedly I penned a note.

Do not let the Corbeau *sail to Saint Helena. This is a
matter of national security. Captain John Fitzhugh died of this
knowledge, and so did Mr. Stephen Whitworth. May they rest in
peace now.*

Since I did not believe that it would encourage Mr. Smith to take any more heed if he knew I had authored it, I did not sign it.

Folding it, I addressed it to Mr. Smith, then hurried into the sitting room. I was surprised to find Cassia absent. Quickly I heated and plopped a blob of sealing wax on the closure, and (since I had none of my own) stamped it with her seal. It wasn't as though Mr. Smith would recognize it, after all.

I jumped as Millie came in from the kitchen. "Miss Whitworth left at dawn, miss; she asked me to tell you she'd be out today."

I reminded myself how unlikely it was for any men with naval boots to be lurking about Flittingsworth; Cassia would be safe enough, wherever she was. Millie set the tea tray on the table, and I handed her the note. "Please make certain this travels in today's post. It is regarding yesterday's matter of importance."

Millie slipped the note into her pocket. "I must run to catch it, then, miss. I'll be back as soon as I can."

She was already flying out the door as I blinked at the mantel clock. How could it be so late?

And where was my father's trunk?

Gulping my tea, I hurried down the short hallway to Cassia's room. As always, it was as neat as though no one lived there, though she moved a book from one stack to another from time to time.

My father's trunk had been placed in the corner. I knelt on the cold stone in front of it, and opened it. All his clothes were still there, all still slashed and shredded.

I took a deep breath in, a deep breath out, letting my cheek rest on the torn, folded clothes. Somehow, this trunk full of clothes no longer worth mending was more final to me than any grave site. My father was dead. He had died from the information he'd learned in his work. I had uncovered the message, discovered its meaning, and sent it to Mr. Smith; that was all I could do. Now it was time to get to my feet, dress myself, and be off to earn our new fortunes with glamours for fashionable ladies, if not for spies.

But I stayed there, breathing in that last faint hint of lavender and boot oil, until Millie came back from the inn.

"It's done, miss," she said quietly, offering me her hand.

Taking it, I climbed to my feet, closing the trunk lid quietly. "Thank you." If Mr. Smith ignored my message, let it be on his head when Bonaparte escaped; not my father's, nor mine.

I let her lead me into my room, obeying silently as she helped me dress and did my hair. It was so cold, these days. I let my eyes rest on the stack of handkerchiefs, noticing how the linen had turned various subtle shades of almost-white over the years: palest blue, green, yellow, violet, as though laundered with garments whose dye had not quite set. They reminded me of that dream, those ships, the dark waters—and the man with naval boots who'd stolen my handkerchief. I shivered. The price of freeing Bonaparte from Saint Helena would be very high indeed; that was no ordinary naval officer. Were we safe from him here? "Millie, if you wanted to hide something where no one would look, where would you put it?"

"Behind the loose cobble in the bottom right of the kitchen hearth," she said promptly. "Unless it was someone who'd worked here looking for it; I'd expect they'd already know about that."

I gathered the handkerchiefs, and added the two I'd kept in my room since London. "Would these fit, do you think?"

Millie rolled them up, studied them, and nodded. "I'll wrap them in a bit of burlap so they don't get covered in soot."

I followed her into the kitchen. She was right; there was a loose cobble, the soot masking the gap in the mortar. When she lifted it, the space inside held only a tiny bag, which she tucked into a corner as she added the burlap-wrapped handkerchiefs.

I thought of my trunk full of gowns I could not even wear, all Cassia's books, even my father's slashed clothes, and then Millie's one worn dress and tiny bag, smaller even than my reticule. I had lost my father, my mother, but so had she, and she had no Aunt Cassia.

"What will you sew for the ball, do you think?" she asked.

I blinked. "The ball?"

She nodded. "You're to go with Mr. Harrington, tomorrow night?"

I stared at her in horror. Somehow, it was already Wednesday, and I'd forgotten all about the ball. "We must hurry!"

Millie followed as I raced down the hallway toward Cassia's room and pulled open her trunk. I chose the gown I'd seen her wear least, and pulled it out. As I did, I noticed the cravats from my father's document case folded underneath. I handed Cassia's gown to Millie to tuck into a bandbox. I stuffed the cravats into another bandbox, along with one of my old ball gowns. Cassia had his trunk; surely I could keep a few of his things too.

Madame Martine was late to open that morning. So many things had happened since I'd left the shop that it was a shock to find the patchwork mess of Millie's shop dress still on the dress form.

"Set that to the side for now, Millie," I said, pulling my old ball gown from my bandbox and shaking it out. "Put this gown on the dress form instead."

She hurried to obey, and I studied the result.

It was a pity to ruin the blue-figured muslin gown, but since my magic transformed gowns more easily than fabric, it must be sacrificed. I could not stop the *Corbeau* from picking up its passenger on my own. I could not force Mr. Smith to listen to me, or find my father's killer, or recover his money. But I could learn to use my talent properly. I would find a way to earn our fortune, no matter what it took.

The sprigged-violet print was very pretty, but pretty wasn't enough to help me now. Grimly, I picked up a hank of black silk and threaded my needle, advancing slowly on the dress form. If we were to survive here, someone must wear a gown that would make all of Flittingsworth rush to order from Madame Martine. First, I would make it black.

I made my first stitch through the front of the bodice, insisting with the full force of my mind that this gown really must be black. Slowly I pulled the thread along the stitch.

Nothing happened.

I made the next stitch, and the next. I would show my aunt that I could succeed, and to do it, this gown must be black.

Yet it was not.

Breathing deeply, I pushed the needle through once more. I let the grief I'd felt at the kindness in Mr. Harrington's eyes fill me, let myself remember that I was in mourning for my father, and therefore, this gown must be black.

But it wasn't.

I paused, the needle clutched tight in my fingers, remembering the way the black had flooded my shawl on that dark day, before the visit to the War Office. I looked straight at the stubborn gown, and in my mind's eye I saw the same black flood this gown, saw it change in my vision, the violets gone, the style cleaner-cut, undoubtedly from London, if not from Paris itself. I took another stitch, and saw myself standing confidently in a crowded ballroom, surrounded by ladies who were sneaking glimpses of my gown.

And this time, this time I felt the fabric tug and change. The black flowed out from the tiny hole around my needle, flooding through the cloth, a faint rustling filling the silent room. I made the next stitch.

And as I pictured the new gown in my mind—gathered and tucked sleeves, and a wider, more elegant neckline, certainly—I distilled all my thoughts into the longing I felt: that this gown would reinvent my life. This gown would allow me to save my aunt from employment with horrid young persons who would never give her a moment of peace for her letters. With this gown, I'd begin to find the truth behind Mr. Harrington's lies. Somehow, even the War Office's spies would learn about the young lady who wore this gown.

Remembering the War Office's long, twisting hallways, the hints of movement just out of sight, I shivered.

But what use was magic if it couldn't help me? I imagined myself quite safe in the middle of the ballroom, so surrounded by admiring young ladies that no man with naval boots could possibly come near me.

I pulled the thread through. The muslin whispered, then sighed like silk, then was silk, rustling as the fibers changed in some unknowable, magical way. I passed the needle through the fabric again, and pulled the thread, slow as a held breath, watching the bodice tighten and change to a more fashionable height as I relaxed, imagining the eyes of every lady in the ballroom, all longing to be in command of this dress, all whispering the name of the talented modiste who'd sewn my gown.

As I stitched my way farther down the dress, I lost track of Millie putting things in their places, of the sunlight falling through the small windows, flowing across the shop as the hours wore on. I didn't notice that no one had come in, didn't worry where Cassia might be. I stitched the fabric of the skirt until it all turned black, until it all turned to silk. I stitched the hem until anyone who saw it would know how it would flare out in the turn of a waltz, until no one could doubt my talent.

A shadow passed through the light, and I looked up. "What was that?"

Millie was staring at the tiny front window. Rose light streamed through; it was nearly twilight. "Someone was looking in, madame."

"A customer?" I asked.

But she shook her head. "A man, I think—I couldn't see his face." She was trembling.

I stood slowly and went to stare out the window. I could see the empty lane in front of the shop quite clearly through the wavy glass. "Whoever it was, they're gone now. Most likely just some curious footman, hoping to see a bit of magic." My back ached, my head pounded, and I felt far more tired than I could ever imagine. Was it the magic running through me, I wondered, that made me feel as though I'd been dancing for hours and hours? Or did every modiste feel this tired at the end of her day?

Millie nodded, but I knew she didn't believe me.

Ah well. At least the sleeves were properly puckered and the fichu was artfully tucked. I asked Millie to lay it aside and bade her put Cassia's old cream dress with the ink-stained elbow on the form for tomorrow.

As we crossed the lane, Millie checked every shadow, I noticed. When would I have time to finish her gown? Was it even salvageable?

We hurried inside, only to be faced at once with another problem. Flittingsworth, it appeared, was not only unaware of Madame Martine's presence; it did not even know that Miss Whitworth and her niece had come to town. Mrs. Spry had not invited us to her ball.

"We can't simply arrive without an invitation!" Cassia put her pen down and folded her arms. "You must write at once to Mr. Harrington and tell him we're unable to attend. It isn't as though we have time for such things anyway, even if they were seemly, which they are most likely not while we are in mourning!"

"As though Mr. Harrington would invite us to unseemly goings-on!" I began to pace, winding around tables, chairs, and piles and piles of books, unable to take so much as one long stride in the tiny sitting room. "It isn't a pleasure jaunt; it's a piece of very savvy business. Madame Martine is certain to have loads of orders after we've shown off our new gowns at a Flittingsworth ball."

Cassia sighed, as though she were the one who required patience. "We have tried it your way, Annis. I cannot make money appear when there is none, and we must have money to continue— you know we were counting on your father's overseas accounts to fund your endeavor. We must find employment, and quickly."

"My shop has only just opened!" I cried. "I am a very fancy modiste, and I will make us more money than we possibly could make as companions. There is no way for a lady to earn her way out of such employment—you taught me that. Once you are destitute, the only genteel way out is marriage. Barring any such offers at present—unless you are writing to suitors as well as to your lady friends?—we must find another way. And we have! What, then, could possibly be the problem?"

Cassia took a very slow, very deep breath, but oddly it was Millie who answered. "Begging your pardons, but when will I be paid?"

I blinked, and looked at Cassia.

Who looked very, very tired.

"It's just that, you see, I have a sister—my younger sister, Betty—and last I heard, she isn't very happy where she is." Millie bit her lip and looked away.

"We'll make certain you're paid, Millicent," Cassia said gently.

∞)(∞

I found myself staring into the fire, still sitting there long after Cassia had kissed my forehead and gone to her room.

I looked out the window, into the black country sky, so full of stars, and so empty of buildings. I had the talent. I knew it was our only way back to a life we'd want to live. Somehow, I must make Cassia see that too.

What if I sewed a gown for Cassia that overcame her own objections? One she'd want to wear enough to attend the ball?

Could I manage to sew such a gown? I bit my lip. It had not been easy to control my magic, even on my own gown, with my own vision. What could I imagine that Cassia would actually want to wear? And even if I could imagine it, could I sew it?

But if I did not have enough talent to manage this, I was already sunk, and might as well become a governess. The only thing left was to try.

Chapter Fifteen

CHARITY; OR, AN INSULT TO THE EYE

It is justice, not charity, that is wanting in the world.
—A *VINDICATION OF THE RIGHTS OF WOMAN*, by Mary Wollstonecraft

I awoke early the next morning, for the sun had made another chilly appearance, and every bird in England was singing in the hedgerow outside my window. I dressed quickly as Miss Annis, pleased with how much I could do for myself, and hurried into the sitting room, full of plans once more. "I know just what we must do," I announced. "We shall temporarily invest your postage money in my dressmaking."

I have never before seen my aunt speechless.

"Oh, you can still accept the letters that come to you, and even write your replies, never fear—all you must do is wait to post them until we've received payment for a few of my gowns. Surely no one will write back until they've received your reply? You must spend pounds and pounds receiving all of those letters you get! There now, see! You always said you could teach me economy, if only I applied myself." I beamed, happy to have proven myself so apt.

Before Cassia could reply, there was a knock at the door. I glanced to make certain my gown was straight, and waited for Millie to answer it. There were no bellpulls in this four-room cottage, but surely she must have heard it, wherever she was?

Cassia rose to her feet and answered it herself, letting in a plain young woman in a walking dress with a very no-nonsense cut. "Good morning, Miss . . . ?"

"Miss Mary Fielde, and you must be Miss Whitworth, and Miss Annis. So nice to meet you." The young woman bustled into the sitting room, pausing to pass her calling card to Cassia.

Her bonnet was probably past saving, I decided as I stepped forward to greet our guest. But once that was replaced, I could advise Miss Fielde to choose a gown that suited her forthright face, instead of emphasizing her square chin. "How very nice to meet you," I said. "We are newly come to town, as you must have heard, and I have been wondering about the modiste down the lane—rumor has it she can sew glamours?" I opened the basket Miss Fielde handed me, and stopped. This was no gift amongst new friends. This was charity, in all its coarse brown bread and homespun cloth, nothing pleasant, nothing nice.

Cassia saw my face. She said nothing.

Miss Fielde saw it too. "I've formed a society to help those in need, you see—"

"Oh, wonderful!" I shoved the basket back at her with a smile that felt as though my face might crack. "My aunt and I are very concerned about the welfare of those less fortunate. You must tell us about it someday, and perhaps we can be of assistance."

Miss Fielde took the basket, her smile faltering. "But—I was led to believe—"

"Oh, I might spend more time than you do on my appearance,

but that doesn't mean I have no thought for others!" I gave a little laugh, though it didn't sound terribly convincing. "Now, tell me: who will we meet at Mrs. Spry's ball? I have never lived anywhere but London, so I have no idea what a country ball is like!"

"I'm sure you'll find it very tame after London," Miss Fielde said, flushing.

"Indeed, it will have to be, since we are in mourning," I agreed. "But even a dull ball is better than no ball at all, don't you think? It gives one a chance to chat with one's friends about fashion, or charitable works, or whatever is on one's mind."

Miss Fielde put her chin up. "I find it difficult to discuss my life's work amidst the din and commotion of all that music and dancing."

I tipped my head, considering. "Do you? Perhaps it isn't your true life's work, then, after all, if it can be interrupted so easily."

I hadn't seen anyone flush so deeply red since Miss Highsmith stepped on the front of her dress during the quadrille and tore the front panel right out. "Excuse me, Miss Annis, but I have several more homes to visit this morning. If you are quite certain—"

"Oh, quite! Just let us know how we may help," I said, leading her toward the door.

"Our thanks, Miss Fielde, and a pleasure to meet you," Cassia said quietly.

Miss Fielde nodded, still red above her unflattering collar, and left quickly.

Cassia folded her arms and glared at me. "That was not kind."

I fairly boiled with the injustice of it. "*I* was not kind! That is the outside of enough, when she dares come here and throw charity in our faces before we've even met! She thought we were poor!"

"We are poor," Cassia said levelly. "We will continue to be poor for quite some time, so you may as well accustom yourself to it. I wish that your father had been better with money—"

"He was not foolish with money!" I said, angry, or crying, or both at once—I no longer cared. "Someone probably killed him and stole all his money, and no one will ever even bother to tell us why, or figure out who, because we are merely the people who must live with the aftermath of it all!" I stormed past Cassia, yanking the front door open. "And her bonnet was an insult to the eye!" I shouted, and slammed the door behind me.

⟿)(⟾

The icy wind cut right through my irritation, leaving me frustrated and sad. I didn't want to be poor any longer, at the mercy of ladies with charity. I didn't want to bow my head and become a governess just because my aunt said I must. I missed ices at Gunter's, walks in the park with my friends, bustling streets of ladies and maids buying gloves, hats, slippers, stockings, lengths of cloth, and everything else one could imagine. Here, there was not even a draper's where one could buy cloth! No wonder Miss Spencer's patisserie was such a success, for what was there to occupy one's time but eating pastries and drinking tea? Not that I had money or time for that either.

I missed my own modiste, Mlle Fillioure, who took each of my designs as a personal challenge. I missed wearing colors that looked well on me, and advising other ladies what would suit them best. I missed musicales and dancing, evenings with Cassia where we had not a single argument, even the wretched ratafia everyone drank at Almack's. I missed wondering when my father would next come to London, whether I saw him during dinner or only at a ball. Everything I knew was gone, leaving me on a muddy country lane with the sun rising unseen behind the clouds, hoping it would all work out somehow.

But I had no time to waste on tears now. I must sew Cassia's gown. There were no other options left.

Millie followed me across the street and into my shop, gently taking the bandbox from my hands and helping me transform myself back into a widowed old shopkeeper.

The sight of Cassia's dowdy gown on the dress form brought me back from my wallowing. Why had I ever allowed her to wear it? I loved my aunt too much to let her be seen in such a gown. I examined it in the morning's chilly light, and wondered where to begin.

It was fusty; that must be corrected. It was stained, dusty, and crumpled; that would not do. But above all, it was simply wrong for my aunt. She was crisp and clear; this gown wobbled with tired ruffles. She was precise and forthright; this gown muddled its lines in puckering seams. Once, when a carriage had overturned almost on top of us, Cassia had had the situation in hand within moments: the footmen obeyed her instinctively, the horses hadn't dared rear, the throngs of passersby made way for her, and she'd stanched bloody wounds with her own hands, completely ruining her best gloves in the process. This gown couldn't command a sitting room, let alone a crowded London street.

What would Cassia want instead? I wrinkled my nose. Why had Cassia never complained about her horrid gowns, or ordered different, better ones?

Two hours later, I had turned Cassia's seventh-best gown into plain black sarcenet, without a ruffle to be found. It was not quite all wrong, but it was hardly inspiring. When the bell tinkled and the door flew open, I jumped in front of the dress form in a most un-Madame-like manner.

Thankfully, it was not my aunt, nor a prospective customer, but Miss Spencer. I immediately examined the lines of her gown. How did she manage to look not at all like a young miss, yet not like a dowager either? Was it the lack of gathers in her upper sleeve, perhaps? The decorative running stitch along her waistband? Then I realized Miss Spencer was staring at me too.

Immediately I straightened my neck and looked down my nose. "*Bonjour,* Miss Spencer. A pleasure to see you again," I said in my best Madame voice.

"You know, it boggles the mind to think that Miss Annis is in there somewhere," Miss Spencer said to Millie, still staring at me.

Millie smiled. "I did my very best," she said modestly.

I bit my tongue on my retort. Millie might not have sewn my gown, but she had done quite a lot to turn me into Madame Martine, and she should be allowed to take pride in her work. "Indeed you did," I allowed, still in Madame's French-influenced tone, nodding my head toward her.

Unfortunately, this allowed Miss Spencer to crane her neck and catch sight of the gown.

"Who could possibly have ordered that?" she asked.

I stepped aside and let her look. "It is for my aunt to wear to Mrs. Spry's ball. Only, it is not quite right."

Miss Spencer snorted (managing to do it quite elegantly, I noted). "Your aunt is hardly some prim old chaperone, even if she has been playing that role since she was your age. Hasn't she earned something better from you?"

I wrinkled my nose. "But what would she prefer?"

Miss Spencer shrugged. "You, madame, are the expert. Or you had better become one. It is not merely young ladies who buy gowns, you know."

I looked down at my boots. And then I remembered that I had designed the very gown I was wearing—which was certainly not for a young lady, nor for just any older woman either. I could do this. I must find a way.

I folded my arms to match hers, and returned her look. "Miss Spencer, what do you look for in a gown?"

Miss Spencer blinked. "Oh, I am not here to order—I only stopped by—"

"No, no," I interrupted, waving her objections aside. "In general, I meant. When you choose a new gown, how do you want Flittingsworth to see you, if not the world?"

"What an interesting question." Miss Spencer gave it some thought. "Not black, and no lace caps; I don't want to dress like some old dowager bat—no offense intended," she said quickly.

I inclined my head graciously. "None taken," I assured her. "What else?"

Miss Spencer stared out the window. "I've had my fill of pale muslins and sprigged flowers and docile, polite small talk," she said. "I'm done with all that. What I want now is a sense of style, a sense of flair—I want . . ." She hesitated. "It's silly, I suppose, but perhaps you might understand by now? I would like the ladies of Flittingsworth to envy my independence and the way I have fashioned my way in the world, even if they would shudder to live it themselves."

I nodded slowly. "When I first met you in London, I knew I should infinitely prefer to be a shopkeeper than a governess, if it meant I could be like you."

Miss Spencer beamed. "Perhaps that is what I look for in a gown."

And what would my aunt want the ladies of Flittingsworth to see in her? Not just an unexceptional chaperone, or an old dowager bat. Not even merely a fashionable lady of London. I closed my eyes. When I pictured my aunt, I always saw her at her desk, with her beloved ledger, or those hundreds of letters she was always writing. Must I embroider quills all over her gown? But no: anyone could write a letter. Few ladies, indeed, discussed mathematics, economics, and the like the way my aunt did.

Slowly I opened my eyes. "I can see it now," I told Miss Spencer. Then I turned back to the gown. "Quickly, my needle, Millicent."

I have no notion how long Miss Spencer stayed, or if she saw the way my magic drew the weave of the gown into something that could pass through the most erudite salons of Europe, each French knot as meticulous as a bead on an abacus, each line as graceful as an equation.

I saw Cassia in my mind's eye, the center of a crowded room, all in attendance impressed with how intelligent she was, as well as how elegant. She was nodding knowledgeably over a lady's accounts; giving a gentleman a pointed look that stopped him in his tracks and sent him back the way he came; telling a young miss that she really must carry a spare handkerchief at all times. I saw Cassia, reaching out to take this gown from my hands, her face filled with wonder and awe.

I hesitated. Could it possibly work? But she who hesitates is lost, I reminded myself; better to choose a path and forge ahead.

At last, I clipped the final thread, handed the scissors to Millie, and stepped back to examine the full effect. The sunlight was already fading, but Millie held a lantern so that I could see.

The gown was most unsuitable for a young girl: too definite, too strong, no hint of coyness. Yet it skimmed over the body as French gowns did, and would reveal more of my aunt's rather good figure than she was accustomed to. What would Cassia think of it?

The church bells began to chime the hour, and Millie glanced out at the darkening lane and back at me. "We must run," she said, snatching the gown from the dress form. "Mr. Harrington will arrive after dusk, and Miss Whitworth will send him away if you are not there."

Chapter Sixteen

IN WHICH MILLICENT O'LEARY
IS A WONDER

Time is everything; five minutes make the difference
between victory and defeat. —Admiral Horatio Lord Nelson

I blinked at her, so tired I could hardly see.

"You must hurry," Millie insisted, slowly and clearly.

So I tossed Madame's wig on the little table in the shop's back room and tore off her gown, raising my arms as Millie threw Annis's gown over my head. I'd barely gotten it hooked when she grabbed my hand and half pulled me out the shop's back door, carrying Cassia's gown.

"You must run now, miss, or your aunt will send him away," Millie cried. So we ran.

Cassia leapt to her feet as we burst into the cottage, looking about wildly, as though she expected half of Napoléon's army at our heels. "What is the matter?" she demanded.

I tried to catch my breath, but I had never been much for athletics, and although the cold air had cleared my head, it had not done much for my lungs. "You must put this on, Aunt Cassia. Please—I shall explain as soon as I am dressed as well—but really, you must!" I snatched the gown from Millie's hands and thrust it toward my aunt, who reached out automatically to take it.

Then I ran for my room. "Millie, please help Miss Whitworth!" I called back, and shut the door behind me.

The water in the washbasin was so cold I was surprised it hadn't iced over, but I scrubbed at my face anyway. It would not do to leave any trace of who I'd just been, not even a touch of powder in my hair, for Mr. Harrington was the sort who noticed things.

I heard Cassia's voice rising, though I couldn't make out her words, and I hurried faster. Off came my usual mourning dress. On went the new ball gown. But here there was a dilemma, for I had not thought to provide myself with a gown whose buttons I could reach. I bent and contorted, strained and writhed, but still the gown flapped open over my upper back. Did I dare leave my room in such a state, when Mr. Harrington might arrive at any moment?

My dilemma was solved when my aunt burst into my room in her petticoat, followed closely by Millie. "Millicent says you will explain to me why I must put on a ball gown." Cassia folded her arms and glared.

I bit my lip, and held out my hand. Wordlessly Millie handed me the gown.

Smoothing the silk with my fingers, I held it up so that Cassia could see it properly. But I couldn't read her face as she stared at it.

"I've worked so hard on this. It would be a shame if Madame's

119

gowns were never even seen. . . . I wanted you to have a gown that really suited you," I said, hating the small shakiness in my voice that sounded almost like tears. "I thought you might like it." This was not at all how I'd imagined this scene.

But slowly, almost as though she couldn't help herself, Cassia reached out for the gown. Then she shook her head and looked at me, raising an eyebrow. "Well, if Mr. Harrington is on his way, as Millie says he is, I cannot receive him in my petticoat."

Quickly Millie helped Cassia into the gown.

"Could you please do my buttons?" I asked, turning so that Cassia could reach them.

She sighed, but her fingers were gentle as she fastened them.

"Miss Whitworth's hair first, please, and then mine," I said as Cassia finished my last button.

Millie pulled out the chair from the dressing table. Cassia took her seat, and within moments Millie was braiding and knotting her hair.

"Really, you are a wonder!" I exclaimed. "Where did you learn to dress hair so quickly?"

The brush slipped from Millie's fingers and clattered onto the table. I caught her face in the mirror. She looked as though she might cry.

But she didn't look away. "My father owned a theater, miss. My mother helped the actresses dress."

And it all made sense: how Millie had helped me learn to look, speak, and even move like Madame Martine.

"What happened?" Cassia asked gently, her eyes in the mirror watching Millie's face.

Millie's voice trembled. "There was a fire. My sister and I were home; my mother didn't want us to help with the evening performances—she was a respectable woman, and she didn't want the gentlemen to assume we were actresses, or, well, you know. They . . . they couldn't get out in time, the others said." She looked up from her boots and met Cassia's eyes in the mirror. "I know it isn't a respectable connection, miss. I know that no lady would hire me, if she knew; I know what she'd think. But I cannot change the past, and I must make my way in the world somehow. You've kept me on this far, despite everything, and I won't lie to you."

Cassia's face had no hint of disquiet as she nodded. "Then no wonder you've learned to work in a hurry. I'm so sorry for your losses. But, Millicent, can we not discuss your disreputable past later, after you've done our hair? Mr. Harrington will arrive at any moment."

"Then—do you mean—you truly want me to stay on, madam?" Millie asked, her eyes wide.

Cassia snorted (and not, I feared, as elegantly as Miss Spencer). "As though there were another maid in all of Flittingsworth—or London, even!—better suited to assist my niece with her preposterous schemes? Really, do I look as though I haven't so much as a feather between my ears?"

We all looked at her.

"I think I look rather smart," Cassia said. "Or, at least, I will once the rest of my hair is arranged. Do hurry, Millicent!"

Millie snatched up the brush, fingers flying with extra speed.

And I thought that I must make one last adjustment to my aunt's ball gown at the earliest opportunity: a softer hand to the fabric, perhaps, for no one could match her kindness just then.

Cassia met my eyes. "I know things have been difficult, Annis. If this is that important to you—well, I'll just have to think up some reason for us to attend without an invitation."

Of course, all this excitement meant my hair was only

half-dressed when Mr. Harrington arrived. At least Cassia was presentable enough to receive him. It irritated me no end to have spent two days on some of the hardest work I had ever done to prepare for this moment, and yet Mr. Harrington might think I was just another silly girl fussing over her appearance, keeping him waiting for no reason at all.

"There, miss; that'll do." Millie stepped back, surveying her handiwork anxiously.

Carefully I shook my head, then rose and hopped up and down a few times. All secure. "Thank you, Millie. My aunt is right—you are a wonder."

I stepped toward the door, and Millie caught my sleeve. "Careful, miss—you're walking like Madame again."

Right. How had I walked before I began this charade? I watched as Millie tripped back and forth as though she hadn't a care in the world. But I was already exhausted from long hours of sewing and rising far too early each morning, and I hadn't even begun my evening. Perhaps that horrid Mr. Smith was right. Perhaps this was all too much for me, even without becoming a spy.

But no; I lifted my chin and gamely tripped after Millie until she nodded that I was fit to leave the room. Picturing Mr. Smith made me want to stab him in the middle with my best parasol. He must be proven wrong. "Best of luck, miss," Millie whispered, and I tripped forth into the sitting room as though I hadn't a care in the world, even adding a gay little "ha-ha!" when my tired feet stumbled over the rug.

Chapter Seventeen

IN WHICH RUFFLES
ARE DEEMED A TERRIBLE DANGER

*Give a girl an education and introduce her properly
into the world, and ten to one but she has the means of
settling well, without further expense to anybody.*
—*MANSFIELD PARK*, by Jane Austen

$\mathcal{M}$r. Harrington wore yet another brown jacket (I was forced
to admit that this one set off his broad shoulders quite nicely)
and the same brown Hessian boots, polished within an inch of
their lives. But he gave me no compliment when he saw my new
gown. In fact, he looked ever so slightly disapproving, and continued to discuss the state of our finances with Cassia (who looked
extremely smart, I had to admit).

I reminded myself that it did not matter if he thought us the
sort of ladies who buy new gowns even when destitute, and followed Cassia out the door.

Mr. Harrington had borrowed Lady Dustingham's coach.
He explained that Lady Dustingham did not commonly attend
balls other than her own, as she was an artist, which I took to
mean something of an eccentric. I hoped she might be the sort

of eccentric who wore wildly interesting (possibly even flattering?) costumes rather than the sort who ran about in nothing at all, as the latter would be unlikely to order many gowns. Cassia assured Mr. Harrington she was quite familiar with Lady Dustingham's work and indeed had already taken tea with her twice.

This was news to me. It had not occurred to me that Cassia might be doing anything other than writing letters while I worked. I stared out the carriage window, imagining Cassia sipping tea with her friends while I spent hours sewing her gown.

Mr. Harrington smiled at me as he helped me from the carriage, but he did not press my hand any more tightly than a footman would. Not, of course, that I wanted him to—especially not when I knew I couldn't trust him.

There was a brief murmur in the crowd when I appeared at Mrs. Spry's ball. I smiled graciously at the young ladies who stared at every line of my gown, making mental notes to tell their dressmakers.

But it was nothing compared to the soft roar that greeted Cassia as we crossed the hall to greet our poor unsuspecting hosts.

"Everyone is staring at my, er, brooch," Cassia muttered, sotto voce, her lips never moving. (This whispering-without-being-caught was a very useful trick she had taught me, once she realized I couldn't be convinced to wait to say whatever I was thinking until after social events were over.)

"It is not your brooch they're admiring, but your figure," I replied.

Cassia shifted uncomfortably. "It is this gown's fault. I am far too old for anyone to be admiring my, er, brooch region."

"Really? But you commented just the other day on what a fine figure Miss Spencer maintains, and you know she is precisely your age," I countered.

"Well, you must admit hers is remarkable, particularly for a lady who owns a patisserie. My figure is quite forgettable, I am sure."

"Or perhaps it's you who's forgotten about it for the past sixteen years," I replied.

My eye was caught by a lady leaning forward to whisper in her friend's ear. I didn't like the look of them at all: something about their smug, self-satisfied faces told me they would be trouble if they weren't dealt with quickly. Oh, I hated to play these games, hated to give ground, but I was here to win orders for several gowns. I glanced at her, then stopped directly in front of her. "Oh, but how simply lovely your pearl earbobs are!" I said, smiling shyly. "They suit you beautifully."

The lady stopped whispering, tricked into a real smile. "Why, thank you," she said, the malice gone out of her eyes.

I gave her a little wave, and hurried to catch up with Cassia, who hadn't paused.

"Follow my lead," she whispered, and I gave a tiny nod, happy she was willing to talk our way out of this one.

I had not expected much, based on Mr. Harrington's description of a quiet country ball. But one glance around Mrs. Spry's ballroom convinced me that yes, indeed, there were ladies in the country both willing and able to pay dearly for a dress.

The ballroom was of modest size, but packed to the brim with fashions to examine: puffed and gathered Mameluke sleeves, intricately knotted cravats on gentlemen, and even a few gowns whose designs I committed to memory, for later use, as we passed through the crowd.

The quartet was playing a waltz, rather than a country dance; it almost reminded me of London. I caught a glimpse of the side-boards, brimming with Miss Spencer's cakes and lemonade, and my stomach growled, reminding me that it had been quite a long time since the morning's porridge.

Then I looked up, and realized how much Mrs. Spry cared what people said about her balls.

For hanging from the gilded beams were two of the most exquisite lumen chandeliers I had ever seen. I stopped, stunned by the beauty as well as the expense. I could not imagine how long it must have taken the lumenist who made them, for every hanging crystal glowed with lumen magic, as did the glass candles. Between the two of them, they filled the ballroom with so much light that Cassia could have brought a book and made out every word on the page. So that was why I could smell the hyacinths that decorated the room: there was no smoke to mask the scent.

Mr. Harrington stopped at last in front of a comfortable-looking lady in a gown of copper-colored brocade, which (I was surprised to see) was neither very fashionable nor very well suited to her coloring, though certainly not an eyesore. This was our hostess? She'd spent far more on her chandeliers and even her refreshments than on her gown, I feared.

And then the young woman at her side stepped forward, and I did my best not to gasp.

If she hadn't been our hostess's daughter, I would have rushed her from the room and covered her with a cloak until I'd found her something else to wear. Someone had spent quite a lot of care and expense creating the most unsuitable gown I had ever seen. Rows and rows of the most terrible leaf-green ruffles clashed horribly with the tone of her skin, causing her to look like a worm emerging from a wilted cabbage. Even her hair—which was a nice enough pale brown—was festooned with ruffled green bows.

A jab in my stomach told me I was staring. One glance at the poor girl's eyes told me she knew exactly how awful she looked, and my heart broke for her. I looked at Cassia, whose eyes were on our hostess, and tried to listen to her words.

". . . so very kind of you to invite us newcomers to your lovely ball! I know my niece was disappointed to leave London just before the start of the season, and I am grateful she will have this opportunity to meet a few young people."

Mrs. Spry was nodding vaguely, staring from Cassia to me and back, as though trying to remember where we'd met and if she'd truly invited us. I dropped my best curtsy to distract her. "Yes, how glad I am to know that you have balls in the country! I have never lived anywhere but London, and life has been very quiet since my father died."

A tiny shake of Cassia's coiffure told me we were to get off that subject at once. Without a pause, I changed course. "And I have never seen such magical chandeliers, not even at court! What a lovely, lovely ball!"

Mrs. Spry beamed. "I doubt that very much, Miss Annis, but it's a pleasure to meet you nonetheless. Now, Miss Whitworth, remind me where you are staying?"

Hastily I turned back to the unfortunate young woman, with only a very small flinch. "It is a pleasure to meet you, Miss Spry."

She was staring at my gown. "Oh, yes!" Blushing, she met my eyes, then glanced anxiously over at her mother.

Oh, dear. So this wretched gown must be her mother's doing. Very well, but how was I to broach the subject, with her mother feet away? Ought I to compliment this poor girl on her gown, to see what she said? No, I could not bring myself to do it. But how could I bring her to Madame for a new one without raising the subject of gowns, one way or another?

I opened my mouth, shut it, and hesitated a moment too long. Before I knew it, Cassia said something to Mrs. Spry that I didn't hear, and grabbed my elbow to pull me away.

Drat! Cassia was absolutely right, as usual: she who hesitates loses her chance.

"I do hope to see you again soon, Miss Spry!" I called back as we beat a hasty retreat.

⚬⚭)⚬(⚭⚬

At least Cassia did not seem to be making for the door, nor did any footmen appear to escort us immediately out, so I concluded her efforts had been successful. "Well done with Mrs. Spry," I whispered under my breath.

"She's decided she would have invited us if she'd heard of us, so she's ignoring our impertinence," Cassia said, her eyes scanning the crowd without appearing to take any notice of the waves of attention following her. "Do you think they might stop staring at me if I removed my brooch?"

"Honestly, Aunt Cassia, this is no time to think about your own appearance—not when there is work to be done! Someone must help that poor girl, only how are we to do it?"

Cassia's eyes snapped back to my face. "Very true. Weren't you able to speak with her, then?"

I looked away. "I couldn't even think how to begin," I confessed. "It was so truly appalling—the green, and all those endless ruffles—and I am convinced that she knows it is all wrong, so why hasn't she addressed the issue? It is dire, I tell you, a terrible danger to her future—it might cost her all happiness if not addressed at once!"

Mr. Harrington (whom I admit I had rather forgotten—he does have an almost frightening ability to blend into a crowd) smiled at this. "Miss Spry, I presume? Your passion for her cause is admirable, Miss Annis, but don't you think you might be overstating the matter?"

I find it quite irritating when a gentleman who seems otherwise intelligent allows such nonsense to pass his lips. Fortunately, I have had quite a lot of experience correcting wrong notions such as this. Folding my arms, I looked at him. "As a solicitor, you must be aware, Mr. Harrington, that daughters do not typically inherit their family's estate, or indeed much more than an allowance? Also, that not only most professions but the colleges are closed to them? How, then, do the vast majority of ladies achieve a comfortable living?"

He blinked, opened his mouth, and then hesitated.

"Yes, through marriage." I nodded at him encouragingly, having helped other less thoughtful gentlemen through these very steps so many times before. "And tell me: on what quality do most gentlemen choose their brides: their skill in mathematics, or their beauty? Which is most likely to be exhibited at a ball such as this?" Carefully I raised one eyebrow, feeling quite pleased to note that it had much the same effect on him as Cassia's did on me. (Practicing in the mirror had been worthwhile after all!) "So, if Miss Spry is expected to secure her future livelihood at an event such as this, based solely on her beauty, does not the dress she is wearing constitute the most dire of emergencies? For I cannot imagine that penniless spinsters who've failed to acquire an offer of marriage find their lives filled with any great happiness."

It was a faint nod, but it would do. He would have plenty to think about. I turned back to Cassia, but before I could speak, a girl in a white dress with masses of dark curls stepped forward and said, "Hear, hear!"

I matched her smile immediately, and raised my eyebrow at Mr. Harrington again.

"Oh, pardon me!" he said at once. "May I present Miss Kalmia Riverton? Miss Riverton, this is Miss Cassia Whitworth and Miss Annis Whitworth, recently arrived in town."

"It sounds as though you've already been introduced to my dear friend Miss Spry," Miss Riverton said, examining my dress.

I could feel my face burning. "I didn't mean—that is, I didn't mean to say—"

"Oh, you were absolutely right!" Miss Riverton assured me, catching sight of my expression. "In fact, I am trying to think how I might spirit her into London to visit your modiste—or must it be Paris? I couldn't help but overhear you, and I will not see my friend married off to some gentleman with an appreciation for cabbages! She deserves better. Now, where must we go?"

I couldn't help myself; it was such a pleasure to find someone asking just the right questions about matters of importance, even in the country! I gave Miss Riverton my biggest smile, instead of the coy little one I'd planned to use, and said, "You'll never believe it, but I found the most amazing modiste right here in town—I am told she can sew glamours, and I believe it! Madame Martine made both of our gowns, from the little shop near the patisserie."

Miss Riverton beamed. "Then I shall drag my friend there at once, no matter what her mother says! Would you care to join us, Miss Annis? I can tell already you'd be a valuable asset when choosing a gown. I can assure you Miss Spry isn't half so tongue-tied when she's out of her mother's eye."

My smile fell before I could stop it. How could I possibly visit Madame Martine with her, when I had to *be* Madame Martine? "I wish I could," I said slowly. But what could I possibly claim to be filling my time with? "That is—I—" I saw Mr. Harrington's eyebrows wrinkle.

"My niece and I are mourning the death of my brother, her father," Cassia said smoothly. "We are leading very quiet lives just now." She managed to completely ignore the part where we were attending a ball anyway.

Miss Riverton was no fool. She stepped back, looking hurt. "I see," she said.

"But I would love to—I mean—perhaps . . ." But what could I offer instead? I couldn't call on her; my shop was open during calling hours. We were not equipped to host a dinner party or some other evening entertainment. And could I risk her discovering my secret identity?

"A pleasure to meet you, Miss Whitworth, Miss Annis." Miss Riverton bobbed a quick curtsy and was gone before I could find my words.

I tried to swallow my disappointment, looking away from Mr. Harrington's concerned eyes. What luck, to find a kindred spirit here, and then immediately be forced to snub her!

I sighed. Madame would be happy with the evening's work. It was only Miss Annis who felt tired, and suddenly lonely.

Cassia pulled her fan from her reticule and put it to immediate use. "It is very warm in here. A glass of lemonade would be most welcome."

As soon as Mr. Harrington had disappeared into the crowd, she squeezed my hand, but said nothing.

I stared at the crowded room, full of blurry movement, all the voices and laughter and music too loud in my ears. It was exactly the sort of soirée I'd most enjoyed in London. Here, now, I wanted nothing more than to go back to my plain cottage room and sleep.

Chapter Eighteen

DEMONSTRATIONS OF SKILL AND TRAINING

Public opinion is a mysterious and invisible power,
to which everything must yield.
—Napoléon Bonaparte

❧)(❧

An unexpected feeling stole over me then: that of being watched. I was quite used to it in London, of course, but why should anyone be studying me here in Flittingsworth, when Cassia's gown had quite outshone my own? As Cassia had taught me, I scanned the ballroom without seeming to . . . There! But why would I have caught Lady Prippingforth's attention? Surely she could not recognize me from her encounter with Madame Martine? Then she turned to argue with the older gentleman at her side as he slipped something into the pocket of his jacket, his shoulders hunched under her tirade. (I regret to say that her gown was not canary yellow, much as she deserved that indignity. At least she did not seem to be enjoying her evening.)

"Who is the gentleman talking with the lady in the fawn gown by the potted palm?" I asked Mr. Harrington, my lips hardly moving. I did not see Mr. Hustlesmith anywhere; most likely the lady's horrid nephew was in the card room. But it seemed only sensible to identify all of that lady's friends and relations; know one's enemies, and all that.

"That is Lord and Lady Prippingforth," Mr. Harrington said. He hesitated. "He is often abroad, so I have never been introduced to him, but if you would like an introduction, I shall do my best."

"Thank you, but no," I said firmly. As I watched, Lord Prippingforth turned away from his wife and began to move across the room toward us, no doubt headed for the banquet tables beyond.

Cassia followed my gaze and raised an eyebrow, giving Lady Prippingforth one of her infamous looks, then turning it on Lord Prippingforth for good measure.

A sharp movement in the crowd of people at the edge of the dance floor caught my eye. Unfriendly laughter followed. A lady hurried out of the crowd, and I pulled myself together, putting a bland smile on my face once more.

Cassia stepped into the woman's path. "Good evening, Miss Fielde."

Miss Fielde pulled up just short of Cassia, blinked, and bobbed her curtsy. Her ball gown was a light-peach muslin, which could have looked nice, but somehow the pale color was too sugary, the flounced hem too frivolous, and the whole effect just too much at odds with Miss Fielde's forthright face. Now, here was another lady who ought to have a different gown at once—however much her attempt at charity might have irritated me. Her face was red and her lips were pressed so tightly together I was surprised she could get the basic courtesies out. "Miss Whitworth, a pleasure." Then she glanced back over her shoulder, and tried to hurry past.

Unfortunately for us both, she ran straight into me.

Thankfully, Cassia had made me practice the delicate art of graceful collisions in crowded ballrooms until I could manage any crush with ease. I braced myself, steadied Miss Fielde, keeping my slippers firmly on the marble floor to avoid damaging either of our hems, smiled without flinching at the impact, and even turned the whole event into a bit of a curtsy, a maneuver of which I was rather proud.

Alas, Miss Fielde was not so skilled, letting out a loud "Oof!" and nearly tumbling to the floor despite my forcefully steadying grip. Nor had she practiced the art of quick recovery, nor of never allowing those around her to see that an error had been made. She turned even redder, gasping some sort of apology. And then her pursuers were upon us.

I had forgotten what it was like to stand in a swarm of young ladies whom I did not know, all examining my gown, my hair, and my figure with varying degrees of obviousness, in order to assess the competition. Here was a test indeed.

Quickly I assessed the group, pleased to see that neither Miss Riverton nor Miss Spry was amongst them, for I did not care for this group's tittering laughs at Miss Fielde's discomfort. I identified the leader at once: a chestnut-haired girl with at least six inches of space all around her. She wore white netted lace over white muslin, with a girl's simple string of pearls and a pair of enormous diamond earbobs, and had a nasty glint in her eye as she smiled. I braced to receive the first blow, trying not to quail as she smiled and stepped forward.

But she turned instead to Miss Fielde, who had no notion of

how to hide her discomfort. "Miss Fielde, how very clumsy of you! Why, rushing about like that, one would almost think you didn't wish to speak with me. I know you do not delight in the simple pleasures the rest of us do, with your very high-minded pursuits, but surely you've spent enough time amongst us to know one does not charge full-on into a lady so finely dressed as this one?" Miss Chestnut-Hair smiled at me as Miss Fielde squirmed and the rest of the girls tittered once more. I felt ill inside (not that I was foolish enough to show it) to be so complicit in her torment.

I hesitated, and Miss Chestnut-Hair saw it. "What a lovely gown," she purred. "Why, it must be from London, or perhaps Paris?"

It was too perfect an opening. I abandoned Miss Fielde's cause and smiled. "Actually, my modiste is here in Flittingsworth. Why, if I'd known you were hiding such a wonder in your quiet little town, I might have come to the country sooner!"

Carefully I judged her reactions. The slight narrowing of her eyes as she considered my answer, then the parting of her lips as she remembered there was a new modiste in town . . . I'd been right; she'd never have believed me if I'd simply told her.

"How happy for you that you found her, then!" Miss Chestnut-Hair's smile did not reach her eyes, but it didn't matter; even if all her gowns came from Paris, all the other girls had heard what I'd said. "Until we meet again."

Having gotten what she wanted from me, she turned to leave, stepping so close to Miss Fielde that the girl shrank back from her—and I could hear the sound of Miss Fielde's hem tearing under Miss Chestnut-Hair's pure white slipper. "My dear Miss Fielde, do try not to be so clumsy." She smiled her triumph, and I (who had, of course, watched her carefully, without appearing to do so) was certain she had executed this maneuver many times before.

Only, this time, as she turned with a smug little smirk, she ran straight into Cassia, who did not look at all amused. Slowly Cassia raised one eyebrow, looking down at Miss Chestnut-Hair with no tolerance whatsoever (and I was pleased to note that her new gown emphasized her fearsomeness in a new, quite fashionable way). "How very strange that you should call Miss Fielde clumsy, when it appears to be your shoe on her hem, Miss . . . ?"

One of the girls let out a nervous titter, which she tried to turn into a cough.

"Miss Whitworth, Miss Annis, may I introduce Miss Brattlesby?"

I jumped (despite Cassia's training) when Mr. Harrington spoke, for I had failed to observe his return; flustered, I stared down at his brown Hessian boots, wondering why I was blushing. When I looked up at last, he smiled and handed me a glass of lemonade.

Cassia examined Miss Brattlesby and gave a little *hmph*, which I recognized as one of her fearsome friend Lady Wendall's finest snorts. "Charmed, I'm sure," she said, in a voice that implied she most certainly wasn't. Then, turning her back on Miss Brattlesby, she said, "Now then, Miss Fielde, you were saying . . . ?"

I turned my back on Miss Brattlesby as well. I didn't care how much Madame might need the business; I was not going to tolerate deliberate, malicious hem-ripping. "Yes, Miss Fielde, you simply must tell us what she said next!" I added.

Miss Fielde gulped, and kept a closer watch than I would have liked over Cassia's left shoulder, but under Cassia's steely eye she tried to rally. "Well, er, after that . . . she said . . ."

Neither Cassia nor I did anything like so silly a thing as to look over our shoulders; besides, there was no need to, as it was perfectly clear from Miss Fielde's slump of relief when Miss Brattlesby had at last gone out of sight.

Cassia pulled around to block the view from the ballroom floor with her black skirts; I handed my lemonade back to Mr. Harrington and crouched at Miss Fielde's hem, plucking my already-threaded needle from my reticule. I hoped she would not notice that the thread was black in my needle eye, yet peach where I whipstitched her ruffle back on. Once finished, I took a few more stitches, trying to convince the gown that on no account must it allow itself to be torn by such a nasty, spiteful girl. It was hard to tell whether the gown quite got the concept, but I couldn't lecture it in front of everyone, and I didn't dare risk Miss Fielde's wrath by testing its strength myself. I knotted the thread, slipped out my tiny silver scissors, and cut it.

Mr. Harrington reached down to help me to my feet, and whispered, "Nicely done," as he handed back my lemonade, which filled me with warmth.

Still, I had not yet had an opportunity to question him about the discrepancies in his story about my father's travel plans, and I reminded myself not to trust him.

Miss Fielde glanced down as well. "Thank you, Miss Annis," she said, not meeting my eyes.

Cassia paused her lecture long enough to nod approvingly, then went back to explaining to Miss Fielde the precise dangers of looking over one's shoulder while fleeing, and how instead to recognize the signs of pursuit while keeping one's eyes firmly in front of one's feet.

I ignored her easily, having long since mastered that particular lesson. Honestly, I couldn't imagine why Miss Fielde's mother, or at least her aunts, hadn't explained such basics as this before setting her loose in such a crowd. But perhaps she had only uncles?

Instead, I turned to Mr. Harrington and smiled. "Do tell me, Mr. Harrington: had you managed my father's affairs for very long?"

"Not long, no—only since my predecessor, Mr. Winchester, was called back to his family's estate. Last spring, I believe." It was smoothly said; did I imagine the note of caution, that tiny hesitation? I wasn't sure.

"Did my father's frequent travels seem strange to you?" I asked.

Again, a tiny hesitation? Or was I simply expecting one? "Oh, no, not really—it was clear that Mr. Whitworth loved travel above all else."

"Quite." I waited until he realized what he'd said, and then, before he could place his foot back into his mouth, I took up my questioning once more. "Have you always wanted to be a solicitor?" I sipped my lemonade so as to avoid letting him see me study him.

"Once . . . Well, but it's of no importance, really. My father lost his fortune, and when he died, we lost the land as well. I was lucky to find work I was well suited for."

Which, I noted, did not answer my question, though it did address why he seemed extraordinarily well-bred, for a solicitor. Or a spy. Perhaps the War Office recruited young gentlemen whose families had such abrupt changes in fortune. Why had they not yet thought to recruit young ladies? I filed it away under a list titled Arguments to Have with Mr. Smith, as Soon as Is Convenient.

But Mr. Harrington had been nothing but kind about my father's death, and I ought to do my part as well. "I am sorry to hear it. What a wretched time that must have been."

He smiled, a little sadly, I thought. "It was difficult at first, indeed, and there are still times I wish that some things might have been different."

Was it the lumen lights' twinkling that made me think he stared at me a little too long, with those words?

He sighed. "But the life of a solicitor is not so hard as all that, after all."

I considered this. "Yes, I would much rather be a solicitor than a governess, if that option were open to me, despite not having my aunt's magnificent head for numbers."

Mr. Harrington stared at me as though he'd never considered such an option.

"But perhaps we shall manage without any of that," I said thoughtfully. "Though I do think it's a pity that Cassia couldn't be a solicitor—she'd be a very good one. Don't you think?"

Mr. Harrington glanced at my aunt, who was lecturing Miss Fielde on the importance of always including at least a small sewing kit in one's ball reticule, as well as a spare handkerchief, just in case of emergency. "Indeed," he said, a bit feebly.

Perhaps Cassia heard her name on my lips—she always seems aware of even the insignificant things around her. At any rate, she asked Miss Fielde to come visit her anytime to go over her society's accounts and look for efficiencies, and then took my arm. "Annis, I do believe you are looking rather tired," she said firmly.

It was not a question. Though it was not yet eleven o'clock, I agreed; morning would come soon enough, and Madame must be ready to sew new gowns for paying customers. But I did manage to divert our course near enough to the refreshments to snatch several pink-frosted tea cakes to wrap up and tuck in my reticule.

When we arrived at our cottage, Mr. Harrington stepped out to help the footman assist us down.

"Thank you for your company," I said, wondering why he had not let my hand go once I was firmly on the ground.

"Miss Annis—may I—would you like to go driving with me tomorrow?" he asked.

It was my turn to blink. Was he ready to confess to his earlier lies? Could I trust him, if he did? "I should love to, only . . ." I hesitated. Madame must be ready to receive customers. Really, how was a person to get anything done when she must work all the time!

He didn't look as though he was ready to share his secrets. He looked like a slightly crushed suitor who's been told a dance is promised to another. Really, he must be a very good spy. Impressed in spite of myself, I nodded. "Yes, but it must be tomorrow morning; I, er, sketch every afternoon, without fail."

Thankfully, he did not appear to hear Cassia's quiet snort. "Would ten be too early?"

"Eight would be better," I said, for I was quite sure neither Miss Riverton nor Miss Spry would arise before eleven, no matter how excited they might be. Millie could watch the shop until then.

He nodded, pressed my hand, and took his farewells.

"Annis, what on earth are you thinking?" Cassia asked.

I simply smiled mysteriously and hurried inside, passing a sleepy Millie a pink-frosted cake before devouring my own.

It was only when I reached my room at last that I found the note left inside my own reticule, quite without my knowledge. *We are watching you,* I read, and shivered. The spies at the War Office? Or someone else?

Chapter Nineteen

IN WHICH MR. HARRINGTON LEAPS TO A FALSE CONCLUSION, AND MISS ANNIS IS NOT WHERE SHE IS NEEDED

Single women have a dreadful propensity for being poor. Which is one very strong argument in favor of matrimony. —Jane Austen (who, I note, never married)

Six o'clock in the morning came quite early indeed. I groaned, sat up, and motioned for Millie to set the candle on my nightstand. Then I slid my bare feet out from under the quilts and onto the cold stone floor before I could hesitate. Crossing the two steps to the clothes cupboard, I pulled out a fresh pair of wool stockings and my old black mourning gown. It was a pity I had nothing better, but there was no time to worry about it. Holding it out to Millie, I explained the circumstances of the morning.

Rather to my surprise, capable Millie did not appear to relish the thought of running Madame's establishment in my absence. She unhooked the gown while I slipped on my stockings, but with the set face that I'd learned meant she wasn't going to tell me what she was thinking.

I frowned. That was the trouble with magic: it always relied on the talented individual to get things done—there was no way of avoiding wearing oneself out or getting one's hands dirty, so to speak. (Or, of making any money with one's talent if one happened to be born a lady, and if one was not willing to resort to the sort of life I was living.)

But Millie was a superb shop assistant, always prepared for anything, and with her skills I was certain she could manage. I stepped into the gown and let her fasten the hooks, then seated myself at the tiny dressing table. In the mirror I could see that her old brown maid's gown had a fresh patch on the shoulder that looked to have been dyed with tea to match. "I am sorry I haven't finished your shop gown yet, Millie, but I assure you, no one will be about so early, especially not after the night of a ball! And it's not as though I need a maid for a country drive in an open carriage. This isn't London, after all."

Millie coiled my braids up and stuck them full of pins. At last, she said, "Yes, miss."

I resolved to finish her gown as soon as possible, and to make certain it gave her the confidence she'd need, for I was going to have to call upon Miss Riverton as well eventually. Millie must learn to manage on her own.

I strode into the sitting room, only to hear a crash and a scream from the kitchen.

"Aunt Cassia!" I cried, rushing in.

Cassia's eyes were dark with shadows. The black iron kettle lay at her feet, spilling porridge onto the bare stone floor. She was cradling her hand, biting her lip quite firmly. "It's nothing, only a bit of a burn," she said.

"Millie—fetch butter and brandy at once to put on it, and something to bandage it!" I said, feeling a bit faint.

Millie grabbed a cloth pad and righted the kettle. She hesitated, her eyes sliding to Cassia, who looked away.

"We've no butter, no brandy, no money to buy any," Cassia said quietly. "It will be fine without."

I felt my eyes sting, and quickly looked out the tiny window set in the whitewashed stone wall. All I needed was a little more time—or a little bit of luck.

"I'm to go driving with Mr. Harrington this morning," I said, my voice hardly trembling. "Millie will open the shop, and I'll join her before our customers are even awake. We shall have orders today, I'm sure of it."

Millie took the wooden spoon from the hook next to the hearth and glopped some of the unspilled porridge into a bowl, which she handed to me. She carried the other two bowls herself, shooing us back into the sitting room as she followed behind.

Cassia sank into her chair. "Annis, this is all simply delaying the inevitable. We must find real work, with real payments, if we're to reconcile our accounts."

I picked up my spoonful of nasty-looking porridge and popped it into my mouth without flinching. Sometimes I wondered how Cassia thought we were going to manage if she did nothing but stand in my way, wringing her hands and worrying. But she was tired, and her hand must sting, and there was nothing she could do to solve our worries.

Thank goodness Mr. Harrington arrived promptly at eight o'clock, though he looked rather bleary. Cassia had settled down to her letters, despite her sour looks, and I knew Millie would hurry over to open the shop as soon as we'd cleared the lane. I'd have preferred more enthusiasm, but she was dependable as a rock.

Still, after Millie's sighs of doom and Cassia's huffs and puffs, it was quite nice to be out in an open carriage, even in weak winter sunlight with Mr. Harrington. Somehow, it banished the sound of Cassia's cry from my ears at last, and even Millie's unspoken doubts. We might not be able to buy butter and brandy today, but surely we would soon.

I checked my surroundings for any suspicious individuals who might be watching me, but there was no one at all about. Then I examined Mr. Harrington covertly. He had much the same air as Mr. Smith, to be sure: of a man going about his business as usual, without any of the skulking or drama one might expect from a spy. But I remembered that from my father too: no matter how many times I tried to catch him in some tiny slip, he never gave any hint that he was anything other than a man who enjoyed travel, even when it took him away from his family for weeks, months, or years. And I never managed to form the question, never dared to simply ask him.

There were waves of blue in the shadows under the trees, and tiny green leaves appearing on every branch; all of that mixed with the spring green of the grass into something that hurt my heart.

"I hope that it was this beautiful the day my father died," I said at last. "I hope he had that, at least."

Mr. Harrington touched my glove, then pulled back so quickly that perhaps he truly hadn't meant to. "I am sure there were stars, that night."

We rode on in silence for a while as I considered this. Stars were beautiful too, but so very far away. I wished that a thousand things might have been different, but none of them were.

At last, Mr. Harrington cleared his throat. "How do you find your new home, Miss Whitworth?"

I managed a weak smile. Part of me had wanted to pretend this drive was only that for just a little longer; part of me had wanted to question him straightaway. After all, I was rather in a hurry. "I'm sure it's very nice, though quieter by far than London. In fact, why haven't you moved to London yourself? Wouldn't it be better for your business?"

He shrugged. "Traveling gentlemen like your father stop more often in the port towns than in the city. Besides, it suits me here." He turned to smile at me. "Your father once told me you had a knack for asking surprising questions."

My father had mentioned me. I caught myself suddenly on the edge of tears. "Perhaps he knew me better than I thought."

He took my hand and squeezed it, and I blushed, though there was no one around to see. "He said how very like your mother you were. She may have died when you were young, but anyone could see how much he still loved her, and you too, of course."

I tried to laugh, but the tears had started to spill over; it was too much, missing him, missing the mother I remembered only as a warm hug and the scent of roses. Cassia said she'd enchanted everyone she met.

Mr. Harrington offered me his handkerchief. "Miss Whitworth, would you do me the honor of becoming my wife?"

I know that a lady ought to be prepared for anything, particularly when alone with a man (though, as Mr. Harrington had always behaved as a gentleman, I had not had my elbows ready in the manner in which I would with certain others). But this quite shocked me out of my tears. "I beg your pardon?"

Mr. Harrington's face grew red. "I do not mean to presume . . ."

I studied him, amazed. Could it be possible that he was not a spy after all? Though who else could be so very plain, so entirely unexceptionable? But surely Mr. Harrington would not propose to a lady without first telling her of his true (most likely danger-ous) employment?

"Only, you do not seem to wish to become a governess—and I am not wealthy, but I can assure you, you would be more comfortable—I am sorry, I ought not—but I hadn't seen, until you explained it all to me last night . . ." Mr. Harrington faltered, staring at me.

Well, this was a fine pickle.

More to the point, it seemed this might be my last chance to sort out the discrepancies in Mr. Harrington's story (it being unlikely he would ask me to drive with him again after I declined his proposal). I cleared my throat. "In the bundle of my father's possessions you brought to us, there was a note, confirming that his passage from Calais to Dover was booked. Did you book that passage?"

Mr. Harrington blinked. He opened his mouth, shut it, and stared out over the field. "I did," he said finally.

At last, we should get to the truth! "Then why did he send his trunk to Hamburg?"

"I don't know," Mr. Harrington said. "When he wrote to me to request passage, he said he'd planned to go to Hamburg but had changed his mind, and to book him passage to London in-stead. He insisted we still meet in Calais—I don't know why." His face was sad. "I have asked myself a hundred times what might have been different, had he not been on that road at that time. I am sorry."

He did sound sorry. Was it possible that he was only my fa-ther's man of business—that he knew no more than the rest of us? But if he wasn't the one watching me, who was? "Then why didn't you tell us he was coming to London?"

"Why should you be haunted by the knowledge he'd died on his way to London, most likely to see you? You had enough to bear." He shook his head. "I should have known you'd simply work it out for yourself."

I nodded. It all sounded awfully plausible. But the trouble was, if Mr. Harrington thought my father was coming to London to see me, he knew very little about my father's work, and nothing at all about the *Corbeau*. My father might have loved me, but I was never his top priority.

It really was quite a pity. Mr. Harrington seemed like a kind man, entirely unobjectionable, in fact, but I had hardly met him, and hadn't even danced with him. I'd heard that love worked in mysterious ways, and had had more than one acquaintance who swore she'd known her true love in only a glance, but then, those girls had been spending all their time *looking* for husbands. I, on the other hand, had far too many things to do as it was; it was not as though I could spend my time gazing into Mr. Harrington's eyes, figuring out what I might see there in time. If only he'd continued to be a kind face, without asking more.

Part of me did wonder what my former self might have felt, hearing those words. But my former self did not need to figure out a way to buy butter and brandy, nor to practice the art of hiding secrets from a man even as I promised to love and to trust him. No, marriage would not do, not for who I was now. I tamped down my melancholy thoughts; it didn't matter that I'd miss the touch of his hand on mine.

"Mr. Harrington, it's very kind of you, but if I had wanted to marry my way out of my financial difficulties, I'd have done so before I left London. I appreciate your concern, but there's no need for it."

He frowned. "But you were right, you know—there are few options open to a lady in your difficulties. You do not wish to be a governess; you have no family to provide for you—what will happen to you? It would not be what you are accustomed to, I know, but I can provide for you, and for your aunt as well."

So could I. Not that I could tell him that. How utterly irritating—to be the object of his pity, and not to be able to set him straight!

We were coming to a wide-ish place in the road, so I took the reins from his hand and guided the horse around in a turn; I was already wishing we were back at the cottage, and I felt Mr. Harrington would soon join me in wanting to end this ride as quickly as possible. I snapped the reins until the horse picked up speed, and lifted my chin. "Thank you very much for your concern, Mr. Harrington, but I'm sure we shall manage quite well. My father's money is bound to turn up, and in the meantime we shall make do with Aunt Cassia's investment income. I appreciate your offer, but may we now pretend this conversation never occurred?"

"But, er—do watch that corner, Miss Whitworth! But I've searched high and low for those amounts—I mean . . ."

Mr. Harrington's *ums* and *ers* grew quieter as the carriage pulled back into town, and fell silent as I pulled the carriage up in front of the cottage. "Thank you for a lovely drive, Mr. Harrington. Perhaps we'll see you again sometime." I hopped down from the carriage and fled inside without looking back.

"Mr. Harrington proposed marriage to me," I announced, still trembling with irritation.

Cassia looked up from her letters and blinked. "Mr. Harrington did what?"

"He told me he wanted to marry me. For my own good, of course, since we're destitute." I paced the small room. "In fact, he didn't seem to think the money from my father's overseas accounts would ever be found. You don't think that Mr. Harrington stole our money, do you?"

Cassia raised one eyebrow. "I certainly do not."

"Well, he didn't seem to think any better options would come my way, so I wondered if he had helped to make certain they wouldn't. If this were a play, he'd have seen me from afar, fallen madly in love with me, and arranged it all so that I'd have no choice but to marry him."

Shaking her head, Cassia went back to her letters. "Honestly, Annis, you are not the tragic heroine you imagine yourself to be. Mr. Harrington is a kind man, not a thief, however much he may have offended your romantic sensibilities." She glanced up at me thoughtfully. "He's right, though," she said. "The next few months will be uncomfortable. If you'd prefer to marry than to live this charade, you could do worse than Mr. Harrington."

I stopped pacing and stared at her. "Truly? I'm to be grateful for the first pitying offer that comes my way, and change my life accordingly? Ha!" Not waiting for an answer, I rushed down the hall to my room to fetch my bandbox.

I cannot think what made me tell Cassia. I suppose it was simply rattled nerves.

Clearly, she did not think Mr. Harrington had been struck by a mysterious bolt of love, or that I was worthy of anything other than pity, at least in marriage terms.

How dare Mr. Harrington assume I could not manage my own life! I wanted to cry, for some reason, and that made me even angrier. How could he think I had no goals, no plan for how to accomplish what I must! I wanted to rush back out and explain to Cassia, and let her soothe me and confirm that of course I could succeed without him.

But Cassia had stopped telling me to make my life worth living. Now she thought I should marry Mr. Harrington because he was kind, or else become a governess. Somehow, my father's death had flattened the pillars of my aunt's philosophies into tired little pancakes, and she had gone from lecturing on why women should be allowed to study at universities to doubting my ability to earn a living.

Picking up my bandbox, I stormed back down the hall. It did not matter what Mr. Harrington thought, or even Cassia. I had work to do, and plans to achieve, and I'd wasted enough of the morning. "I declined," I said haughtily as I passed her.

Wordlessly she handed me a sheet of paper. I took it; the gossip column. Biting my tongue to keep from shouting at her that I had far more important things to worry about, I stuffed it into my bag, and stalked outside. Pulling the door shut behind me, I rushed across the lane to the back door of the shop.

It was locked. I hesitated, then pounded on it. No one answered.

That was odd. Surely Cassia would have said something if Millie hadn't been able to open?

Cautiously I circled the shop, glancing up and down the street. No one was in sight. I pressed down the latch, and the door easily opened, the tiny bell tinkling.

Inside, the shop was a disaster. My table was overturned, pins strewn everywhere, and my scissors were stabbed into the bosom of my dress form. The pieces of Millie's new dress had been torn to shreds. The door swung shut behind me with a last sad chime.

As I stared at the wreckage, I heard a sound from the back room, muffled, like someone crying.

I ran to the door of the back room. "Millie? Are you hurt? Millie? Please answer me, Millie!"

All I could hear was crying, then the scrape of something heavy being dragged across the floor. She opened the door partway. "It was—he—" She began to sob again, her shoulders shaking.

I squeezed through the opening and hugged her. "It was Lady Prippingforth's nephew again, wasn't it? Millie, I'm so sorry he scared you. Tell me: did he hurt you?"

She shook her head, still sobbing, and pointed to the washstand, still half in front of the door.

I gave her a weak smile. "Well done." Then I squeezed back out and ran to lock the front door.

I gave Millie a clean handkerchief and insisted on bathing her face with clean water. Thank heavens he hadn't caught hold of her.

Then I sat her down with my smelling salts, quickly garbed myself as Madame, and began to clean up. The table was easily righted, and the pins were soon swept up. I'd need to mend the dress form, but with any luck my talent could do that, and at least the scissor edges weren't harmed. But all through the everyday motions my rage boiled like a furnace. How dare he come into my shop when I had told him to go? How dare he intimidate my assistant—how dare he mistreat my tools, destroy my work? I felt my rage lock into a pinpoint of focus. I was going to find some way, somehow, to help Millie.

Chapter Twenty

OF SHREDS AND MAGIC

It had much of glamour might,
Could make a ladye seem a knight
—*The Lay of the Last Minstrel*,
Canto Third, by Sir Walter Scott

∞)(∞

*W*hen I reached the pieces of shredded lilac muslin that were to
have become Millie's shop dress, I stopped. The dress had been
a mess from the beginning. Now the fabric was so torn I wasn't
certain I could make it whole again, let alone as lovely as Millie
deserved. But my anger filled me with purpose. She would not
lose the one bit of beauty I could give her to that horrid young
man's fit of pique and destruction. I set the pieces carefully down
on the table, folded my arms (noting that I had not padded Madame's bosom anything like as evenly as Millie always did), and
gave them a long, thorough glare.

That they reminded me of my father's slashed handkerchiefs
only made me angrier.

Without letting myself think about it for too long, I picked up
the scraps and a handful of pins, and began tacking them to the

dress form. I tacked longer shreds to the form's shoulders, letting them drape down over the arm stubs for now. When I had no more strips left, and no areas left to cover, I picked up my needle, threaded it with a long length of silk, and examined the feathery effect of the overlapping fabric. I needed it to grow a bit in width, or Millie wouldn't be able to bend at the waist. I needed it to look less like a ragbag and more like a gown as well. I breathed in, breathed out, not allowing myself to doubt. I slipped the needle through the top edge of the neckline and began.

One stitch flowed into another, silk thread sliding through cotton muslin, muslin blending into something thicker, more textured, more elegant. The needle slipped through the next tear, into the next strip. Another stitch. Another. Fraying threads brushed against each other, held, fused. I blinked. Was it my eyes, or was the fabric growing darker? I didn't dare take my eyes off the gown, for fear it would drift back into fraying chaos. I took the next stitch, following the neckline, watching the fabric shift and change as the thread pulled through the weave.

When the neckline was stable, I ran a thread down the back, then began again at the waist. The neckline was solidly aubergine, but the bodice was mottled with lilac, the fabric a mishmash of textures. As I stitched around the high waist, I willed the gown to pull itself together, and watched the color shift and the texture thicken as I sewed my way around.

What if one could sew one's way out of a dreadful situation in this manner? Not only sew a disguise, but transform it: repair damage, even cover wounds—could I repair skin with my stitches? Or only fabric? (It would be useful for a spy, no doubt, but I did hope I could put that lesson off for a while.)

As I pulled the thread through the darkening fabric, I pictured

Millie confidently facing down her horrid attacker, with no hint of the fear that haunted her now. I saw him splutter, step back, and turn to flee from her. I smiled, straightened, and put a bit of extra sturdiness into my thoughts for the next few stitches. No one would ever wreck this gown again.

Of course, then when I went to trim the edges of the sleeves, the scissors would not cut through them. I sniffed in annoyance, set the scissors down, and decided Millie would look lovely with a little extra ruffle in her sleeve hems. So I gathered up the ends of the strips of one sleeve onto the point of my needle, held them at the height I wished them to be in the end, and pulled the thread through. The fabric flowed up into an elegant little puff, trimmed with just the sort of ruffle I'd had in mind. Mr. Smith might turn up his nose, but I knew the value of a well-turned sleeve, and I was quite pleased. Hurrying around, I did it again on the other side, before I became distracted—and smiled in delight when they matched perfectly.

Stepping back, I considered the hem. Would repeating the ruffle be pleasing and harmonious, or merely expected and dull?

A tiny cough came from just behind my left shoulder. I gave a most un-Madame-like gasp and whirled around.

Thankfully, Millie caught my arm before I knocked the dress form over. There were tears in her eyes.

I glanced at the door; still locked. "Don't you like it?" I asked.

She reached out, just her fingertips touching the frayed edges of the strips that made up the skirt. Then she nodded, the tears coursing down her face.

Hmm. I examined the gown. The top was really rather lovely—much prettier than Madame's gown, though of course not at all suitable for a widow of Madame's years. Perhaps Millie was worried that the skirt wouldn't be wide enough in the end?

I ran the thread down the front until I reached the point where her hips would be widest and began to thread my way around. "Millie, what is your favorite color?"

When there was no response, I looked up over my shoulder.

"It's . . . It's so beautiful . . . ," she sobbed.

I straightened. "Yes, of course, but do you like the color?" I studied her face. True, she was rather red and blotchy, not to mention dripping, but I felt the aubergine would do at least as well for her as the lilac.

She nodded, still dripping. "But, madame—it's not for someone like me."

"Who on earth is it for, then—Cassia? This is hardly her color, and she would never wear a ruffled sleeve!" I put my hands on Madame's padded hips. "No. Whether you agree or not, I am the glamour modiste here, and my talent knows what's needed. This dress is for the bravest, most competent woman I know—someone who has dared make a life for herself no matter what stood in her way and, somehow, has still kept her kindness and her loyalty." I turned her to face the gown. "Can't you see that in its lines?"

Slowly Millie nodded.

"Then it's for no one except you," I told her. "I'm only sorry I didn't finish it sooner." I turned away, trying to set aside the memory of Millie's terrified face, replacing it with my new vision for her. I crouched down by the gown's hips again and began stitching once more. "I'll need you for a fitting in an hour or so. Until then, why don't you wash your face and then find something to tidy?"

"Yes, madame." She bobbed a curtsy and disappeared into the back again.

She'd reminded me that I was expecting customers, though. I glanced at the clock, thanking all that was good that the drive with Mr. Harrington had ended so early. Then I began to thread the strips of the skirt onto my needle, yanking the thread through as I crawled around the dress form. I left the front door locked and hoped no one would see me through the small shop windows. It would never do for Madame Martine to appear so undignified.

Even with my needle flashing around the gown willy-nilly, the skirt flowed into the same aubergine, the tattered muslin into the thicker, more textured cotton; the hand was rather like a poplin, I decided. But the drape of it was really quite extraordinary: somehow, the new fabric kept the graceful flow the strips had had, even as the edges and tatters disappeared into a new, confident cloth.

At last, I tied my knot and bit off the thread (thankfully, it had not taken on the impervious properties of the cloth, or I might have lost a tooth in my hurry). Slowly I rose from my crouch, groaning at the stiffness in my legs, to find Millie already supporting my elbow. "Do try it on," I said, rubbing my back.

She settled me into a chair, and then carefully removed the gown from the form. As she held it up, I thought the aubergine suited her perfectly, despite the slight redness of her eyes and nose. She disappeared into the back room.

I tried not to fidget while I waited, tried not to worry that I had no idea what had worked this time, or why it had failed to work when I'd tried to sew her a gown before. To keep busy, I tottered over to the dress form and began sewing the gap shut, pleased to see that whatever magic had driven my needle caused the gouge to vanish without a trace (and didn't turn the dress form to aubergine).

I heard the back door open and whipped around, and this time, I must confess, it was I that began to cry.

Lest you think I'm prone to that sort of nonsense, let me assure you that when I lived in London, I transformed all manner of young ladies of quality from dubiously dressed victims of the fashion papers into radiant gems of the first water, and although I was quite pleased with the results, I never wept over any of them. And although I cried plenty of tears of rage and despair during my own ignominious lettuce *d'orange* period, I shed not a tear when I was finally dressed as befitted my looks and station.

Neither did Millie. No, she floated across the shop floor, her new skirt swirling about her feet (really, I must find a way to replace her ancient boots—could slippers be sewn?). Taking a clean handkerchief from her sleeve, she patted away my tears, carefully smudging the powder back into some semblance of its former self. She bobbed a curtsy, gave me the most confident smile I'd ever seen on her face, and went to unlock the front door.

And it was a very good thing that she did, for within the hour, the bell tinkled, I jumped, and in came Miss Spry and Miss Riverton. I held my breath as they entered, but they stared at me with wide eyes and not a glimpse of recognition.

Chapter Twenty-One

IN WHICH MISS WHITWORTH MANDATES A PLAN, MISS ANNIS UNCOVERS A PLOT, AND MILLICENT O'LEARY LEARNS KNIFE-FIGHTING

He who is afraid is half beaten.
—General Aleksandr Suvorov

By the end of the day, Madame was moving as if she were her supposed age, and I was exhausted. But, having assured my dear aunt countless times that I was equal to the challenge of dress-making, no matter how hard the work, I could hardly show it—particularly not when I was about to earn us some proper money at last. I pasted a bright smile onto my face, and felt it become a real one as I thought of the gossip Miss Spry's transformation was certain to cause.

Neither young lady had so much as blinked when I'd told them the price of their gowns, which assured me they'd be back soon for more. Miss Riverton would shine, and Miss Spry would no longer look like any sort of vegetable at all. It was enough to make me pleased I'd lost my fortune—well, almost enough. It was a pity that I could not spend time with them as myself—but then, I had no time as myself, not really.

My smile dimmed when I watched Millie stiffen as she stepped out into the dark lane behind the shop. Apparently, I couldn't even sew in enough confidence for her to walk these few steps in my company without fear. One could hardly blame her, of course; still, I wished it could have been otherwise. I tried to turn my thoughts to happier topics, imagining Cassia's face as I told her how much Miss Spry and Miss Riverton would pay for their gowns. She had always been so proud of any accomplishment, however tiny—but this time, she'd be not only pleased but impressed. There'd be no need to discuss Mr. Harrington's silliness any further.

Cassia was seated at her desk, surrounded by stacks of papers, looking as tired as I felt. She rose as we came in, and went to the tea table. As she poured from the silver teapot, the spout chattered against the rim of the cup. If she had been anyone else, I would have been certain her hand was shaking, though I couldn't fathom why.

I sank into my chair, waiting for Cassia to compliment Millie's new gown. After several minutes passed without comment, I frowned. I could not recall the last time any important detail had escaped Cassia. (In fact, after being lectured on how a young lady must not allow a gentleman's lips anywhere near her own, my former friend Miss Tittlevrim called Cassia an interfering old witch with a hatful of eyes—"like that one in that play about Hamblurt, or MacDougal, or whoever that gentleman was who did not behave as he ought"—which made Cassia positively howl with mirth, for she does have a fine sense of humor. Or, at least she did before my father died.)

Well, Millie appreciated her new gown, and I could point it out to Cassia later. I pulled the gossip column out from my bag, and began to read it as I sipped my tea. Cassia might as well start noticing that I spent my days working, not reading gossip!

Miss K.T. wore a most unfortunate watermelon jacquard gown to last night's Assembly . . .

How maddening! Kitty had ignored my advice again. I was tempted to write to her, but she'd hardly listen to me now.

. . . and was passed over for several dances by the newly promoted Cptn. C.K. of the Paloma, formerly first mate of the Corbeau, who is to set sail for China next Tuesday. . . .

I froze. Captain C.K. was Mr. Kent, the former first mate of the *Corbeau*. It could be no accident that he'd now been promoted and given his own ship, the *Paloma*. The treasonous wretch who planned to free Bonaparte would be sailing by Saint Helena, despite my best efforts. Someone had set all this in motion— someone wanted Bonaparte's armies to attack England. Someone who knew the British fleet, and perhaps even wore naval boots . . . Someone who might know what message was hidden in my handkerchiefs, and that I still had them.

I shivered. And Mr. Smith's men were busy rerouting the *Corbeau*, not knowing it was Captain Kent who must be stopped, or the name of his new ship. . . .

"Annis, I am afraid I must go to London at once, to attend to some business," Cassia said abruptly.

I beamed at her in relief. "Why, so must I!"

Cassia stared at me.

"I mean, um, it would be the perfect opportunity to select

a few more lengths of muslin, and other supplies—Miss Spry brought me the most ghastly length of green organza today, and I had to promise her that of course she should not wear it, poor girl. And some scraps of leather could be helpful if I'm to experiment with matching shoes—or should I begin with gloves, I wonder?" I breathed a sigh of relief as Cassia looked back at her cup.

"You've been invited to stay with Lady Dustingham."

I blinked. "But she's your friend, not mine. I don't believe we've ever met. Why would she invite me to stay with her? How can I work as Madame Martine if I'm staying with Lady Dustingham? And why would she know you'll be going to London even before I do?"

Cassia turned a page in her ledger, paused, and made a note. "Lady Dustingham is a well-known illusion artist. Madame's shop will close indefinitely. Instead, you will stay with her, and in return, you will assist her with any small tasks she might not find time for—mending stockings, perhaps, or reading aloud as she works—"

"In other words, I will act as her companion." I stared at Cassia, too furious even to cry. "How long have you been planning this? And why is it that every time we agree on a course of action, you change it behind my back?"

"Annis, it will not be so bad, really, it won't! Your friends in London need never know; they are certainly not in the habit of calling on Lady Dustingham, and she rarely travels anymore. You may even find the work of interest—"

"I already have work that is of interest!" I shouted. "Did you even notice Millie's new gown?"

Cassia remained silent as Millie stepped forward.

"I made that gown today from a pile of shredded strips of lilac muslin," I said, trying to control my voice, if not my temper. "In anyone else's hands, it would have been pitched into the dustbin. Then I took orders for two more gowns, for outrageous sums, no less, from the young ladies we met last night—and they will be back for more, or I'll eat my old dancing slippers. Tell me, why can't my plan work? I shall make back our fortune within the year!"

Cassia turned to meet my gaze, her eyes terribly sad. Then she passed me the ledger.

I held on to my anger even in the face of her sadness, but I took the ledger. I ran my finger down the page and stopped, shocked. "But weren't my father's recent travels already paid for?"

Cassia shook her head. "The bills just arrived."

"But we haven't got anything like that much. . . ." I checked her sums—or, rather, her subtractions, for there was no income coming in. The rent on the shop and the cottage, our moving costs, even our groceries, all flowed out in a steady stream of bills, followed by this huge new expense. And Millie had still not been paid. The orders I'd taken today couldn't begin to cover this.

"I must go to London to speak with our creditors. . . ." Cassia's voice trailed off into my shocked silence.

It was Millie who stepped into the gap. "Miss, Lady Dustingham's nearest neighbor is Lady Prippingforth."

I turned impatiently, then stopped as I saw how white her face was. "You'll be safe, Millie. Miss Whitworth will need you to accompany her to London."

Millie said nothing, her eyes wide.

Cassia looked at her sharply. "What on earth has happened?" she asked me.

"Lady Prippingforth's nephew, Mr. Hustlesmith—that horrible man who attacked Millie when she was a maid there—came to the shop today."

"Well, why didn't you ask him to leave?" Cassia shut the ledger abruptly and set aside her pen.

"I was out," I said shortly.

"He looked in the window," Millie said, so quietly it was almost a whisper. "He saw me, I know it. He saw I was alone. And then he came in."

She was trembling now, trembling so hard I wondered if I ought to slap her, or figure out where she'd put my smelling salts, but I couldn't bring myself to interrupt.

"I saw him come to the door. I didn't know—I wasn't sure what I ought to do—but when he came in, I ran into the back room and slammed the door. I put everything I could move in front of it. And . . . then I waited."

I watched her shiver, and for a moment I could almost feel it too—how it would be to wait in the dark, knowing someone would try to break in, no matter what you did.

"I could hear him in the shop and, miss, I'm so sorry, but even when I heard him throw things and tear things, I couldn't—I just couldn't . . ."

Cassia snatched a blanket from the chair nearest the hearth and wrapped it around Millie's shoulders. "Quite right to stay where you were," she said briskly, pouring Millie a cup of tea and pushing her firmly down into the chair.

I met Cassia's eyes. "When I came in, things were everywhere, but Millie was safe in the back room—and you must know that's what matters most, Millie! Anyway, you'll be safe in London."

Millie looked up at us. "But, miss—will you be safe?"

It was ridiculous, of course; her fear of the horrid Mr. Hustlesmith was causing her to imagine all kinds of things. Why should Mr. Hustlesmith attack Lady Dustingham's guests, however depraved he might be? Only, I realized . . . I wasn't to be a guest. I would be a servant.

"I see." Cassia rose to her feet, looking first at Millie, then at me. "Perhaps it is time for lessons." She walked slowly around the small desk, hardly ruffling the stacked sheets in her passage.

Then, moving so fast I lacked time even to scream, she whipped her paper knife off of the desk, twisted my arm up behind my back, and forced me to my knees. I could feel the cold brass against my throat.

"Did you see how that was done, Millicent?" Cassia asked, without taking her eyes off of me.

I managed to clear my throat, resisting the urge to shrink away from the metal. "Really, Aunt Cassia, was that quite necessary?"

Millie set her cup down on the table and came to stand beside Cassia. "Not precisely, madam," she said, studying me intently.

I noticed how tall she was standing, how, finally, she seemed to be here in the room with us, no longer in the tiny shop room, alone. I wondered how Cassia had known what to do for her.

"Then we shall do it again, after which it will be Annis's turn." Cassia helped me to my feet, patting my shoulder. "Do find a cushion to put on the rug, Annis—it will be far more comfortable on your knees, and then Millicent won't have to worry about hurting you when she tries it for herself."

So off I went to find a cushion.

Millie learned quickly, though whether it was due to her innate grace and many other skills or to her unusually high motivation, I cannot say. Whatever it was, I did not share a whit of it. I failed to disarm either of them as they came for me, and did no better when Cassia shook me awake the next morning, nor when Millie leapt out of my wardrobe.

"You really must put your mind to it, Annis!" Cassia insisted, deftly resisting as I grabbed for her arm in what must have been my thirtieth try before breakfast. "Your safety could very well depend on it, you know."

I opened my mouth to explain that of course I knew that. But Cassia pulled away, and Millie came out of nowhere and struck my knuckles with the clothes brush, causing me to lose hold of my aunt altogether.

Then she promptly snatched a butter knife from her boot, pulled Cassia down to her knees on a cushion, and held the knife to her throat.

"Very good work, Millicent," Cassia said, smiling.

I sighed. "I am trying, my dearest aunt, but I have not yet mastered it. How long did it take you to become such a prodigy, may I ask—and why did you never teach me before?"

Cassia stiffened. Then she flipped Millie over her shoulder onto another nearby cushion, taking the knife from her hand as she flew, all while rising to her feet without so much as a crease in her gown (though she did already have an ink smudge on her nose, I noticed). "Approximately two weeks, for the basics; I insisted your father teach me while he was in London, when I first came to care for you." She hesitated, looking at Millie. "Just in case," she added. "I had a much more vivid imagination, back then."

Reaching down, she helped Millie to her feet. "Very well. Annis, as you cannot yet defend yourself, you will accompany us to London. After I meet with our creditors, we'll discuss what happens next."

I said nothing. I must see Mr. Smith at once, and this was my best opportunity.

"Miss Whitworth, may we practice in the carriage?" Millie asked.

"Certainly not—there won't be room," Cassia said. "Instead, I shall teach you how to untie knots that bind your hands, behind your back as well as in front. But it must wait until we are packed."

Chapter Twenty-Two

A DREADFUL CARRIAGE RIDE, AND ANOTHER MESSAGE

I have very rarely met with two o'clock in the morning courage. —Napoléon Bonaparte

*P*acking was rather more complex than I'd expected. I might need Madame's clothing and accessories as well as my own, not to mention tools and supplies for the gowns I had on order. I had Millie retrieve the stack of my father's handkerchiefs from behind the loose cobble as well, and packed the reticule he'd sent me, and the cravats I'd taken from Cassia's wardrobe, for who knew if they would be safe in our absence, or whether I should ever return to the cottage? All of this added up to a trunk that caused Cassia's eyebrows to fly toward the heavens.

"You are aware that we are not, in fact, moving to London?" she asked.

I nodded. (If only!) "But we are not quite certain what comes next, correct? So I had better not leave wigs and great wads of padding in the shop's back room, just in case. And you know I must finish the gowns that have been ordered, whatever happens. My customers are counting on those gowns, and we shall need the money!"

Since Cassia hates it when she does not know what happens next, the subject was changed almost at once, and my trunk was strapped to the back of Lady Dustingham's carriage without another word. (I do wonder why Lady Dustingham maintains a carriage she clearly never uses, but thank goodness for her eccentricity!)

Once in the carriage (and with the shutters safely closed), I was found to be no better at untying ropes than I was at knife-fighting (it will surprise no one that Millie excelled yet again).

"Oughtn't your magic to work on this too?" Cassia asked as I struggled.

"I don't see why it should—it's not as though one can free oneself with a needle," I snapped, my fingers beginning to throb.

Cassia sniffed. "Just find the end of the rope, Annis, and then tease it free."

After that, Cassia declared Millie could practice pulling knives from her boots, but that, until we arrived, I could not even hold the wicked little blade she'd given me, in case I was tempted to practice, as I was far too erratic even for her to disarm. (I thought this ought to be counted a good thing, as perhaps I'd be too erratic for an assailant as well, but she insisted that unpredictability was never a good thing.) Millie continued as though she'd been born to whatever trade whipped sharp knives out of their boots, until I began to worry she might take up work as a highwayman (er, highwaywoman).

Luckily, this reminded me that I too had work to accomplish, so I begged Cassia to untie my hands, pulled out my workbag, and began Miss Spry's gown.

It would have been better to begin with a new piece of silk, or at least muslin, I felt. But Cassia had been quite clear that there honestly, truly was no money at all, that it was immoral and dangerous to make purchases on credit without knowing where the payment would come from, and that it would be extremely odd for Miss Annis Whitworth to suddenly return to town and buy fabric on credit when word had already gotten out that she had left town to recover from straitened circumstances.

So I was attempting to sew a gown from the horror that Miss Spry had brought me.

It was organza, which was far too stiff yet had no backbone at all, neither of which would do for Miss Spry. And (alas) it was that shrill green that she'd worn before.

First off, it had to become a better color, if only to prevent me from being sick in the jolting closed carriage. Miss Spry was fair and rosy-cheeked, with brown eyes and a quiet, sweet manner. I was certain she'd be delighted with a simple white muslin, if only because it was not the horrid green, but I could also envision her mother putting a horridly colored sash on it within two minutes flat, and spoiling everything. Also, really, what is there to be said about white muslin, aside from that it is unexceptionable?

I took a stitch, then another, pulling my thread along as I thought. As a general practice, I'd always designed my gowns to cause the viewer to compliment my looks, not my gown's. And yet . . . Now I must cause some notice to be paid to the gown as well, or how would Madame incite more business?

I glanced down at the fabric and shuddered. A wash of grayish blue had overwhelmed one edge of the green, clashing so horribly that my stomach lurched.

"Do you intend it to look quite like that?" Cassia asked as she pulled four knives from her boots in quick succession, without even a flash of ankle.

I shuddered. "Certainly not, in the end. But magic takes time, you know." My words did not sound quite as all-knowing as I'd intended, and I reminded myself not to attempt to attach the sleeves while Cassia was present, no matter how distracted she might seem.

All in all, the journey to London felt far longer than I could have imagined, and yet I still completed less than I'd hoped.

That night, in the stuffy room at the White Owl, my thoughts whirled about like Millie learning knife-fighting, though with far less direction and success. My duty regarding the *Paloma* was clear, but how best to convince Mr. Smith of the danger? I had no faith in his perceptiveness any longer, nor in his good sense, as he'd ignored all the assistance I had offered. Part of me wished to simply present Mr. Smith with the news and be done with it, for what else could I do? But, deep down, I suspected that my father would have handled it differently.

What did Mr. Smith see in me? The same girl Mr. Harrington did, I suspected: destitute, orphaned, alone. But that was not everything I was. I was a glamour artist, with her own magic, her own shop, her own disguise. I wasn't going to become a governess, not even to please Cassia. I'd uncovered messages of the greatest importance. Perhaps, someday, I'd be a spy like my father, so I needed to start thinking like one.

Cassia would be busy with her negotiations the next day, so I could visit whomever I chose, as long as I returned before she did. Would Cassia take Millie along? No, I decided; she would want to look like a threadbare lady who's lost even her maid, in hopes of sympathy. I could count on Millie's assistance then.

I must tell the War Office that the traitor was Mr. Kent, and to reroute his ship. But Mr. Smith thought me a foolish girl to be brushed off and sent home.

Then there was the man with naval boots, who might be lurking about London. I could not believe it was a coincidence that he'd stolen my handkerchief immediately after my last visit to see the spies. Granted, I'd seen no sign of him since then, ominous note aside. But I had also learned that knife-fighting was not a skill I possessed. Ought I to send another note, instead of calling there myself? But it would be so easy for Mr. Smith to dismiss a note, or to fail to understand the need for immediate action! And Millie would be with me.

I lay there for a while, listening to Cassia's restless tossing and Millie's deep breathing. Mr. Smith thought me a fool, but what might he think of Madame Martine?

⚬⟊)(⟊⚬

Cassia was up at dawn, not so much to take pains with her appearance as to pace about aimlessly.

I'd woken from another nightmare, this time of a ship sailing ever closer to the rocky prison of Saint Helena while a handsome man waltzed with Kitty Tittlevrim on the deck, and I threw knives that immediately turned into fish. Suddenly afraid, I brushed the sleep from my eyes and crept over to where Cassia stared out the window. "I need to ask you something," I said. Cassia would know what to do.

"This is hardly the time for questions, Annis," she said. "Millie, do my hair at once, or I'll be late."

I stared at her. Cassia never snapped at the servants. She wouldn't meet my eyes. Was my fearless, knife-wielding aunt afraid of what the creditors would say? I wasn't sure, but I said no more.

Millie did Cassia's hair in braids that looked both respectable and careworn, and I offered to make her gown a bit more or less attractive, depending on her strategy. (She declined both, which made me worry that perhaps she did not yet know her strategy.) Grabbing her bonnet, shawl, and reticule, Cassia rushed out the door.

I watched her from the window of our room as she hurried down the street (unfortunately, she headed south, the same direction we'd need to take, but surely our routes wouldn't coincide for long in a city as large as London). "Millie, if you were Miss Whitworth, trying to convince our creditors to grant our loan, how might you go about it?"

"Same way she will, miss," Millie said promptly. "You've noticed that she took her reticule that's near-impossible for cutpurses, didn't you? Pawn all she's got, use that to give them a taste of what they could have if they'll wait for it, and then talk vaguely about investments coming due. They'll fall for it." Millie studied my face, and I closed my mouth hurriedly. "When we come back from the War Office, don't ask her where that ring that she always wears is. You won't want to remind her just yet."

I nodded, trying to get my feet back under me. Cassia's jade ring had been a gift from my father, to thank her for caring for my mother and me. She would never willingly sell it. How was it possible that Millie knew my aunt better than I did? And how did she know we were to visit the War Office again? "I shall go as Madame Martine, this visit."

"Of course, miss," Millie said, already holding Madame's wig. "That Mr. Smith might recognize me, so I packed the shawl you wore last time. May I wear it?"

"Certainly," I agreed, removing my dressing gown and holding my arms out while she wrapped the corset and padding around me.

I decided I might as well tell her everything, since she'd hear it soon enough, and would be better equipped to act if some danger appeared. "It seems the first mate of the *Corbeau* is now the captain of the *Paloma*, and since we cannot count on Mr. Smith to have sorted it out himself, we must do our best." Pulling the gossip column from my bandbox, I showed Millie the relevant portion. (Somehow, I did not think that showing it to Mr. Smith would advance my cause, but it would be foolish to leave behind such evidence, even if he did discount it as mere gossip.)

She read it through, and nodded, returning to my corset-lacing. "We'll have two to three hours, I expect, plus you'll need to get some sewing done, or she'll ask what you've been doing." Quickly she tied off my laces and began on my dress.

Two to three hours, tops, to prevent Napoléon's escape and keep England from another war. No, a note would not do; I'd have to deliver this message myself.

To calm the pounding of my heart, I pulled the stack of hand-kerchiefs from my bandbox and idly smoothed the tears with my fingers. There'd been no time to try to mend them.

Millie finished doing up the hooks on Madame's gown, and began to braid my hair.

If Mr. Smith did not believe me, what else could I try?

Rummaging through my bandbox, I pulled out the two hand-kerchiefs with their hidden message and stacked them neatly on the table next to the others. He hadn't paid any attention when I had showed him my father's message.

I pulled out the rose handkerchief my father had bought for me. Did it make him smile, to buy me a handkerchief when I'd sent him so many? I stacked it on top of the two with their message, the color just barely pink against the white. I'd never know.

I pulled the palest peach handkerchief out of the stack of shreds, wondering what it could have been washed with to yield such a lovely color. It might be worthless to anyone else, but I remembered every stitch. The monogram was lumpy and unsure, and I smiled a little sadly. Once, when I was small, I'd made my father come see a rainbow through the sitting-room window, no doubt to delay his departure. He'd taken my hand (funny, how the memory of that touch made my eyes burn) and explained how light swept through raindrops and caused the colors to appear, lined up just so.

Idly, I placed the peach on top of the rose. Even in these shreds, there was some beauty left—beauty that might be mended, the way Millie's dress had been. Thumbing through the stack, I found a pale primrose-yellow one, adding it on top of the peach, and then the lightest spring-green. It made me think of the fields I'd driven through with Mr. Harrington, and I sighed as I added the palest blue. Perhaps there was a time when it could have been that simple: a man I liked well enough had proposed marriage, on a spring day in a bluebell wood.

Then again, I thought as Millie powdered my nose vigor-ously, things might have become just as complicated, for what would Mr. Harrington have thought when I needed to call upon the spies to prevent a war? I put the last shredded handkerchief on top as soon as she finished, pleased it was violet, and admired the spectrum they created.

Then I stared.

The way the holes lined up, I could see flashes of the colors beneath. Which could mean . . .

Millie stepped back as I jumped to my feet and ran to the small window, carrying the stack of handkerchiefs. "Come quickly," I said, holding them up to the light. Scattered letters shone through from the embroidery below, making no sense until I read them in spectrum order.

FOG IS FOR FRANCE

Who had this message been meant for? Surely not for me.

"We will need the sturdiest, most thief-proof reticule we have," I said, trying hard to keep my voice from trembling.

Millie grinned. "Yes, madame." A knife appeared in her hand as if from nowhere. She hesitated. "If you ever become a spy yourself, you know . . . Well, you'd need a maid."

Slowly I lowered the handkerchiefs from the window and met her gaze. "And not just any maid."

Chapter Twenty-Three

IN WHICH MADAME MARTINE PAYS A CALL ON MR. SMITH, AND EVERYTHING (ABSOLUTELY EVERYTHING) GOES QUITE WRONG

Truth is a point of view, and so is changeable.
—Hypatia

This time, I knew the way, though it was a bit unnerving to catch glimpses of a woman I didn't know striding along next to me. I wasn't sure how it had looked on me, but the shawl made Millie difficult to look at directly; as I tried to assess her hair, her face, and her figure to see exactly what had changed, I felt my eyes slide off her instead, only to find myself admiring a window in a storefront, or the bonnet on a lady in an open carriage. I did worry a bit that it might give the game away too early, but she kept her apron on over her aubergine dress, and anyone who wore an apron must be a maid. How many people really looked hard at maids, anyway? Especially in the presence of such a fascinating person as Madame Martine.

Outside, the horse guard paused for Madame, showing none of the arrogance he had with me. (Of course, it could have been a different guard; they all looked alike in those outfits, with the hat and all, not to mention being so high up.)

"I have business with Mr. Smith," I said in Madame's voice.

He paused for a long moment, during which I had an uncomfortable realization that people speaking in French accents might not be welcome in the War Office, even though I was well aware that no one would take me for an actual Frenchwoman. (Then I remembered that, technically, I was half French, which complicated things.)

Then he nodded, and Madame marched up the front stairs without a moment's hesitation, her shopgirl trailing behind by just a step or two.

We went through this rigmarole again with the butler (oddly, the butler spent far more time inspecting Millie than he did Madame, and delayed us both for so long I felt ready to throw open the door and announce us myself, but he did at last allow her to accompany me).

We were led to the same room as before, staffed by the same young man—James, that was it. The only change was in James's behavior, and I did hope for Mr. Smith's sake (not to mention mine, if I was to be working with these people eventually) that his training had finally taken. When the butler announced me, James neither yanked cords nor lurched about. "Is Mr. Smith expecting you, madam?" he asked, making no move to do anything at all.

"Well, he will be very shortly," I replied, nodding to Millie, who slipped over to the desk and yanked on the correct cord before James could do anything about it, just as I'd known she would. (I was quite pleased to be working as a proper team at last.)

I felt a bit sorry for James, whose look of horror and sudden spluttering took him right back to our previous visit. But really, oughtn't the War Office to entrust their secret bellpulls to a better guard than James, if they didn't want to be notified that people were here to meet with them? It was not as though I'd asked Millie to pull a knife on him.

As before, Mr. Smith arrived at a fast clip. He stopped, looking very slowly from Millie to me to James and back to Millie (who stood properly at my side as though she had never pulled a bell cord in her life), then back to James.

"Madame—Someone-or-Other—to see you. I am very sorry, sir—it will not happen again!" James babbled.

I smiled at him. "*Bonjour*, Mr. Smith."

Mr. Smith shook his head slowly and sighed. Then he held the door open and beckoned us after him, without a word of introduction.

⟞⟊) (⟊⟝

I am nearly certain he took us to a different room than before, although it looked very much the same, for I followed the memory map I'd made during my last visit and noted a few changes toward the end. It would have been preferable not to need one this time around, but I have found that life does not always follow my preferences.

Today the twisting dark hallways reminded me of the catacombs in my favorite gothic novel, for we saw no one (although I did think once I heard a woman's voice, very faint). But I didn't flinch when Mr. Smith closed the door behind us, for the small, plain office did not resemble a crypt at all, and even if he were possessed by an evil spirit and driven to do terrible deeds, no one ever does terrible deeds to widowed French modistes, not even in the very best novels. And, although I was not willing to bet my knife skills against Mr. Smith, I was certain that Millie could defend us both, and probably quite enjoy herself in the process.

So, when he glared at us, I gave him my most mysterious smile. (I considered raising an eyebrow too, but thought I'd best save that for later in the game, as he was certain to say something ridiculous.)

Somewhere out in the hallway, something rustled. Millie glanced at the keyhole, ever alert.

Mr. Smith exhaled very slowly through his teeth. "As you are no doubt aware, madam, the French are watching our offices, and are particularly interested in French citizens who visit us. I must warn you, whatever relative you are searching for, however long you have lived in England, you have made our job immensely more difficult by coming here today. Yes, the war has been over for three years now—but wars do not end so neatly in people's heads."

Which irritated me enough to put all thought of eyebrows from my mind. "I am quite aware of that fact. I am here to inform you that the first mate of the *Corbeau*, a Mr. Kent, now commands the *Paloma*, and that the *Paloma* must not be allowed to sail near Saint Helena."

"Captain Kent of the *Paloma* is sailing instead to New South Wales."

I blinked. So Mr. Smith already knew everything I'd come to tell him. Captain Kent would be detained in the penal colony, or face hanging or the firing squad. I wished I could feel some relief at this, but instead I felt only a deep loss: was this all that my father had died for?

Millie nudged me out of my reverie, and I remembered that I must push forward with my success. It did not matter that he had already known of the treachery; it only mattered that I had known of it too, and therefore he could not discount me. "You are very well informed, Mr. Smith." I tried to smile. "I wish to assist in your efforts. I would like to become a spy for England."

He yanked the door open and said, "No. Out."

I was startled, I admit, but I stood my ground. "But I shall wear a disguise—I do not have to appear French, you know. Why, I could even fool—"

"Anyone who shows as little sense as you have in coming here today, appearing in such a manner, is not worth training, no matter what connections in France you have. Leave at once, or I shall call the guards."

Millie tensed by my side, and that decided me; however badly things were going, I did not think they would be improved by Mr. Smith bleeding all over the place. I swept from the room, Millie followed, and I turned back to give Mr. Smith one final glare. "Fog is for France," I said. "When you come to your senses, you may find me in Flittingsworth. Good day."

Did he flinch, just for a second? Before I could be certain, Mr. Smith closed the door behind us.

"What now, madame?" Millie asked. "Do you think we ought to—"

"Not now, Millie," I said. What we needed was a moment to regain our composure privately, somewhere where I could get out my needle without being seen, and without the bother of encountering that James again. I led her down the corridor to the right, past the painting of Lord Nelson, where one eye was significantly larger than the other, and turned into a hallway that, oddly, had a whiff of the same rose water that Cassia favored. I was certain that I heard footsteps behind us, but every time I turned to look, no one was there. Quickly we hurried past three more doors, and pushed open the door of the room where I'd spoken with Mr. Smith on our first visit.

Unfortunately, a dark-haired lady of perhaps Cassia's age, or even older, was seated at the desk, reading a folded note by the light of the lantern. And, despite her unusual location, she really did seem to be a lady; I would have sworn that her high-necked walking dress cost as least as much as I'd charged Miss Spry, and her black lace mantilla put Madame's to shame. I was willing to bet that her skirt as well as her spencer had secret pockets sewn into the lining to keep valuables safe when traveling, and the small reticule on her desk had a strap so sturdy I was certain even Millie would approve. As I stood there, she raised one eyebrow, tucked away her note, and got to her feet. "Charmed, I'm sure, Madam . . . ?"

Quickly I studied her. Yes, I would bet Madame's dress form that the embroidery on her spencer was by Mlle Fillioure's top assistant, and I had to admit she was perfectly dressed to be a spy—which surely she must be, to be at the War Office unaccompanied? At last, a lady who would understand the true value of the services I could provide! Why had I not met her before? "Madame Martine, my lady," I said with a curtsy. "I have come to offer my services, as a glamour artist, and as a spy."

The lady snorted (a sound that, I regret to say, did not match her elegant appearance) and turned away. "Thank you, but no."

I frowned. "Now, just you wait a moment, madam—"

Millie stepped in front of me, interrupting. "Excuse me, madam, but you've a loose thread." She took hold of a thread on the lady's sleeve that I hadn't even seen, and gave a little tug.

And, quite suddenly, the lady's fashionable black dress lost some of its shine, becoming merely a not-too-shabby black gown, of no particular merit.

I stared, from her to Millie and back. Was it my eyes, or had the lady's nose grown a bit more prominent, and her hair a little less glossy? (The embroidery on her spencer remained the same, though, so she did have good taste, and the funds to support it.)

The lady glanced down at her sleeve, curious. "You can remove glamours?" she asked Millie.

I gaped at Millie. In all my reading, all the stage plays and fairy tales of glamours, I'd never heard of such a talent. Why, everyone knew you could wear a glamour for years, and no one would know until the fabric tore to shreds. . . . How had Millie come by such a talent? And why hadn't she told me before?

Millie stepped back, clutching her hands together, staring at the floor. "I didn't mean to, madam—I didn't know, I swear it!"

The lady rose to her feet, smiling. It wasn't a very nice smile.

"Not at all, my girl." Slowly she walked a circle around Millie, who stood perfectly still, never raising her eyes. "Now, you, we might have work for."

I regained my voice all at once. "My shopgirl is not for sale, not under any circumstances. Leave her be, or you will have me to reckon with."

The lady chuckled, but didn't bother to look at me. "Oh, those who assist me join of their own free will, madam. There's no need to defend her so fiercely, for I'm convinced she is able to take care of herself."

I did not deign to reply, though I did reach into my reticule and grasp my knife.

The lady stopped circling and faced Millie. "I have need of someone who can disappear. Are you interested?"

This was really too much. "You ought to know that I sewed the shawl that is making her disappear!"

"Remove it," the lady said calmly.

Millie took off the shawl, becoming herself once more.

"Now disappear," the lady said, and somehow, Millie became less noticeable, without so much as changing her hair.

The lady looked at me. "My dear, *you* will always be the center of whatever you are part of. You could not play a maid if you tried."

"I most certainly could!" I said hotly.

"Then stand as a maid stands," the lady said quietly.

Dropping my knife back into my reticule, I crossed over and snatched the shawl from Millie's hands, wrapping it around myself. Then I stood as I imagined Millie might stand, ready to assist.

Millie sighed.

The lady studied me, then shook her head. "Thank you for your offer, Madame Martine, but we have no need of you. Best wishes in your current occupation."

"But I bring a message." Furiously I dug in my reticule for the stack of handkerchiefs. Quickly I arranged them in the pattern, and held them in front of the lantern.

She studied it for a moment. "How interesting," she said at last, as one might when one's hostess has told a tediously long story about her young grandson. Then she turned back to Millie. "Did you do her hair and face as well?"

Millie nodded modestly, not looking at me.

Slowly I folded the handkerchiefs and tucked them back into my reticule.

"Excellent." The lady smiled. "It would be dangerous. Do you have family?"

"A sister," Millie said quietly.

The lady nodded. "Would she come work for us in a more . . . usual . . . occupation, do you think? We would need to be certain no one could be used against you."

"Oh, yes," Millie breathed, her face lighting up. "At least, as soon as I'm paid, I could send for her. . . ."

"We would handle that." The lady nodded. "Very well, then, I will begin making the arrangements. Until then, you must go about your usual business, with no signs of change. Where will we find you?"

Millie hesitated, looking at me.

I thought quickly. If Millie left us, Cassia would insist we go into service at once; there was no way I could convince her to trust another maid with Madame's secrets. But if the War Office spies came to find Millie at my shop, I might convince them to take me as well. . . . "You will find Millicent at my establishment in Flittingsworth," I said, nodding graciously as Millie beamed.

The lady shook her head. "Too risky. Flittingsworth, though . . . I'll need about three weeks to arrange things." She turned. "I will find you at Lady Dustingham's masquerade; no one will notice us in that crush. You'll receive further instructions."

Millie bobbed a curtsy. "As you wish, madam."

The lady smiled. "You may call me the Honorable Miss Smith."

Millie glanced at the door, and then I heard the footsteps too.

"*Au revoir,*" I said, and threw open the door, sweeping out with Millie at my heels just as Mr. Smith arrived.

Chapter Twenty-Four

ON THE VALUE OF KNIFE-PROOF GOWNS

Augustina rushed forward over the wounded, and
slain, snatched a match from the hand of a dead
artilleryman, and fired off a 26-pounder,
then jumping upon the gun, made a solemn vow never
to quit it alive during the siege.
—*NARRATIVE OF THE SIEGE OF ZARAGOZA,* on Agustina of Aragón,
Wellington's only female officer, by Charles Vaughan

An icy mist had filled the streets outside the War Office, adding to the gloominess of my mood. How had things gone so terribly wrong? But that idiot James, at least, would be watching me
from the windows, so I forced my feet into Madame's stately pace
as we walked down the steps once more.

A flash of black caught my eye, and, for just a moment, I
thought I saw Cassia's bonnet in the crowded street ahead. But,
of course, when I studied the woman, it was someone older, a
stranger; it was only that her shawl looked somehow familiar.

Slowly I set my feet toward the White Owl, already dreading
the conversation with Cassia. I wondered why I did not feel at all
victorious. We had done our part to keep Bonaparte in chains,
far away from England, even if the War Office already had it in
hand. I had passed on the mysterious message. And I would no

longer have to worry about my duty toward Millie. At least she had a future.

But why must spies always be so difficult about things, so unpredictable? If they had work for one more, why not two? And how had Millie come to have such an exceptional talent? Had I known, I would never—

I stopped myself. *Truly, Annis?* I thought. *Have you become the sort of person who would hide her maid from a better employer, while you fail to pay her? Would you hide her from the very work your father gave his life for? The same work you want for yourself?*

I hoped not. I could not deny that it was very disappointing. But Millie had proven herself time and time again, and if anyone deserved a better life, it was her, not me. I'd had years of perfectly comfortable living, and if it was not to continue, well, I would not submit without a fight, but I could not claim fairness as a defense. I raised my chin. Very well. I would do everything I could to make certain that Millie would be employed by Miss Smith. She deserved no less.

Though rows of carriages still lined the streets, they were shuttered against the weather, and there were fewer passersby as we hurried along. I could not help but shiver, no doubt from the fog, or from remembering Millie's past troubles. It was not possible, of course, for a city as large as London to resemble a gothic windswept moor, but if it could have, it would have looked like this.

And then I grabbed Millie's arm. A large man in a greatcoat and a pair of worn naval boots had just turned the corner and stepped into the street two blocks ahead of us.

I wanted to freeze, wanted to run, but I forced my feet to carry me forward, my pace unchanged. Without turning my head, I examined the nearest carriage lantern's reflection of the street behind me, as Cassia had taught me to do (so useful for avoiding inebriated gentlemen at balls). I could not be certain about their boots from that glimpse, but two more large men in greatcoats bore down on us from behind.

"I smell the sea," Millie said, her lips hardly moving. Her hand was hidden in the folds of her skirt, but I knew she was ready.

"Retreat is impossible," I replied sotto voce.

Carriages blocked the street to our left, no gaps in between; if we ducked beneath them, we'd be crushed by the wheels when they moved. There were no shops we could enter, no Bow Street Runners in sight, nor anyone I knew.

We still had a chance of escape. "Turn right at the next street," I told Millie, dropping her arm.

But just as we reached it, a hackney cab overturned, blocking our way. "It's them," Millie breathed, and I glimpsed a man in a greatcoat just behind the thrashing horses, holding a whip.

I yanked Millie to the left as the carriages that lined the street began to move, and stopped dead as I glimpsed a man in a greatcoat on the opposite side of the street. How many of them were there? This was no simple robbery, not this time.

I could see the fear in Millie's face. "We won't make it to the next one," she whispered.

There was an alley ahead, but no lamplight shone from it. Most probably they meant to herd us there—as though we'd walk quietly into a trap! I reached into my reticule and grabbed my knife.

As I looked up, the front of the building before the alley came into view, and I recognized it at once: the Countess Lieven's townhouse. I recalled again how at my very first ball, she had found me hiding from the ladies who'd laughed at my gown and had asked, "Will you retreat? Or will you come forward and learn how to fight?"

This time, I had no choice but to fight. I only hoped she would still assist me.

"Run for the townhouse before the alley when I scream—the one with the iron gate in the stone arch. If I am not with you when you reach the door, send help." I bit my lip as Millie gave a tiny nod. "And tell Cassia everything." For how many times had I feared my father might disappear, like so many during the war, and I would never know what had become of him? How I wished I'd insisted she listen that morning!

I kept my knife at my side, careful to hold it so that it would not catch the lamplight. I strode forward, Madame's skirts gliding along silently, three steps, four, listening for any change in pace from the boots behind me, watching the man ahead as he stood on the other side of the alley. I could just make out the smile on his face, though the rest was obscured by his hat. There was no one else walking along this street. No one would help us.

We passed the fourth house before the alley, and the boots behind us increased their pace. Were there still only two pursuers? I checked another carriage mirror, and flinched when I glimpsed a third. No doubt a fourth would join us soon.

I let my steps grow a tiny bit faster, my hand shaking so hard I thought I'd drop my knife.

We passed the third house. I tried to breathe. A few more steps, another, and another . . .

I screamed.

We ran.

I could hear the boots pounding ever louder behind us as the man in front of us rushed forward. I could not see his face in the dim, misty light, but I was close enough to smell the sea. Instead of retreating, as I'd hoped, he'd gauged our direction and distance and moved to block our path, his arms reaching wide.

But we did not slow, barreling toward the gate until he loomed above us. I swerved just a touch, and Millie followed. We struck as we ran.

I didn't hit him nearly as hard as I wanted to. My knife pierced the sleeve of his coat, then skittered out of my hand. He roared in pain or surprise as we hit the gate. I was certain Millie's knife did not miss.

The gate opened at once, and I pulled her inside and slammed it shut behind me. Something flew through the air toward us, over the gate. Millie cried out. I pulled her up the path to the door, and pounded on it frantically.

It opened at once.

I could not help myself: I glanced behind me. Three men in greatcoats, their hats pulled low, were pulling at the gate—which would not open. Two more loomed behind. One looked up, and saw the open door. He said something to the others, and they turned and disappeared into the mist.

"Who may I say is calling?" asked the Countess Lieven's very proper butler, showing no interest in the situation.

I hesitated. Surely they would not try again? Cassia would return soon, and she would not be at all pleased to hear that I'd paid a call on one of London's premier hostesses, dressed in my disguise. . . . I smiled at the butler. "Oh! *Pardon*—I seem to have mistaken the address—we shall just be on our way. . . ."

The butler cleared his throat. "I should not recommend continuing past the alley to the north, until the lamps that were broken earlier are replaced." He raised one eyebrow. "And her ladyship will be most displeased if I fail to give a proper accounting of her visitors' names and purpose. It would be best if you were to come inside, madam."

"If you please—when were the lamps broken?" Millie asked.

The butler regarded her. "Approximately ten minutes ago."

Just after we'd left the War Office. This was no random attack. Whoever that man was, he'd followed us despite Madame's disguise and Millie's glamoured shawl, and brought far more men than he'd need just to steal my handkerchiefs. Could he see through glamours? Or did he somehow know who I was? No, we didn't dare leave, not yet.

The butler coughed. "Your name, madam?"

As the Russian ambassador's wife and a patroness of Almack's, Countess Lieven held sway over society, of course—but the rumors said she moved in the shadows of governments just as easily, and that many an arrangement had been brokered according to her direction. I didn't think she'd appreciate a guest impersonating someone else in her house.

I raised my chin. "Miss Annis Whitworth and her maid, here to see her ladyship," I said, noticing the butler had no trouble looking straight at Millie, though I still could not manage to keep my eyes from sliding off her shawl, not even to assess the damage to the shoulder she was clutching. He held the door open, and we followed him inside.

"Are you injured?" I demanded as we entered.

Slowly Millie took her hand from her shoulder and moved aside the shawl. There was no blood, no visible damage. "That man threw a knife at me," she said, her eyes wide.

"Thank goodness he missed," I said, squeezing her hand.

She shook her head and held up the edge of the shawl, revealing a wide slit through it. "He didn't miss."

I swallowed, remembering how my scissors had failed to cut through the material of her gown, and vowed to sew such impenetrability into all her gowns from that point forward. She'd have even more need of that protection once she became a spy.

A footman took his eye from a peephole to the courtyard and nodded to the butler. "All clear?" he asked.

The butler inclined his head. "Indeed. You may unlock the gate."

The footman nodded. He raised an iron latch and let it swing down to hang free, then hurried along the hall.

"It wasn't magic, then, but mechanics?" I asked.

The butler merely smiled. The countess's servants all had a reputation for being utterly discreet; her butler, Ivanov, however, was legendary. I reminded myself that I ought to be grateful for this as I followed him down the hall.

⁓◎) (◎⁓

Countess Lieven received us in her library. She was dressed in a dark-green gown and cinnamon pelisse robe, and she raised an eyebrow as the butler announced us.

I sank immediately into a low curtsy. "Please forgive my unusual appearance, my lady," I said, my eyes on the lovely Oriental carpet.

She waited until the door closed behind her butler. "You do not resemble the Miss Annis Whitworth who was presented to me," she stated as I rose and took the seat she directed me to.

I nodded. "It was better that I not be recognized on my errand."

She acknowledged this with a tilt of her head. "Yet I prefer to be certain of those with whom I am speaking."

Carefully I lifted Madame's wig and mantilla off my head, setting them on the gilt table beside me.

"Surely you have learned by now that appearances are not to be trusted?" The countess smiled. "Tell me something only you and I would know."

I returned her gaze. The countess was a trusted ally to England—all doors were open to her—and yet, she was not English. Picking up the wig, I placed it back on my head, waiting until Millie kindly straightened and pinned it for me.

"When I was first presented at Almack's, I wore the worst imaginable orange-ruffled gown; you must remember it."

She nodded. "But so would everyone present, I imagine."

I shuddered to think it, but had to agree. "You complimented my embroidered slippers, in spite of it—or perhaps because of it. I remember that kindness, but no one else would."

She nodded, pleased, but still thoughtful.

"And I have long wanted to thank you for colliding with Mr. Ives while holding a full glass of Lady Bethany Chadwick's grape punch, which I have since learned you despise," I added.

She smiled. "It is a pleasure to receive you at my home, Miss Whitworth. I see you've decided to learn to fight at last."

But I was no longer that tearstained girl at her first ball. I returned her gaze steadily. "Please do me the honor of reminding me which necklace you wore that evening."

She laughed. "Touché, Miss Whitworth! I wore no necklace that night. I did, however, carry a beaded reticule embroidered with a wreath of French knots, which I imagine would have caught your discerning eye, though few others'. Tell me: have I passed your test?"

I nodded. Cassia had always claimed that the countess did have a sense of humor; I was relieved to find her correct.

She rose to her feet. "Follow me."

But when Millie followed after me, the countess stopped. "Your maid will wait in the kitchen, where she can warm up with a bowl of soup."

I met her eyes. "I trust her with my life."

The countess's eyes were sad. "And whom, I wonder, did your father trust with his?" she asked quietly.

I swallowed. No. I would not believe it wrong to trust Millie. What life would that be, to trust no one at all?

Countess Lieven pulled a bell cord. "You may trust her with your life, but I do not know her, and shall not trust her with mine. I assure you, she will be quite safe in Lizzie's company." A maid appeared almost immediately at the door.

Millie looked to me.

I sighed. It was the countess's home, and we were in need of her help. "Millie, please do as her ladyship requests," I said, and she nodded.

I knew that Millie would never leave me if she truly felt I was in danger. So, after the door closed behind the maids, when the countess pulled a lever and a section of bookcase swung open, I followed her inside without hesitation.

Chapter Twenty-Five

IN WHICH SECRETS ARE REVEALED
(THOUGH NOT NEARLY ENOUGH OF THEM)

It is a pity Countess Lieven wears skirts.
She would have made an excellent diplomat.
—Russian emperor Alexander (1801–1825)

*T*he room inside, though tiny and plain, was furnished comfortably enough, with space for three or four chairs near the countess's writing desk. It was warm, and the large lantern the countess held lit the space brightly.

Placing it on the desk, she indicated for me to seat myself, and sank down in her chair with a sigh. "I hear rain has followed the breeze," she said.

Rain leaving field . . . "Rain was my father," I said slowly. "Who is the breeze?"

"For someone dressed as you are, you know less than I thought," she said, studying me. Her face gave nothing away. Then she sighed once more, looking tired. "I suppose there can be no harm in it now," she said. "Breeze was your mother, Lisette. They teased her that she went where the wind did, that no one could be certain of her. France thought she worked for them, but in truth, she served the English, with your father."

"My mother was a spy?" I said, staring at her.

She nodded. "Until her true allegiance was revealed to France. She barely escaped with her life."

"Thanks to my father?" I said, imaging how it must have been. He would have been so young, stationed in France with his brigade. . . .

The countess laughed. "Thanks to me. I smuggled her out myself as my lady's maid. Your mother was wonderful with hair, I suppose from having to do her own so often in the field."

I added these facts to the tiny treasure box in my heart of things I knew about my mother, marveling, as always, how very few they were. But now I knew why. I resolved to ask Millie to teach me how to do hair at the earliest opportunity.

The countess reached out and touched my hand. "I am sorry," she said softly.

I blinked a few times, to clear the dazzle of the lantern from my eyes. "Who is fog?" I asked. For I no longer believed that just anyone was following me—nor that this would be the last time I'd face him.

Countess Lieven grew quite still. "Someone you should not know," she said. "I do not know myself, and if I did, I could not tell you." She caught my frown, and laughed. "Do you think your spymasters tell everyone their secrets? Even your own spies do not know each other's names. It is safer that way."

I waited. Whoever he was, he'd thrown a knife at Millie. I was not leaving until I knew more about the dangers we faced.

Finally, she looked up. "It is said that fog is everywhere, and death follows behind it."

I shrugged, tired of the secrets. "Death followed my father as well. But he said 'Fog is for France.'"

"Did he," the countess said, and smiled. "When did he tell you that?"

Something about her smile made me oddly uneasy. It was the expression of someone with power, who knew exactly what she wished to do with it. She could be trusted, couldn't she? My father had often danced with her. But did he trust her? Or was he watching her? I moved my reticule full of handkerchiefs down by my feet, and did not answer.

Countess Lieven studied my face and chuckled. "Good; finally, you are cautious. Perhaps you realize now that it is not dance cards we play with, not here." She folded her hands on her desk. "Tell me, then: what did you call here to learn?"

Could those men have herded me here, instead of down that alley? Well, if they had, it would do no harm to see her reaction. "I did not mean to call upon you, my lady. My maid and I were attacked by five men, all in greatcoats and naval boots, as we were returning from . . . an errand."

"Who knew of your mission?" she asked.

She did not seem surprised. I hesitated.

"Oh, use your head, girl! If I had wanted you dead, I would hardly have had you attacked in front of my house, particularly not by men incompetent enough to let you escape!"

That did show sense. "Only myself and my maid knew."

She nodded. "You were not sent, then. I thought not; this— whatever you are—does not seem their style."

"I am Madame Martine, glamour modiste," I said, rather irritated.

I thought I saw a flicker of surprise in her face; then she laughed. "And, madame, you were returning from . . . ?"

"From the War Office," I admitted, chagrined.

"Where the spies overhear all news as a matter of course. And you did not bother to double back, nor to shop along the way, nor to send someone else to confuse whoever saw you there." She sighed. "You are very poorly trained, my dear." She studied me awhile longer as I tried not to fidget. "But you have your mother's frown. I trusted her, you know, though few did. Often have I wished I could have done more for her—at the very least, could have discovered which of her allies put her life in danger. But, try as I might, I could not, no more than your father could, though he has—though he spent the rest of his life trying."

She rose to her feet, and I did as well, clutching my reticule. "In her memory, I will tell you all I have learned of Fog. He is a man; of that, I am nearly certain. He is valued by his employers. He is said to rarely leave France. He cannot see colors."

I thought of the spectrum of handkerchiefs. My father had known Fog could not see colors. He had sliced up his own handkerchiefs to send a warning. I wondered if he had sliced up the rest of his clothes as well, or if the mysterious Fog had, and why. "And he works as a spy for England," I said softly. "But why do they trust him? Why don't they know he's a traitor?"

The countess shrugged. "How do we ever know whom to trust?"

"I trust my father's word," I retorted.

Smiling, the countess leaned forward. "And you will swear he has never been wrong? You think the War Office should condemn a man to death based purely on your father's say-so?"

"He attacked me outside of your home, with four men!" I said.

She nodded. "Yes. He is becoming sloppy, and you may find

some true proof at last. Until then, trust no one, Miss Whitworth. And do try not to tell the entire War Office what you've learned."

"Thank you, my lady," I said, curtsying low. Then I met her eyes once more. "What did you learn of my mother's betrayal?"

The countess glanced at the secret door. "*Betrayal* is a complicated word, don't you think? For was your mother not betraying her country, spying for England? Then again, it was France that killed her family, so perhaps they betrayed her first." She smiled sadly. "I learned very little of what truly happened, so I will tell you the story as I lived it, instead.

"In the summer of 1801, her imperial majesty the dowager empress Maria Feodorovna—she was a dear friend of my mother's, you know—sent me to Paris. Bonaparte disliked our ambassador, Count Morkov—oh, but I can see from your face that, unlike your aunt, you do not enjoy politics. Well, the empress wished for me to judge the situation, under the pretext of ordering new gowns for her." She smiled. "And perhaps a few for me as well. There is nothing like Paris for fashion!

"I met your mother, Lisette, at a dinner party one evening in Count Morkov's home—she was the guest of the duc de Cadore, who was also seen talking to—ah, very well; no politics. I noticed her lovely white gown and red overdress—so striking!—and the way she managed to find herself near a window whenever one of the servants brought a message in." She chuckled. "Oh, she was very skilled, your mother—but so was I.

"The next time it happened, I found myself at the window too. I saw the closed carriage waiting across the road, and I saw that the lock on the window had been broken. Count Morkov noticed nothing, of course—though at least he was keeping the duc busy with his arguments. And I saw the flash of panic on your mother's face when the servant brought the message not to her, but to the duc. The duc opened it, read it, read it again—and stopped arguing with Count Morkov altogether."

"Enough about the duc!" I said, clutching my reticule. "What about my mother?"

The countess looked disappointed. "Must I spell it out? Very well! Your mother was waiting for a secure escort out of the country—that sort of thing is far easier to arrange from an ambassador's home. But, instead, someone sent a message to the duc, telling him your mother was a double agent. Which, in case it isn't clear to you, put her in immediate danger of a horrible death."

"Oh!" I said. "I do beg your pardon. Please continue!"

The countess sighed in a manner that quite reminded me of Cassia. "Very well. Now, recall that I had only just met your mother, and although I had my suspicions about her, I didn't know what kind of trouble she faced. But I did not care for the duc, nor for his politics, and I saw no one leaping to her aid as he crossed the room toward her. So"—and here she grinned at me—"I stepped quite firmly on my skirt and ripped it in a way that no one could ignore—why, you could very nearly see my knee! In my confusion—I was only about your age then, and confusion is so believable in the young!—I grabbed your mother's hand and insisted she come with me to repair my gown. I had to drag her away from the window—I don't know why she assumed that carriage was still safe, when I was certain it was not—but we made it to the retiring room at last."

"Do you still have that gown?" I asked, before I could stop myself.

"Of course not!" the countess said. "It was completely ruined! Let me tell you: your mother was brilliant with hair, but she could hardly sew a straight stitch. Though I suppose she was too busy fearing for her life to properly mend my muslin just then."

Apparently, my mother had not shared my talent.

"Anyway, I had more important things to worry about—such as our escape. 'Are you carrying intelligence?' I demanded at once. She was silent, which answered my question. Whatever it was, my dear empress would want to know more—and, besides, I really did not care for that duc! So I broke the lock on the retiring-room window, sent your mother up the tree outside to the window of my room, still in her ball gown—your mother never said no to a daring scheme!—and then left the room myself, to run up the stairs in a fit of embarrassed weeping, absolutely refusing to allow the duc to search my room."

"But he can't have given up so easily as that!" I exclaimed.

The countess laughed. "He most certainly did not! Luckily, my maid was about your mother's height, with some of her daring spirit as well as her coloring. She switched gowns with your mother. I hid your mother under my bed, and sent my maid off with Ivanov—you've met my butler? Together they led the duc around the Continent for nearly three weeks!" The countess smiled. "Meanwhile, I left France to return home to Russia, telling Count Morkov I could never show my face in Paris again, not after everyone had seen my stockings! He believed me—which went into my report to the empress, I assure you—and I made arrangements along the way to send your mother off to safety in England with an acquaintance of mine."

"My father," I said, and she nodded. "But—who sent the message to the duc? It must have been Fog!"

The countess took my hand and squeezed it. "I've wondered, over the years, if there was some way I could have stolen the message from the duc, and traced it to him—but even looking back, I cannot see how, not while saving your mother."

"But the War Office—surely they would have found the truth, and told my mother later. . . ."

The countess shrugged. "Mistakes happen, and messages fall into the wrong hands; perhaps he claimed that was what happened. And spies rarely know the identity of other spies, for everyone's safety. Your War Office would not tell me which of their spies were in France, let alone who knew Lisette was a double agent, no matter how persuasive I was. And I think they did not tell her, or your father—for every time I saw him, he asked me what I had learned. I do think he suspected Fog of treason, not carelessness, but did he ever learn Fog's true identity?" She smiled, a little wickedly. "I wonder if they would tell you."

Much as I wanted to run back and demand that they tell me at once, I had to admit they most likely would not.

"But why would an English spy work for France?" I asked.

The countess shrugged. "Love, money, revenge—what does it matter, in the end?"

The clock in the library began to chime, the chime muffled by the bookshelf wall. I started. "My aunt—she will be frantic if she returns and does not find me there. . . ."

"I will send you back in my carriage. My coachman will see that you arrive unharmed," the countess said.

"Thank you," I said. Impulsively I reached out and squeezed her hand. "And thank you for saving my mother as well."

Chapter Twenty-Six

ALAS

Employment is the surest antidote to sorrow.
—*THE MYSTERIES OF UDOLPHO,* by Ann Radcliffe

⤫)(⤪

*C*assia was not at the White Owl when Millie and I returned. I was relieved, then fearful. I had no idea where she had gone; what if the men who had attacked us had followed her as well? As Millie scrubbed the powder from my face and did up Miss Annis's dress, I quickly explained what the countess had told me. Then I settled myself down by the window, turning the fabric of Miss Spry's gown to catch the last of the daylight, trying to focus on my work once more.

Before, I had known what to do: I must warn the War Office, prevent Bonaparte's attempted escape. Now things were confusingly muddled. Bonaparte would stay safely imprisoned, at least until some other captain was found and bribed—but what caused the man with naval boots to attack me now? Why did the spies ignore the message my father had so carefully sent, while the countess did not?

Why did Miss Smith want to hire Millie instead of me? And how had I forgotten Millie's sister, or how much Millie worried about her? I looked out the small window at cold, gray London, and wondered how it would feel to be separated from Cassia for weeks, even months, worrying about her safety. How did Millie bear it?

I frowned. It was not as though I wished Millie any less success, if this was what she wanted. It was merely that things would have been much easier if Miss Smith had hired me as well. I did have to admit that Millie would make an ideal spy, though, even without her unusual talent.

Bending closer to the window, I stitched on, then stopped as I noticed movement outside. "Millie, where are the lenders and pawnshops located?"

"Charing Cross Road, miss," said Millie, coming to look out the window too.

So why was my aunt approaching our hotel from the opposite direction?

◦◦)) ((◦◦

Cassia entered our room just as I finished sewing up the back seam of the tube that was to become Miss Spry's new ball gown. Sewing always helped me think.

Quietly Cassia closed the door behind her and dropped a parcel onto the small table. Her jade ring was gone. I was startled at how tired she looked as she sank into her chair. Could our creditors truly have refused her request? But Cassia always got what she wanted.

I could not regret the time I'd taken to try to save England.

And I was glad that I'd spoken with the countess, and learned the truth about my mother at last. But nothing I had done would help us pay our debts.

Cassia nodded at Millie, who promptly tucked her embroidery into the sewing basket and went to unwrap the parcel. I set my sewing aside as well as Millie handed me a cold meat pie. A month ago, I'd have turned up my nose; now I tucked in, waiting until I'd eaten every crumb before I asked Cassia my question. "Bad news, then?"

Cassia shook her head. "It's not that simple, Annis—there is no possibility of good news when one is indebted. I am not to go to the debtors' prison today, so there's that." She caught the look on my face and smiled. "I have hopes that it will not come to that; there are still the books to sell, and our remaining jewels. Our creditors have given us three weeks to assemble the remaining owed."

The meat pie sat like a lump of lead in my belly as I pulled my bandbox onto my lap and sorted through it. Pearl earbobs, strung garnets, tiny topaz ring . . . I handed my mother's jewelry over to Cassia silently. "What is the full amount?"

Cassia wrapped my jewelry up in a clean handkerchief, folding it carefully into a flat package, and tucked it into a secret pocket sewn into the lining of her reticule. (I caught Millie's eye, and she nodded; we would need to make a similar modification to my own reticule, in case I ever had something of value again.) "Three hundred and sixty-four pounds, ninepence," Cassia said, staring into the smoldering grate. I noticed her own pie was untouched.

I swallowed. More than we'd earn from selling everything we still owned—with the possible exception of Cassia's investments, which I never followed closely. I could not make so much as that in ten years of working as a governess, I was nearly certain. I blinked hard; I must begin work on Miss Spry's dress once more, and it would never do to spot the silk, not when it would earn us twelve pounds as soon as delivered.

Cassia sighed. "Not including the salary we owe Millicent," she added.

Millie said nothing, but I could see the slight tremble in her hands. She wiped her hands clean on her handkerchief and picked up her embroidery once more, without meeting my eyes.

I felt a rush of shame flood my face. I had hired Millie, but never paid her, had begrudged her offer of new employment— why, there was a society in London set up to help maids recover funds from employers just like me! I knew, because Cassia had made me help her and the other ladies address their mountains of correspondence when I had overspent my account on five French hats. I had never dreamed to fail so completely that my name ought to be on their list.

I picked up Miss Spry's gown-to-be once more. I would finish the gown and pay Millie immediately. Then I would help ensure her employment with the Honorable Miss Smith in whatever way I could. Quickly I began to hem the neckline, absently encouraging tiny pleats to form as I passed (for a pleat is not at all the same as a ruffle, and no one wanted Miss Spry to look like a Spartan at her next ball, however thorough a change was needed; she had neither the face nor the hair for such severity of dress, and she deserved something pretty at last). I would finish these gowns as quickly as I could, I would let Cassia sell all my novels and gowns and hats, and I would hear out her next terrible plan without a word against it, as long as she would give us enough time to see Millie settled into her new employment, properly appreciated and paid at last.

"We must return to Flittingsworth," I said.

Cassia broke her pie into halves and offered it to Millie and me, but we shook our heads. "I suppose we must, if only to pack the books for sale," she said quietly. "The rent is paid on the cottage through the end of the month."

I kept quiet, kept my needle sliding through the pleats, over and over, but she said nothing more. Alarmed, I looked up; still she sat there, pie in hand, staring into the fire as though searching for a way through.

I swallowed. Cassia did not know what to do.

My plans to become a spy had failed miserably. My dressmaking plans had promise, but were moving far too slowly for this new timeline; Miss Spry and Miss Riverton would hardly have time to attend the next ball before our funds came due, and perhaps it would not even be a ball—perhaps it would be the masquerade, instead?

I stopped, narrowly missing the tip of my finger with my needle. The masquerade.

Then I grasped at the rope that the Honorable Miss Smith had thrown us, all unknowing: Lady Dustingham was giving a masquerade. It was an annual event, one even I had heard about, the talk of all the area. Everyone would be trying to outshine everyone else, and to outdo last year's notorieties. Everyone would be wearing disguises, or at the very least domino masks and their best gowns, yet dying to be seen. If this was not an event made for Madame Martine's talent, what was? (And, yes, I could not help but remember that the Honorable Miss Smith would be in attendance, observing every example of my skill. All the more reason to make certain there were many of them. Perhaps there could be one last chance for me as well. . . .)

I opened my mouth to fill the silence, to let Cassia know that all would be well—and then I closed it. I had already assured Cassia countless times that I would make our fortune, yet today she'd had to visit the creditors alone, without a solution. This time, I would not put my efforts into words. This time, I would make things happen.

Chapter Twenty-Seven

IN WHICH MISS ANNIS
UPDATES HER ACCOUNTS, AND A
THIEF IS DISCOVERED IN FLITTINGSWORTH

There never figured on the Courtly stage a female
intriguer more restless, more arrogant, more
mischievous, more (politically, and therefore we mean
it not offensively) odious and insufferable than this
supercilious Ambassadress. She fancied herself
"a power." —*THE TIMES*, on the Countess Lieven

⚬⚬))((⚬⚬

*I*t seemed no time at all before we were back in Flittingsworth, opening up Madame's shop once more. I yawned as I unlocked the back door and stumbled inside. But once the lamps were lit, I emptied my bandbox out onto the worktable.

Millie picked up Miss Spry's gown and began to arrange it on the dress form. I'd sewn half the night and all the carriage ride home, and Millie had spent hour after hour embroidering the hem. It had sleeves now, and was no longer such a horrid green. Surely it wouldn't take much to finish it?

I touched the pile of handkerchiefs, running my fingers over the deliberate tears. Napoléon was safely imprisoned, but Fog was not. And Napoléon did not kill my father, nor steal his money.

Carefully I folded them once more, tucking them back in the bandbox. I would ask Millie to hide them again. Idly I picked up one of the cravats I'd taken from Cassia's trunk, days before, and tried to catch a hint of my father's scent. But all I could smell was starch.

If Fog was a spy for the War Office, and my father did not trust him—

"Millie," I said suddenly, "what if the Honorable Miss Smith is working for Fog? Or Mr. Smith is?"

Millie nodded calmly. "Yes, madame. In fact, even if she isn't, I'll be in danger, for I can't imagine a spy who wouldn't be. But it seems to me we've been in danger since your father died anyway, so I may as well make something of it."

It was an excellent point. Well, at least once Millie was in the War Office I'd have an ally who believed me.

I stopped. I already had an ally who believed me, and who was in a position to avenge my father, should the opportunity arise—or at least convince those who could. No one ignored the Countess Lieven. I ought to thank her properly for everything she'd shared with me—and it wouldn't hurt to show her what my talent could do either.

Glancing around the tiny shop, I wished we'd had time and money to stock it with at least a few lengths of fabric. Should I send Millie back to the cottage for something I could cut up? But no; Cassia would put her to work at once packing books, and I needed her here for the rest of my plan. I could not change what had happened, and no magic could bring my father back to wear his cravats once more. Slowly I ran the silk fabric over my cheek one last time. Then I threaded my needle and began to sew.

Countess Lieven was Russian, haughty and cold in manner, and I'd been terrified when I'd first been presented to her at Almack's. As I stitched the two cravats together, end to end, they blended into a single ice-blue length of silk.

Now I thought she wore that manner as part of her political strategy. She'd been married at fourteen to Count Lieven—she must be younger than Cassia, I thought—yet Cassia claimed she was a better ambassador than her husband, and no one dared ignore her opinion. I had never heard anyone dismiss her as only a lady. She was thin and angular, no true beauty, yet her smile drew every eye in every room.

For the first time, I wondered if that effect was truly hers, or done with glamours.

The silk took on an extra shimmer under my needle and thinned to gauze, and I smiled. If the countess had a secret spy name, it would be Ice.

I imagined her standing in a ballroom, surveying the crowd from the center, with the most intelligent, most powerful people in the room close at hand, smiling her knowing smile. She would wear a white gown covered in this shawl, dripping in silver lace icicles, with a silver domino masking her face, but everyone present would know her name.

When I looked at my hands, silver thread fell in icicles off the hem of the shawl.

I realized Millie was standing next to me, hardly breathing. "What is it?" I asked.

She shook her head wordlessly. "It's nothing—I only—I can almost see the thread, as you sew in the magic. . . ." Her eyes never left my fingers.

I looked down, but I saw no magic. Talents ran in families—one couldn't simply learn to sew glamours. But with her never-before-seen talent for removing them, how was I to know what Millie could or could not do? She excelled in everything.

I had promised myself that I would do anything I could to

help her. Carefully I handed her the shawl and the needle. "Now, pay attention. You must hold this picture in your mind: the countess is standing in the center of a ballroom, admired by all. . . . Go on, try it."

Her eyes shone with wonder. I turned away, back to Miss Spry's dress, as she took the first stitch.

It was only right, I thought as I studied the progress on Miss Spry's gown. Millie would be the spy, and ought to sew such things. But I could still save Miss Spry from a life of terrible gowns. It was important work, and would pay well. I threaded a new needle, and began to stitch.

Fifteen minutes later, Millie handed me the shawl, her face set.

I examined it. There was where I had stopped, the silver thread forming the last icicle. There were Millie's tiny, neat stitches, continuing along the edge. But there were no icicles, no sparkle. "Hmm. Perhaps sewing my vision in won't work for you? Try envisioning your own picture this time. See the countess clearly in your mind. . . ."

Millie listened carefully, nodding as I explained. She took a deep breath, and took the shawl and needle back once more.

This time I watched as she took stitch after stitch, her face screwed up in concentration. But after twenty more stitches she stopped. "It's no good, madame; I can't sew the magic in. I know yours is there—I can feel magic running all through that fabric—but there's none in my stitches at all."

I picked up the shawl and began to stitch again, doubling back to fill in the icicles, then skipping forward in great swaths of looping thread that promptly vanished when I tugged the needle through. "You mustn't be discouraged, Millie; after all, you still have the rarest, most valuable talent of them all." I turned the corner of the fabric, envisioning it stretched to a more practical shawl-width, and smiled as it stretched into place. At least I had learned some things since my father's death. "Why don't you sew Miss Riverton's fabric up into a tube? It will be easier to get it on the form once I've finished with Miss Spry's, and you don't need a magical talent for that."

I continued to stitch, the vision strong in my mind. The countess turned to say something to a nearby lady; whether it was fashion or politics, the lady raised her eyebrows. The countess smiled, her hair dressed just so, her slender bosom accentuated by the silver sash on her gown. . . .

My fingers reached the end of the fabric. Carefully I stitched the last icicle into the first, knotted off my stitch, and smiled. Swishing the shining gauze over my shoulders, I turned to Millie. "How do I look?"

Millie stared at me, her eyes wide with something—could it be fear? "But . . . You look exactly like her," she said at last.

I frowned. This was a masquerade costume, not a disguise. . . . I tilted the cheval glass until I could see myself in the mirror.

Countess Lieven's face, under her brown curls, looked back at me.

I pulled the shawl off, marveling as her face changed to Madame Martine's. What had I done? "Millie, put this on." I handed her the shawl.

Millie disappeared as she swung it around her shoulders, replaced by the Countess Lieven, looking exactly as I'd looked a moment before. She stared in the mirror for a long moment, then quickly pulled the shawl off and handed it back to me.

For a minute I stood there, the light silk pale in my hands. If

I wore this shawl, I could open any door in England, and half the doors in the rest of Europe as well. I could try to find Fog, learn what had truly happened to my father. . . .

Then I folded it carefully and set it down. The only person with any right to wear that face was the countess herself, and I could not, would not leave Cassia to fight our difficulties alone. I picked up my pen, and wrote a note.

To the Countess Lieven
Honored Lady,
Please accept this gift with my thanks, for everything you've done for me and my family. It would be my great pleasure to meet again and further discuss the weather—at Lady Dustingham's masquerade, perhaps?
Respectfully,
Madame Martine

PS Ask someone you trust to wear it, so that you can observe its effect in greatest secrecy. If you do not wish to keep it, cut it up.

Surely that would give her warning enough not to let just anyone wear it. I tucked the note in with the shawl, wrapped it up, and addressed it to the countess.

Then I stopped. True, my gift might impress the countess—but was I certain I could trust her? Everything I knew about Fog came from her. I wanted to believe her—she'd saved my mother's life! But I had only her word for that too. Ought I to send her such powerful magic, without knowing more?

"Millie, would you please take this to the cottage and hide it in the usual spot? I'm too tired to sort it out properly today."

As Millie stepped out the door, I took out the ledger that

Cassia had given me for the shop accounts. There was so little time, so few opportunities to earn our fortune—no, not even our fortune, I reminded myself, merely enough to repay our debts. Even if I somehow managed that, we would still be destitute. I picked up my pen, biting my lip. Therefore, I was going to have to charge a very large sum of money for every single costume. I performed several calculations in the margins, crossing them out until I reached a figure that made even my eyebrows rise a bit. Then I circled the figure, set the pen aside, and stood up to continue sewing Miss Spry's gown.

Moments went by. Where was Millie? I hurried to the window and looked out, but the lane was quiet.

⚬◗)(◖⚬

Millie returned almost an hour later, clutching a note, her face filled with fear.

I dropped my needle and rushed toward her. "What is it? Are you hurt?"

"It's been stolen, madame," she said, her voice breaking.

I blinked. "Stolen? In Flittingsworth?"

Millie nodded, and I saw her tremble.

"Sit down, and tell me," I said gently.

She sat, staring at the note in her lap. "I was walking toward the cottage, madame, when I heard a carriage. I looked, and it was Lady Prippingforth's nephew." Her face took on that bleak look it got when she remembered.

I put my hand over hers, squeezed hard. "You are safe. Go on."

"I ducked into the patisserie," she said. "I didn't mean to—but my feet just . . ."

I nodded. "I would have done the same."

"No, you wouldn't have, madame. But, as soon as it passed, I stepped out again, as fast as I could. I hurried back toward the cottage, but a horse and rider came down the lane—and it was him, madame. I know it was."

"Mr. Hustlesmith?" I asked.

She shook her head slowly. "No. It was Fog. The man who chased us in London. You'd have known him too—he wore a greatcoat, and those same black boots, and even though it was bright daylight, his face was all in shadows, though I wouldn't have thought the brim of his hat was so wide."

I gasped. Our assailant—or at least one of them—was here.

"So I turned and ran," Millie said. "I know you didn't mean to send it, madame, but I didn't want him to see where we live! So I ran for the inn—and I made it, just as the mail coach was preparing to leave. I gave the package to the innkeeper."

"But then how was it stolen?" I cried.

Her smile faltered. "That man—Fog—he grabbed the package right out of the innkeeper's hands," Millie said. "Before I could think what to do, he rode away."

I sat down hard. "You are saying that the man who has twice attacked us in London—most likely the traitor known as Fog, who betrayed my mother and may have murdered my father—you're saying he's here in Flittingsworth? And that he has the countess's shawl?"

Millie nodded. "Yes, madame."

"The glamoured shawl that can disguise anyone as the countess—perhaps even Fog."

Millie nodded, her eyes filling with tears.

"It isn't your fault, Millie—and thank heavens you're safe! Now, help me think: where is Cassia?" I demanded.

"Taking tea with Miss Fielde—Miss Fielde sent her carriage this morning. I saw her get in."

I thought hard. Part of me wanted to rush out to check on Cassia—but even I couldn't imagine Miss Fielde as an enemy agent. Cassia was safe enough where she was, for now—and that gave me time to try to put at least some of this to rights.

I forced myself to take a deep breath. "For an intellectual, Miss Whitworth is awfully good with knives," I reminded Millie. "She may be safer than we are."

She nodded and slid a knife from her boot, sniffing back her tears. "Right after Fog stole that package, the innkeeper—who was even angrier once the man disappeared—yelled out that he was calling the constables, and that there'd be no more stealing of the Countess Lieven's gowns on his watch."

"So all of Flittingsworth knows that Madame Martine sewed a gown—well, what they think is a gown—for the countess." The gossips would spread that like wildfire. It would have been a stroke of luck, except for the part where it had all gone horribly wrong.

Millie nodded. "I imagine every lady whose maid overheard him will be here just as soon as their invitations arrive, to place their orders."

I rubbed my temples. This was no time for the headache. "But no one knew about the shawl—I'd only just sewn it. Why would someone steal my package? Unless . . ."

Millie nodded. "Unless Fog thought you were sending someone those handkerchiefs."

I frowned. "If Fog knows what the message says—and those fools at the War Office may even have told him themselves, since he's an agent—he'd want those handkerchiefs back. They're the only clue we have that he's a traitor, who may be connected to my father's death."

Millie bit her lip.

I made up my mind. "Our assailant will be disappointed to have a silk shawl rather than a pile of handkerchiefs, but at least they're still safe. You'd best put them back in their hiding place tonight."

"Maybe he'll think you already gave them to the countess, and are thanking her for taking care of them for you," Millie offered.

That cheered me up a bit. "Perhaps! I'm quite sure the countess can fend for herself. But I suppose I must write to her and explain why there is a rumor that she ordered a gown from me, and to warn her what that shawl can do." I wondered. Could that shawl disguise a man in naval boots as the Countess Lieven? She would not be happy about this situation, but perhaps she would know what to do. Was the greatcoat glamoured too? If so, who sewed it for him? And what did he look like the rest of the time? There were so many unknowns, so many risks.

First things first. "Who has written to me?" I asked, holding out my hand for the note.

Millie looked away. "It isn't for you, madame. It's addressed to me."

I blinked. "From your sister?"

She shook her head.

Who would write to Millie? I wondered—and then I knew. The Honorable Miss Smith. I forced myself to get up and walk away from her, back to the dress form. That note was Millie's alone.

When I glanced up next, she was frowning over it, but she said nothing.

At last, she rose to her feet, tucking the note into her sleeve.

I cleared my throat. "Millie, we must learn whether Lady Dustingham has sent the countess an invitation to her masquerade." I began to pace the floor of the shop. "Lady Dustingham is an eccentric, rich enough to have a carriage she lends to whoever requests it; she herself doesn't seem to go anywhere, so we shall have to go to her—or, rather, you will have to go to her." I paused, trying to think what else Cassia had said, or was it Miss Spencer? "Oh! And she is an illusionist, and a collector of illusions." I crossed to my desk and took out my ink bottle and a sheet of paper, then absently sharpened the nib on my pen with the knife Millie had retrieved for me. Quickly I wrote a note, and handed it to Millie. "There! We need the money, so Cassia can hardly object to my telling Lady Dustingham that I have a small illusion for sale, can she?"

"Do you?" Millie asked, her eyes round.

"Of course I do," I replied. "Just because we are living a life of deceit is no excuse for lying, Millie. At least, not unnecessary lying. I'll look for it this evening—some horrid man sent it to me when he thought I'd make a good heiress for him to marry, but when I tried to send it back, he'd already skipped town. But you don't need it now—this is just to help you in the door, so that you can gossip with the housekeeper."

"Oh, no, madame," Millie said, shaking her head. "Housekeepers do not gossip."

"Really?" I asked.

Millie shook her head. "Not within the hearing of their staff, at least—not the good ones, anyway."

"Then who does gossip? Someone must." I picked up my needle and began to pick at Miss Spry's nearly-there gown once more. Despite our dire predicament, I could not help but smile at how the tiny pleats at the neckline just barely caught the eye, causing the viewer to look closer.

"Parlor maids," Millie said, with great certainty.

I turned to look at her. "But do parlor maids accept messages for the lady of the house?"

Millie tilted her head, looking pensive. "Parlor maids do not know who is on the guest list. But I shall find a way. What else must I learn?"

"I suppose you'd better let them learn from you: that the countess placed an order for a masquerade costume from Madame Martine, glamour modiste. That ought to warn someone that she ought to be on the guest list, if she isn't already." I hesitated. "The trick will be that you must somehow cause them to ask you all about it, while you very properly refuse to gossip about me, until somehow they are able to worm it out of you. Can you manage, do you think?"

Millie thought for a moment. "Yes, I can, and I shall," she said.

I bit my lip. "Perhaps you'd better wear the shawl you wore to the War Office."

Bravely Millie shook her head. "Fog has seen that one, madame."

I got to my feet. "An excellent point. Well, then, I shall sew you another." I began to search the shop for something else I could sew into a disguise. Perhaps a hair ribbon?

But Millie glanced at the clock, and her face cleared. "I'll ask Miss Spencer's deliverywoman if I can ride down and back with Lady Dustingham's pastry delivery. It's nearly time for that now, and I can see them drive up from the window."

"How do you know that?" I asked. I didn't even know Lady Dustingham had a pastry delivery, let alone when it took place.

"I heard Miss Spencer tell the cook it had to be ready in an hour, when I was there earlier," Millie said, shrugging. "I remember little things like that." Setting her eye to the window, she waited a moment while we listened to the cart roll up the lane, and then, in a flash, she was out the door and gone.

Chapter Twenty-Eight

IN WHICH MILLICENT IS STUMPED AT LAST (THOUGH NOT FOR LONG)

Nothing is to be left to conjecture where the art shews
the way of proceeding with certainty.

—*CRYPTOGRAPHIA; OR, THE ART OF DECYPHERING,* by David Arnold
Conradus (a dusty old book that Lady Scovell gave to Cassia)

When Millie returned and saw Miss Spry's finished gown on the dress form, she gave a very satisfying gasp. I patted it on the shoulder fondly; it really was some of my better work: a sky blue, filled with the peace and happiness I'd envisioned for her, shot through with silver sparks of confidence. As long as she put it on before speaking to her mother, I was nearly certain it would work. (Also, I'd tried it on myself, and it did not make me look anything like Miss Spry.) "No need for dramatics, Millie—we have work to do! Please pack this gown, but don't deliver it; I must finish Miss Riverton's first."

"Yes, madame," Millie said, bobbing a curtsy. "It's just so perfect for her, madame." Carefully she undid the gown and lifted it from the dress form.

I waited, but Millie said nothing further. Well, as I was her employer, it was only proper that she wait until she was asked. "Do tell me about Lady Dustingham's housekeeper, Millie."

"Mrs. Davenport was not available to see me, as there'd been a mix-up about the fish delivery," Millie said, carefully laying the gown on the table.

I sighed. "Well, I shall just have to spare you again later, then—we really have no time to lose, you know."

Millie nodded. "That's what I thought too. So I made arrangements to speak with Lady Dustingham's cousin, Miss Faversham."

Lady Dustingham's cousin lived with her? Why did Cassia try to send me there, if Lady Dustingham already had a companion, of sorts? "And by 'made arrangements,' you mean . . . ?"

Millie smiled, just a hint, but I saw it. "Well, I was very reluctant, of course, but when I happened to mention to Vicky—she's one of the parlor maids—that a great lady from London had ordered a shawl from Madame Martine, she did prod me, so . . . finally, I agreed to tell her who had ordered it, though nothing more, of course, in exchange for a quick word with Miss Faversham."

"Well done, Millie!" I said, greatly relieved.

"Miss Faversham is supervising the invitations for Lady Dustingham. When I gave her your message, I told her how exciting it was that a great lady like the countess might be coming to her ladyship's ball. Oh, she wasn't very happy, madame; told me that the countess and Lady Dustingham had been friends for years, and of course the countess always received an invitation—though, me being new here, I wouldn't know that—even though she so rarely leaves London, and that Lady Dustingham is a great lady too, and I oughtn't to forget it."

"At least she sent the invitation! She can be as disgruntled as she likes!"

"No, she hadn't, madame," Millie said positively. "But she'll send it tomorrow, quick as she can."

How did she know these things? I could not begin to guess. "Excellent work. And you saw no signs of our mystery assailant, nor of that horrid Mr. Hustlesmith?"

A knife appeared in Millie's free hand. "No, more's the pity."

"Er, very good," I said. "As always, I am deeply indebted to you."

I picked up Miss Riverton's tube of fabric once more, then became aware of Millie's hesitation. Slowly I turned back. "You have my attention, Millie."

"I'd like permission to tell the Honorable Miss Smith how I helped you create Madame," Millie said quietly. "So she knows what I can do."

For just a moment I hesitated, my stomach filled with squirms. Millie had taught me how to dress and how to act as Madame Martine—what to say, even how to walk. I'd made my double life work, but only because she had helped me. I couldn't be a spy without her—why, I couldn't even maintain Madame's disguise on my own.

And that meant I owed her all the help I could give, even if losing her meant I would lose my shop and everything else. I raised my chin and met her eyes. "Agreed," I said. "You've earned the right, a hundred times over."

She bit her lip. "But, madame—I can't read the note she sent."

I frowned. "What do you mean? Is it in another language?"

Millie pulled the folded note from her sleeve and handed it over.

I smoothed it out on the table, scanning the contents. "Ah! A numeric cipher."

4 5 1 18 13 9 12 12 9 3 5 14 20

13 5 5 20 13 5 1 20 14 9 14 5 15 3 12 15 3 11 9 14 12 1 4 25
4 21 19 20 9 14 7 8 1 13 19 12 9 2 18 1 18 25 15 14 20 8 5 14 9 7 8 20
15 6 20 8 5 13 1 19 17 21 5 18 1 4 5

23 5 12 12 4 15 14 5
20 8 5 8 15 14 13 9 19 19 19 19 13 9 20 8

I looked up at her. "Cassia taught me this one years ago; you know how she loves numbers. Miss Smith didn't think much of your ciphering skill—this one is quite easy. Do you want to puzzle it out yourself?"

Millie looked down at the numbers. "But . . . it's just numbers."

"It's meant to look like just numbers, true enough. Here, I'll show you."

Quickly I wrote out the alphabet on a sheet of paper, adding a row of numbers below it:

A B C D E F G H I J K L M N O P Q R S T U V W X Y Z
1 2 3 4 5 6 7 8 9 10 11 12 13 14 15 16 17 18 19 20 21 22 23 24 25 26

"See?" I handed her the sheet. "Try it—you'll soon see the message." I picked up my needle again and turned resolutely back to Miss Riverton's gown. This was Millie's message, not mine, even though she hadn't been able to read it on her own.

"What an odd thing for a lady to know." Millie was staring at me.

I laughed. "A lady, perhaps, but not a mathematician. I prefer novels, but there's nothing Cassia likes better than to work out a puzzle. Once in a while her friend Lady Scovell sends her a truly difficult one, and then it's all I can do to convince her to stop and eat!"

Millie stared at me a moment longer, then nodded and bent over her work. At last, Millie looked up from her message. "What does the underlining mean?" She turned the paper to show me, so I leaned in to look.

D E A R <u>M</u> I L L I C E N T

M E E T <u>M E</u> A T <u>N</u> I N E O C L O C K I <u>N L</u> A D Y
D U S T I N G H A <u>M S</u> L I B R A R Y <u>O N</u> T H E <u>N I G H T</u>
O F <u>T H E</u> M A S Q U E R A D E

W E <u>L L</u> D O N E
<u>T H E</u> H O N <u>M I S S</u> S M I T H

"It's to separate words, so the whole thing doesn't run together into mush," I told her. "Cassia taught me to alternate two colors of ink, but perhaps Miss Smith didn't have two colors at hand? Anyway, it serves the same purpose." I ignored the sinking feeling in my stomach. Miss Smith really did mean to hire Millie. "If you'd like to reply with a more difficult cipher, you can reverse the order of the numbers, so that *A* equals twenty-six, and write it that way. I'm certain we can borrow another color of ink from Cassia."

She nodded, but said nothing until I'd begun sewing once more. "Madame? What will happen to you, once I'm gone?"

I shrugged, without turning around; I didn't want her to see my face. "Cassia and I will find a way. You must know by now that we always do."

"I think you should come to the library too," she said quietly. "You'd be good at this, madame."

I leaned my forehead on the dress form, trying not to cry. "Millie, I'd be a disaster. I'm useless with knives, I've only just learned to walk as Madame, I sewed a dangerous glamour and immediately lost it, and it took me years to even notice that my father was a spy."

"But you solved that cipher in no time at all," she said.

"Only because Cassia taught it to me." I shook my head. "Who knows if Miss Smith would even speak to you if I turned up too. No, I won't ruin your chances. You earned this, Millie, and I wish you great happiness."

Millie turned the cipher sheet over and began to write, the scratching of the pen echoing in my ears.

I looked away, determined to preserve her privacy.

But instead of folding it up to mail to Miss Smith, she passed the sheet to me.

10 15 9 14 21 19 1 20 14 9 14 5 6 9 6 20 5 5 14 20 8 5 14

I blinked back the tears and smiled at her. "Millie, you really are a wonder, you know."

She smiled, and nodded as we set back to work.

Chapter Twenty-Nine

IN WHICH MADAME MARTINE DISCOVERS THE CHALLENGES OF SEWING FOR MASQUERADES (AND ECCENTRICS)

Age cannot wither her,
nor custom stale / Her infinite variety.
—ANTONY AND CLEOPATRA, by William Shakespeare

$\mathcal{I}$ spent the rest of the afternoon so absorbed in Miss Riverton's gown that I hardly noticed when dusk fell—and by then my feet were dragging as low as my eyelids. Therefore, I was wholly unprepared for the sight of Miss Spencer at our sitting-room table.

Cassia's somber mood did not appear to be affecting Miss Spencer one bit either.

"Invitations to Lady Dustingham's soirée!" she cried, rising to her feet and passing us both cards. "It's in just three weeks, so you'd best begin your costumes."

Millie held out her card to Miss Spencer, her face blank. "But, madam . . ."

"Lady Dustingham is an eccentric, you know—an extremely wealthy eccentric," Miss Spencer said. "The ladies of

Flittingsworth pestered her for years to give balls, and when she finally obliged, she decided to invite not only the proper people, but all the rest of us too!" She smiled wickedly. "So, of course, those same ladies refused to bring their daughters, in case they should dance with a fencing master or some other unsuitable person— but all that changed when the daring Miss Levy attended and caught the eye of some baron or other, who promptly married her. Now it is the marriage mart of the year, at least outside of London, and even the matrons all do their best to outshine each other."

I examined my invitation: gilt-covered and heavy, with plenty of flourishes. " 'Lady Dustingham requests the pleasure of your company—yes, you—at her annual evening of social unity, where all classes will mingle as one amidst a joyous celebration,' " I read aloud. "Ooh, and do listen to this: 'Costumes are never optional. Do your part!' "

"She hates it when young ladies wear a beautiful gown with only a plain mask, without any real attempt at a costume," Miss Spencer said. "Though I can't remember the last time Lady Dustingham wore a mask herself."

Cassia glanced up, dismayed. "I'd forgotten it is a masquerade," she said.

But I certainly hadn't.

I couldn't help the anxious feeling in my stomach as I watched Cassia make her way to Miss Spencer's patisserie the next morning, nor stop myself from searching the lane as we hurried to my shop.

Once inside, I wrote to the countess.

Honored Lady,

I regret to inform you that a gift intended for you has fallen into the hands of which we spoke. If you should happen to hear of yourself attending any events for which you were not actually present, I apologize most profusely.

If it is convenient, I should greatly appreciate your presence and your wisdom at Lady Dustingham's masquerade.

Respectfully,

Daughter of Rain and Breeze

Millie posted it without a word, and without incident, and I had almost stopped feeling sick by the time our first customer arrived.

∞◯)(◯∞

By the end of the day, I had orders for gowns for six Cleopatras (each with a different color of sash, and with no idea there would be more than one—but that hardly mattered, for each one would feel like a unique bright-and-shining jewel of the East at the masquerade); one Helen of Troy (this was after I'd run out of sash colors and was at my wit's end—and did you know that girl had never heard of the Trojan War and did not believe me that Helen could possibly have started it, until I explained all the important bits? And even then she wasn't convinced, until Millie told her that of course Helen must wear gold sandals and agreed that she probably had gilded toenails to match!); one Eleanor of Aquitaine (she'd wanted to be Queen Elizabeth, but I was certainly not going to have time for such an ensemble, nor would she have managed it at all well); one cinder girl minus any hint of cinders (and how anyone was to guess that she was the cinder girl without cinders was quite beyond me, but I supposed I'd have to manage somehow); and an extremely resolute potted plant, who could not be talked out of pot, or foliage, but did allow that a flowered hat might prove acceptable.

Remembering, I caught myself staring out at the shadows, as though I could tell from this distance whether someone in a greatcoat loomed in the darkness, waiting to grab us. I shook my head, forcing myself to look down at my work once more. Millie did not need any further cause for nerves. Besides, I finally had a piece of news worth celebrating.

"To think that each of those ladies will pay fifteen pounds apiece for draped bedsheets!" I said, sinking into my chair. "And not a hint of imagination amongst them. It's enough to make one feel like a criminal."

"Oh, no, madame," Millie said, tidying up the measuring tapes and carefully placing my notes from our last fitting with the customer's length of plain white muslin. "They could make their own well enough, only how would anyone know they'd spent such a vast sum on bedsheets? No, they're not paying for what you'll sew, madame; they're paying to be the star of the ball. They're paying for their dreams."

I stared at her. "Even I can't make them *all* be the star of the evening!"

Millie smiled. "But you can make each and every one of them feel as though they are, madame. That's what they've really paid for."

I picked up the first length of muslin thoughtfully. Miss Allen wished to be a dark and mysterious shining jewel of the East, which was going to be a bit difficult, as she was currently rather pale and bland.

"She wants Mr. Godalming to notice her, but he's chasing

after that Miss Crawley now," Millie said. "Really, though, she'd be better off noticing Mr. Miller, who's been trying to catch her attention for years. They both take a great interest in tulips."

I stared at her. "Do you have a secret life I'm not aware of, Millie?"

She smiled. "Oh, no, madame. I just hear things, when I fetch the post and all. No one stops talking when I come along; why would they?"

"I'll see what I can do for Miss Allen," I said, examining my notes. "It seems wrong to encourage her to marry someone else, though, when she's paying me fifteen pounds."

Millie shrugged. "Mr. Godalming has terrible taste in waistcoats, and Mr. Miller's farm is very prosperous."

"Perhaps I could bring out her own unique beauty and love of tulips, and let her and the fates handle things from there," I decided.

"That should do it, madame," Millie said, beginning to stitch up the sides of the other muslins. "Now, there's Mrs. Carlyle, who wants to dress as a witch, but Mrs. Stephenson, her stepmama, shudders at the very thought. . . ."

⚬))((⚬

The next day was much the same: another Helen of Troy (Millie told her where to order the gilding for her toenails), one Titania (I told her she was going to have to sort out the wings herself), another Eleanor of Aquitaine (this one had to be convinced that dressing as the Empress Josephine would be in very poor taste, even if she was said to have been a very beautiful lady), and a lady who only wanted a pink dress and to gild her toenails too. She lacked vision, but she agreed to the amount without complaint, so I told her she could wear a golden domino to hide her face and tell everyone she was the Dawn, and then wear it to as many other balls as she liked, only without the mask, of course. She seemed pleased.

I, however, was exhausted. I'd spent all the previous night sewing Miss Riverton's gown, and could hardly keep my eyes open wide enough to see the smile on Millie's face when I paid her. Between us, we could hardly keep up with taking in the orders, let alone sewing the costumes. In desperation, I raised Madame's prices yet again, and insisted that half my fees be paid immediately.

But even more customers came, along with a note from the countess.

Miss Damp Wind,

It is not at all convenient. I cannot imagine what you were thinking, to take such risks, but surely you've realized the consequences. I expect you to handle your own difficulties yourself, at once.

Please do not disappoint me.

Dorothea, Countess Lieven

PS Do not contact me again until this has been resolved.

I did not have the energy to think what to do, so I handed it to Millie. "No one has seen the countess in Flittingsworth, have they?"

Millie shook her head, looking worried, and handed it back.

How did the countess think I could possibly solve such a problem?

Hearing the rumble of a carriage, I got up and peered out the window to see Lady Dustingham's familiar landau. I waited to see who would get out. Perhaps I could set Millie to embroidering patterned sashes, if there must be more Cleopatras?

Quite to my surprise, the carriage's occupant was a distinguished gray-haired lady with a silver-topped cane. I caught Millie's eye; she nodded, and went to open the door.

I stood behind the desk as Lady Dustingham herself swept in.

"*Bonjour*. What a pleasure, my lady," I said, dropping a low curtsy.

"Madame Martine," Lady Dustingham said, nodding as she looked me over. "I've heard quite a lot about you of late. Is it all true?"

I raised an eyebrow. "That depends. What do you wish to be true, my lady?"

Lady Dustingham smiled, and took the chair Millie held for her. "Oh, a foolish whim, no more. Still, I am here now. . . . I can paint an illusion, madame: birds that sing and flutter their wings on the page, delighting eye and ear. Yet that is hardly all my magic can do. What about yours?"

Slowly, thoughtfully, I examined Lady Dustingham. Togas did not seem her style, and she would never want to look like a potted plant. But why, then, was she here?

She returned my stare, and I felt as though the air was charged with tension. Lady Dustingham had a reputation, a formidable presence, and I had no doubt that everyone in the area knew her appearance as well as they knew her silver-topped cane. . . . *Ah.*

"You wish for a disguise for your own masquerade," I said slowly. "So that you can see it as others see it."

She nodded. "For ten years I've patted myself on the back

for this opportunity for all classes to come together and enjoy each other's company, but every year I wonder: How well does it work, just outside of my sight? What do my guests say, outside of my hearing? And I cannot help but wonder if this might be my chance."

I studied her. I could not say no. Yet sewing a costume to fool the entire town, all of whom knew this lady's every step . . . I nodded, before I could frighten myself out of it. "I can give you that chance, my lady. Only, we will need a distraction."

Lady Dustingham tilted her head. "Intriguing. Tell me more."

"We shall need someone to play Lady Dustingham and preside over the masquerade," I said. "Only then can you stand at the sidelines. Now, I know of a young lady who dreams of good works, but hasn't much experience with actually doing them. If you were to ask her, as a personal favor, to step into your shoes for one evening . . ."

Smiling, Lady Dustingham opened her reticule, counting my fee out into Millie's hand. "I believe I know the lady of whom you speak. You are correct; it will do nicely. Make of me whatever you like, madame; I trust your judgment wholeheartedly."

As she rose from her chair, I cleared my throat. "My lady, have you seen the Countess Lieven of late?"

She stilled, looking at me sharply. "I have not."

I met her gaze. "Someone stole a package from me, addressed to her. If you should see her, I would appreciate it if you would send me a message."

Very slowly Lady Dustingham nodded. "I see."

Chapter Thirty

LADY DUSTINGHAM'S SOCIAL EXPERIMENT

Desperate affairs require desperate measures.
—Admiral Horatio Lord Nelson

∞◊)(◊∞

*N*ineteen days and twenty-six gowns later (if you counted all those togas), Millie and I delivered the last costume for the masquerade. I had not slept properly in ages—had hardly eaten a bite—and when I reached the cottage, I realized I had failed to account for how we would get to Lady Dustingham's masquerade.

Thankfully, Miss Spencer had not. She arrived promptly at seven-thirty to await our passage in one of the carriages Lady Dustingham had arranged, and was just in time to assist me with Cassia's preparations.

She frowned a little when I opened the door, and then suddenly smiled. "How clever! If you are in costume, you can't truly be Millicent—is it Miss Annis wearing Millicent's old dress?"

"Yes, it's me," I answered, making a mental note to take a few more stitches in the old brown dress so that no one else would see through my disguise. "It seemed appropriate to the event, and I have not had a moment to sew anything else." I ushered her into the sitting room and shouted down the hall. "Here, now, Aunt Cassia, come see how lovely Miss Spencer looks, and do let me finish your hair."

"Absolutely not!" came the muffled reply.

Miss Spencer raised an eyebrow.

I shrugged. "She doesn't like her costume—she wanted to be some mathematician that no one has ever heard of."

Cassia's door burst open, and she rushed into the sitting room in her dressing gown. "Émilie du Châtelet is not just some mathematician! She would be at least as well known as the extremely peculiar Isaac Newton if anyone in academia had a whit of sense!"

I bowed my head. "I stand corrected, of course, and I promise I will try to figure out some way of disguising you properly next year—as soon as you can tell me what she might have worn! Now, will you please put on your toga so that I can do your hair?"

Cassia wrapped her dressing gown more tightly about her. "Certainly not. It is completely inappropriate, as well as indecent." She turned to Miss Spencer. "Can you believe she sewed me a Cleopatra costume?"

"I did not!" I said, indignant. "Really, my dear aunt, it is a wonder you have any costume at all—it's not as though I've had time to spare! How can you argue with Minerva, goddess of wisdom? Just choose some heavy book to clasp to your bosom all night, and let's be off. Although it is a pity we don't have a stuffed owl."

Miss Spencer tipped her head thoughtfully. "Minerva, hmm? No, I must respectfully disagree. If Miss Whitworth wishes to be a mathematician, and if you've sewn her a toga, I believe she must be Hypatia."

Cassia's mouth was already open to protest, but her eyes widened at this. "Hypatia?" she breathed. "Really? Do you think? Of course, it really ought to be an Ionic chiton, not a toga, then. . . ."

As though anyone would identify an ancient Greek lady mathematician by her sleeves, amidst a roomful of Cleopatras! But she could argue as much as she liked with the other guests, once we'd arrived. "Just put it on and tell me where to gather the fabric," I said wearily.

Cassia hesitated. "I am sorry, Annis—I know you haven't had time for anything else, but it really is completely inappropriate for a lady of my age. Why, it is a good thing it isn't raining, or I'd have no illusions left at all! But perhaps Hypatia wore a large shawl at all times."

Miss Spencer laughed. "My dear Miss Whitworth, what is the fun of a masquerade if one cannot be at least a little bit inappropriate? Put on your costume at once, so that we can compare." And with that she removed her own cloak.

Cassia's mouth fell open. I immediately began to make mental notes—how, for instance, did Miss Spencer's seamstress cause her gown to fall like a river over her hips?

"The water spirit Melusine, of course," Miss Spencer said, smiling at our reactions. "Now do get ready, Miss Whitworth, or we shall miss the carriage."

I had to admit her long red hair—left loose just this once—was absolutely perfect with the swinging sea-green drapes of her gown. What a pity Madame had not received any such interesting, daring requests! But perhaps next year . . .

Thanks to Miss Spencer's assuring Cassia that Hypatia's braids could be wrapped and pinned in the carriage, and that she would not allow me to pin them in a historically inaccurate manner, we did reach the masquerade at last.

Oh, I have known marvelous wonders at London balls: ballrooms sparkling with flameless lumens, a pianoforte that would play all by itself (though every so often a pillow would have to be stuffed inside the works as it struck up a highly inappropriate song the string master had learned at sea, startling all the officers in the room), even an extremely famous African siren who made everyone first rapturously in love, then positively ill with the sorrow of her song (well, I was not actually present at that moment, as Cassia had insisted we leave as soon as the siren was announced, but I heard all about it). But in all my years of London parties, I had never seen a crush like Lady Dustingham's ball. Of course, I had never stood next to a housemaid in a red domino sipping a glass of champagne either, nor seen a lady in her leaf-green domino dancing the minuet with a man who seemed to be dressed as a shrubbery. (I did hope the potted-plant lady got a turn with him as well, for they might share some tips.)

But perhaps the most amazing sight of all was the walls of Lady Dustingham's ballroom. I knew she was an illusionist as well as an eccentric, but I had never seen anything like this. I let the crush of the crowd press me toward the far wall.

It was like a patchwork of wallpaper, of sketches, watercolors, and oils, all blended together into an enormous ocean scene. Here, an inked fish swam toward a bit of waving watercolor seaweed, and as I watched, a tiny watercolor sardine swam across the seaweed's paper to join a shining school, heading for the south wall. I could not help but gasp at the beauty of it. As I looked more closely, I noticed that the styles were quite different. Lady Dustingham had not created every illusion herself, but had combined many illusions into one greater illusion. . . . It was enough to make me believe the tales of illusionists who'd painted the navy ships so cleverly they could disappear into nothing but sea and sky (with perhaps an occasional highly indecent mermaid popping out of the waves to lure sailors to their doom, and cause them to doubt their sanity). Not that anyone would dare press Lady Dustingham into service for the navy, the way they might some hapless sign painter.

I followed the edge of the wall, heading for the south, which seemed to be forest or jungle, dawn through night. Unfortunately, half the guests seemed to be swimming upstream from me, and my progress was minuscule at best.

"I was told Lady Dustingham added a dragon to the illusions this year!" a lady in a vastly inferior toga cried, hauling her companion forward, just missing my boots. "Do you see it, Lady Pennworth? Perhaps near the cranes . . ."

Her companion sighed behind her simple black domino, but turned her head obediently toward the cranes as I tried not to mind the press of flesh around me.

Then again, it was not as though it mattered; I had more than an hour before Millie was to meet the Honorable Miss Smith, and no desire to dance in the meantime. At least the pace allowed me to examine the crowd at my leisure.

Many of my Cleopatras were missing (probably waiting to make a dramatic entrance, I guessed). But I spotted the potted-plant lady wearing a rather spectacular corsage and being ogled by a gentleman dressed as a prize heifer (or, that was my assumption, for who else would wear a cow's headdress and carry a trophy?).

Lady St. Gregory of the Royal Society for the Beaux Arts was there, dressed in a chiton whose sleeves differed from Cassia's; no doubt she was impersonating some sculptor she admired. She seemed deep in argument with a young lady who I feared might be dressed as William the Conqueror, complete with the blood of his enemies. I shuddered, and hoped that Lady St. Gregory prevailed. Miss Spencer was talking and laughing with a group of admiring gentlemen, while Cassia seemed to have forgotten her discomfort long enough to argue vehemently with a lady in a turban who was carrying a (hopefully, false) serpent. (I did hope she did not think she was Cleopatra, for her gown was not at all Egyptian, even if one excused the turban.)

There was no sign of the countess. I could feel my shoulders begin to relax from the hunched tension of the past weeks. All those costumes, the late nights—I could not bear to think about how many times I'd muttered "Queen of the Nile, exotic and beautiful" over a piece of white cloth, trying to remember exactly which glamour to add to each particular toga! But we'd received the last of the payments today, and this very evening, after I saw Millie safely settled with Miss Smith, I would give Cassia the remainder, and she could pay our debts and decide what was to become of us. If, that is, Miss Smith did not decide to hire me as well, for really, why shouldn't she?

Across the ballroom, I saw Millie at last: dressed in Madame Martine's gown and wig, nodding thoughtfully at a gushing Miss Spry, who was wearing her new blue gown with a simple silver domino. I could see the peace and happiness shining right out of her from across the ballroom, and so, it seemed, could the rather pink young man hovering nearby. I smiled with pleasure, and continued to scan the crowd.

Lady Dustingham was presiding over all, of course, nodding and smiling at her guests, her hands resting on the knob of her cane. But there: off in the corner were two ladies in the black gowns of housekeepers, having a quiet conversation. They were the only people I'd seen who were making no effort to be noticed, thereby catching my curiosity.

Feeling a little woozy with weariness and the sudden heat of the room, I threaded my way through the crowd, slowly realizing that people did not make way for a girl in a maid's dress the way they made way for Miss Annis Whitworth. I raised my voice a little louder, excusing myself, and got an elbow to the ribs for my trouble. Gasping, I stopped, and a lady bumped into me, spilling punch all down Millie's dress, and did not even bother to apologize. I pulled a handkerchief from Millie's pocket and tried to wipe the worst of it off. Just my luck, to bargain with the Honorable Miss Smith at last, all sticky with punch and smelling like a wine vat. Then again, perhaps it would prove I was not too particular to be a good spy? After all, I'd heard that travel could be dirty and uncomfortable as well as outright dangerous at times, and I could not imagine things would be any more pleasant for a spy than for a gentleman on a grand tour.

"I have been meaning to speak with you about one of my neighbors. . . ."

I was close enough to hear the two ladies now, and I smiled; one was the true Lady Dustingham. But who was her companion? The countess, having changed her mind, perhaps? The Honorable Miss Smith? I crept forward, ears strained for the lady's reply.

Only to bump into none other than Mr. Harrington, in a well-cut naval uniform.

"I do beg your pardon, miss," he said.

"I'm afraid the fault was mine, Mr. Harrington," I said, dropping a curtsy before I remembered I was disguised. His brow wrinkled, and I shrugged. "Miss Annis Whitworth, presently disguised—er, costumed—of course."

His eyes widened, and he bowed at once. "Miss Annis! I hardly recognized you—I mean, I had not heard that . . ."

I frowned. Surely Mr. Harrington did not think I'd been forced to become a maid immediately after refusing him. "Mr. Harrington, I must say . . ." But then I caught the eyes of the nondescript ladies on me, and remembered the Honorable Miss Smith's claim that no one would ever take me for a maid. I'd show her. I raised my chin and said, "I must go, Mr. Harrington." Then I turned and pushed my way through the crowd, slipping under elbows, trying to ignore Mr. Harrington's voice behind me.

I reached the punch tables, and made for the hallway.

Earlier that day, Millie had told me that the library was across the gallery and up the grand staircase, then three doors down the hallway. The crowd had already spilled into the gallery as well. I heard Mr. Harrington call out behind me, and I made my move: I opened the door to the servants' staircase, and slipped into the dim light, hoping for a moment to calm my thoughts and prepare for my meeting.

For all Lady Dustingham's efforts at social equality, there was no comfort here in the cold and echoing stone. But it was quiet. I began to climb the stairs, wondering why Mr. Harrington's pursuit had so rattled me.

I reached the top of the stairs and opened the door just a crack. There was no one around. I slipped into the hallway and hurried down the passage toward the top of the grand staircase, where I began to count doors.

I was almost to the library when I heard a sound in one of the rooms. Strange; who but the spies would be up here tonight? The door was open a crack, and I pushed it open a tiny bit farther, just far enough to see inside.

It was horrid Mr. Hustlesmith. He had a maid's arm twisted up behind her back, her pretty dress was torn, and she was crying.

Chapter Thirty-One

ALL MANNER OF ATTACK

When I see a fellow-creature about to perish through
the cowardice of her pretended friends, I wish to be
allowed to speak, that I may say what I know of her
character. —*FRANKENSTEIN*, by Anonymous (but everyone knows it
must have been written by the scandalous Lord Byron)

"*N*o!" I shouted, and I ran straight for them, my head filled with
the memories of Millie's fear and rage.

I hit his outstretched arm with the full force of my momen-
tum. The maid broke free and ran for the door.

And Mr. Hustlesmith smiled, and grabbed me by the arm
instead, dragging me closer to him.

I forced myself to remember Cassia's lessons on effective
ways to defend against improprieties. I screamed, but Lady Dustingham's walls were thick stone. I could hear nothing but my
heart pounding; no one was close enough to come to my aid.

Time to come forth and fight. Of course, I had not a single
knife on me, nor could I properly use one. Why hadn't I realized
I could be at risk, disguised as Millie? But it never occurred to me
that Mr. Hustlesmith would be here. So I screamed and stomped

on his foot, which did at least wipe the smile from his face. I promised myself that I'd sew knife sheaths into all of our gowns if only I could break free.

I yanked my arm back, but he only held tighter, smiling once more. I tell you, I did not care for that smile.

So I whipped a threaded needle from my waistband and sank it into his thigh.

His roar filled my ears, but he did not let go. Instead, he pulled me around, trapping me tightly against his body by my own arm, so I could not see what he might do next. His breath was hot in my hair, his other hand already tugging at my gown, however I struggled. I remembered the maid's eyes, and I understood her fear.

Then I reached up, grabbed his arm with my free hand, forced my body back hard and low against his, and executed the only attack Cassia had managed to teach me thus far.

Mr. Hustlesmith flipped over my shoulder and landed with a crash on the ground, taking most of my sleeve with him.

Not allowing myself one bit of self-congratulation for actually defeating an enemy, I took advantage of his moment of shock and ran.

I raced back toward the grand staircase and down, trying not to hear Mr. Hustlesmith's longer strides behind me. Where was Cassia, or even Millie? Where was the maid I had freed? Where was the real Lady Dustingham? I could see no one I recognized through the crowd, so I pushed on, begging pardons with every gasped breath. Why was he still chasing me? Didn't he know this was no way to behave? Then I caught sight of the worn brown dress I was wearing. Who would step forward to defend a maid?

He caught me again in the middle of the ballroom, just as

I glimpsed the temporary Lady Dustingham. "Unhand me, you brute!" I shouted, loud enough that the musicians stopped, and stomped on his other foot for good measure.

Anyone who hadn't heard my yell certainly heard his. Slowly the crowd turned and cleared a circle around us as he gripped my arm tighter, his face flushed with rage.

"I found this man threatening a maid," I said, my voice projecting clearly through the room.

A lady whose bejeweled asp matched her golden domino and gilded toenails turned slowly, the crowd parting before her, as Mr. Hustlesmith spluttered. "Surely there must be some mistake," she purred. "My nephew is hotly pursued by young ladies, to be sure, but he has never been other than a gentleman."

I could feel my face go red, and then white. Lady Prippingforth. Who would take the word of a shabby maid with a torn sleeve against hers? Already I could feel the crowd turning their backs to me, turning to face her, nodding along. This was how Millie had been dismissed without a reference; this was how he would slip free of any punishment, over and over.

"That is not true, as you well know," I said, trying to keep my voice from shaking.

Mr. Hustlesmith was smiling again, his eyes hard. "I shall take great pleasure in telling Lady Dustingham how her maids behave behind her back, you little hussy," he said, rubbing his thigh. "No, you won't escape, not until I've handed you over to her." He took a step closer to me.

I took a step back, searching the crowd for anyone who might help—but I knew so few people here, no one who would vouch for me. My heart wobbled in the depths of my stomach. Where could Cassia be, or even Mr. Harrington?

But it was Madame Martine who nodded firmly at a pale Miss Riverton and trembling Miss Spry, and stepped forward. "This man attacked my shopgirl and destroyed my property," she said, and her firm voice carried throughout the room without a quaver. She came forward to stand beside me.

Mr. Hustlesmith took a step back under her glare.

"As though the word of a shopkeeper—and a nasty, spiteful one besides—would stand against that of a gentleman!" Lady Prippingforth cried.

Madame raised an eyebrow, staring down the crowd (which included quite a lot of her clients). Without seeming to move, she reached out and touched my sleeve, and I knew what I must do, for her sake, whether it ruined my reputation or not.

"Then perhaps the word of a lady will, for I am not a maid, but Miss Annis Whitworth," I announced. And as the words left my throat, I felt her pull a thread free, and knew my glamour was broken. I grabbed Millie's arm to steady myself, and to keep her from knifing Mr. Hustlesmith in front of a crowd.

There was a gasp from the ladies around us, but they shrank back from me as well as from him. I looked at them, incredulous. I might still be wearing Millie's old gown, but they must recognize me from the ball. I was one of them. Why would they take this man's word over mine?

Then Miss Riverton stepped forward. "Miss Whitworth speaks the truth. You, sir, have not behaved as you ought." Next to her, Miss Spencer gave a trembling Miss Spry a small shove, and she stepped forward also, nodding vigorously.

Mrs. Spry looked from her pale daughter to Mr. Hustlesmith, eyes narrowing, pulling her pleasant face into a fierce frown. Around her, waves of mamas took note, all squaring up against Mr. Hustlesmith, muttering angrily amongst themselves.

Reluctantly the temporary Lady Dustingham stepped forward into the circle. "Er, now then, let us hear the issue from the beginning," she said, her voice drowned out by the crowd.

But a lady in a black housekeeper's gown patted the arm of a teary maid in a torn pretty dress, and stepped forward into the circle, turning to face the crowd. "Apparently, this evening's entertainment will begin early," she said dryly, beckoning the temporary Lady Dustingham forward to stand beside her. "You see, I thought I might join you all in costume this year."

And as the words passed her lips, Millie stepped forward and pulled a thread from each of their gowns, pretending to take a stitch, so that the audience might think it some part of the glamour. Miss Fielde stood beside Lady Dustingham, passing back her cane.

The crowd gasped. The true Lady Dustingham waited for the sound to die before turning to Mr. Hustlesmith. "As you can see, sir, I have a very good idea how my maids behave behind my back, not to mention my guests. As there is not a shred of doubt in my mind that you have attacked two of my guests tonight, you are no longer welcome in my home."

Mr. Hustlesmith lost his grin. He took a step back from Millie's fierce glare, and seemed to see for the first time the anger of the ladies surrounding him. He turned toward the entrance and tried to push his way through the crowd.

Miss Riverton stuck out an elegant slipper to trip him.

A woman dressed as a highwayman grabbed his arm as he stumbled forward, and a girl with lovely painted butterfly wings punched him in the nose. "That's for Peggy!" she shouted as Mr. Hustlesmith's nose gushed all over his cravat.

"Nice punch, Vicky!" Millie cried. "Give 'im another!"

But Vicky the parlor maid had given way to Mrs. Spry, who

knocked Mr. Hustlesmith to his knees with her very expensive, very large Venetian reticule. It looked quite heavy.

"Mother!" her daughter gasped.

"It's about time you learned to defend yourself, Beatrice," her mother cried. "Now observe!" She swung her reticule high in the air and brought it down on the villain's head with another good whack.

Miss Spry watched, her eyes wide. Then she took off her kid slipper, with its sturdy little heel, and joined in, providing counterpoint to her mother's blows, rhythmic as a country dance.

Another voice roared out above the crowd: Miss Spencer, shouting "Take him away!"

I ducked aside as a diminutive lady dressed as a Highlander and brandishing a wickedly sharp dirk and a burly man in a very well fitted puce ball gown rushed forward at her cry. They hauled Mr. Hustlesmith to his feet and began to march him from the room. As I stepped back, I heard the Highlander say something about improper financials. Lady Prippingforth frowned. She threw back her glass of punch and abandoned her nephew, disappearing into the crowd. The new Duchess Tremontaine (dressed as a swordsman) kept her hand on her hilt as she followed Mr. Hustlesmith and his guards out.

It wasn't until I noticed Millie was holding me up by the arm that I realized how hard I was shaking. "Begging your pardon, miss, but I do think we might need to have another go at those knife lessons," she said.

Nodding, I scanned the crowd for Cassia, but saw no sign of her. Then I noticed the time on Lady Dustingham's painted clock. "You must hurry—you'll be late for your meeting!"

She hesitated. "Miss Whitworth must be here somewhere, or Miss Spencer—"

"Don't be such a goose," I said, pulling away. Millie must not miss her chance. "Now hurry."

Millie glanced at me, reading my face. "Fix your dress first," she advised, and I knew she wasn't talking about my torn sleeve. "I'll see you soon." Glancing back just once in the direction where Mr. Hustlesmith had gone, she smiled. Then she slipped off and ascended the stairs, a black shadow disappearing into the night.

Chapter Thirty-Two

THE (SOMEWHAT) HONORABLE MISS SMITH

Gold is the only suitable reward for spies.
—Napoléon Bonaparte

∞)(⌒

I took Millie's advice, stepping back into the servants' stairway to fix my dress. I won't pretend that my heart was not pounding, nor that I did not keep my ear to the door, still half expecting the sound of footsteps in pursuit. My mind wasn't fully on my work as I mended the tear in my sleeve. A stitch for the way my eyes had slid off of Millie as we walked to the War Office that second time. A stitch for her look of concentration as she'd pulled the glamour from Miss Smith's gown. And a stitch for the way she'd disappeared, after Miss Smith had insisted she remove my shawl, in the tiny, plain War Office room. She could have disappeared just as easily tonight, and gone off to make her appointment, leaving me to sort things out alone. But she hadn't.

How could I ever repay Millie? She'd faced down her personal nightmare for me, armed with nothing but the two customers she'd badgered into helping.

Still, it was a surprise when I saw the result of my mending. The candlelight hit my dress when I stepped back through the doorway and into the gallery, revealing a copy of Millie's aubergine gown. I frowned. When would I learn to fully control my talent, or at least remember to pay attention to what I was thinking as I sewed? Still, I had to admit I'd far rather call on Miss Smith in this gown than the other. If Millie wanted the old brown one instead, she would have no trouble stripping out the glamour.

I glanced at the ballroom, then doubled back to the punch table, selecting two punch cups, which I carefully balanced as I threaded my way through the gallery and up the stairs. I could not help but glance through the crack in the door at the room where I'd found Mr. Hustlesmith. There was no sign of him. Would I be checking each alley and doorway for him for days to come, the way Millie did?

I steadied my punch cups and stepped forward, catching sight of my reflection in the glass of a framed watercolor. A shadow of Millie's face looked back at me.

Had Millie had enough time alone with Miss Smith? Was I already too late?

The next door was open just a crack, and a flicker of movement caught my eye. An old lady wrapped in a shawl walked over to a sewing table, sat down, and scribbled something. Surely Lady Dustingham did not demand that her companion miss the festivities? Or, I thought as I studied her, perhaps she was too old to enjoy them properly, and preferred the quiet.

The third door was shut quite tight. I swallowed, looking up and down the hallway, but no one was in sight. Then I put my ear to the door.

"What have you done with Millicent O'Leary?" I heard the Honorable Miss Smith say.

"It is not as though I control the girl's every movement" came the reply. "Perhaps she decided to enjoy the party and let you cool your heels."

I stiffened. I never sounded so arrogant! And my French accent wasn't nearly so appalling.

But it didn't matter. Millie hadn't revealed her true identity yet, and she'd fooled Miss Smith. She was hedging her bets—there'd be no backing out, not once Miss Smith realized she, a trained spy, had been talking to the girl herself and still hadn't recognized her.

I took a deep breath, then looked at the doorknob, and at the cups in my hands. What would Millie do? She would find a way to carry both cups in one hand without spilling a drop, I was certain. So I rearranged my fingers until I found a way, turned the knob without making a sound, and slid inside the library.

"There you are." Not a flicker of surprise crossed Madame's face, at seeing Millie's face on me.

"Your punch, madame." I handed each of them a cup, bobbing a curtsy, then stepping back.

The Honorable Miss Smith smiled. "We meet again, Millicent."

"Yes, madam." I bobbed my head, losing myself in a flood of memories of Millie, standing in corners, not speaking until spoken to, always so still, always waiting. I let it wash over me and fill me up.

Miss Smith stepped forward and studied me. I kept my eyes on the floor. "I expect punctuality from now on, Millicent."

"Yes, madam." I kept my voice level, gave nothing away.

She nodded. "I suspect that tonight's tardiness may not have been your fault." She shot a dirty look at Madame. "Still, you are here, and that is what matters." She folded her arms. "Everything has been arranged. We'll pay you twenty-five pounds per year. Wait fifteen minutes, then follow me out. Find the hackney coach pulled by a chestnut with a blaze on the right, and a bay with two white socks on the left. Do not enter the coach until the footman mentions the bluebells in the woods."

I glanced at Madame, who gave a tiny nod. Millie was satisfied.

But I wasn't. Without raising my eyes, I asked, "Madam, when will my sister's passage be arranged?"

"Ah, yes—you have an excellent memory for detail, Millicent. I shall arrange it once I've returned to London; she should arrive in three or four days, and we shall bear the cost ourselves."

"And her living arrangements too, madam? And what about her wage—how much will she earn as a maid for the War Office?" I pressed.

Miss Smith frowned, and Madame stiffened.

"It's so that she isn't tempted to find other work in London," I explained diffidently. "You can't tell her why she's there, I assume—so how should she know not to find a place that pays better? And if I'm not there to keep an eye on her, well, I shouldn't like it to complicate things for you."

Miss Smith nodded, reluctantly. "Very well, Millicent. She'll be paid fifteen pounds a year, plus her room, board, and uniform. Will that do?"

Madame's wide eyes told me the answer.

Did Millie have any other relatives to take care of? I wished I could remember for certain, but I could not think of any. So I nodded. "She'd like that," I said, smiling a little.

Miss Smith smiled in return, softening a bit. "I'm glad to hear it. Now, I have a long journey ahead of me, and I must be off."

I dropped my eyes to the floor again, narrowing them. I was not Cassia's niece for nothing; I knew how much my father had been paid as a spy, and he had no such rare talent. If this woman thought she could steal my maid without even paying her properly, she had best prepare for a fight.

I waited until Miss Smith stopped gathering her things and noted my silence. Then I looked up at Madame, ever so hesitantly. "Madame, do you think you could offer double my sister's salary, as well as mine? And her passage, and room and board too? It's a lot, I know."

I don't think Miss Smith caught the brief flash of shock, only the way Madame pressed her lips together disapprovingly (and that didn't hurt, so I didn't worry about it for long).

I widened my eyes. "You did say you might manage fifty pounds a year, madame, now that the shop is doing so well?" I clutched a fold of my skirt, silently urging Millie to play along, for her own good.

Slowly she narrowed her eyes, tipping up her nose. "For you . . . I offer to triple both the salaries Miss Smith has proposed. Will that do?"

I nodded. "Oh, thank you, madame—after all, they do say talents run in families!"

Miss Smith stiffened, just as I'd intended. "One hundred pounds per year for you, and fifty for your sister. Refuse that, and I shall have you declared a matter of national security, which I doubt you'd enjoy."

I gulped, eyes wide. "Yes, madam." I turned to Madame. "I'm ever so sorry, madame, but you can see I must accept."

Madame nodded slowly. "I suppose you must." She raised her chin and stared right at Miss Smith. "Now then, I have another matter to discuss with you."

Miss Smith narrowed her eyes. "I have my eye on you, madame. One peep about any of this out of you, and you'll find yourself turned back to France without a moment's hesitation— and you might not like the assumptions they make when we hand you over." She smiled.

"Then there is something you must know," Madame said, slowly crossing to my side like a ship sailing through the sea. "We are not always quite as we seem."

I held out my arm, and she felt for the thread. Then she yanked the glamour from my dress.

Miss Smith's face froze. I turned to Madame. Carefully I lifted the wig from Millie's pinned hair and smiled, turning back to Miss Smith. "May I assume I shall receive the same salary? You've seen we work best in partnership."

Miss Smith glared at me, with not so much as a hint of a smile. I hoped she would not be a poor loser. "You are not Madame Martine. Who are you?"

"Well, I am Madame Martine more often than I am myself these days, it seems—and that was my name when you met me before. But I was born Miss Annis Whitworth. Rain was my father, and Breeze was my mother."

She did not stop glaring. "And you do, in fact, sew glamours?"

I nodded. "Such as the one this dress had, as well as Madame's gown, yes."

She studied me for a minute longer, then snorted. "Very well, Miss Whitworth. I do not recommend that you try such a trick on the War Office again—but, in order to prevent you from doing so, perhaps it would be best if you came to us. One hundred pounds per year." She crossed her arms and waited, her eyes never leaving my face.

"One hundred will do, as long as you'll pay my travel expenses as well—and Millie's, of course? And any expenses we might need for disguises too."

Miss Smith pursed her lips. "Yes—with the prior approval of your commanding officer."

I nodded. I was certain I could help such a person see reason. "Now then, I may not have a sister, but I do have an aunt, and sixty pounds per year will just about keep her in postage, as long as you'll provide her with room and board as well. And she can share the coach ride with us to London—no passage needed."

Miss Smith smiled tightly. "Oh, but a grown lady in society cannot come work for the War Office as a maid might—people would talk! No, she must go about her life. You will not contact her again. Don't fret, I shall send your excuses myself, once there's no chance she'll follow." She tapped her chin thoughtfully. "Let me think—perhaps you'll elope to Gretna Green with a dashing young fellow. . . . So romantic, don't you think? You seem the type. Goodness knows you're reckless enough."

I stared at her. "But I can't just vanish without even saying goodbye!"

Tipping her head, Miss Smith regarded me. "I see. Did you plan to tell everyone you know you're becoming a spy?"

I swallowed. "Of course not. But my aunt will never believe you. She'll guess the truth at once, when I visit her!"

Miss Smith raised an eyebrow. "Perhaps. But you'll spend the next year at least on the Continent, so that won't be any time soon." She glanced at my face and chuckled. "Oh, don't be so dramatic! Isn't this the life you wanted?"

I stared at Miss Smith, unable to allow the words to form sense. Oh, I had planned to leave Cassia behind during my adventures, certainly—but to disappear? To let her think for more than a year that I'd abandoned her, without so much as a visit?

What would happen to her? I had imagined it might be hard, living as my father did, but this . . .

"No." The word choked past my lips before I realized it. "No, I cannot—I cannot. Please. I'm sorry." I scrubbed at my burning eyes with the handkerchief Millie pressed into my hand.

Miss Smith raised her eyebrows. "I shall tell my commanding officer that you refused. You do understand there will be no second chance? And of course you must say nothing of this to anyone. We are spies, after all; we will find out."

I swallowed and nodded, not trusting my voice. No, she did not have a nice smile at all.

She turned to Millie. "Follow me to the coach in fifteen minutes, and do not forget to wait for the bluebells. And tell your employer goodbye; you will not see her again."

Millie nodded.

Miss Smith smiled and left the room, closing the door behind her.

Chapter Thirty-Three

IN WHICH THINGS ARE NOT AS THEY SEEM

There are secrets in all families, you know.
—*Emma*, by Jane Austen

∽◦) (◦∾

After a few minutes, Millie opened the door once more, and I followed her out. There was a bench across the hall; I sank down onto it. I had earned my place in the War Office—and had refused it. Millie would be leaving in only a few moments. I would never see her again. Madame's dressmaking fees would barely cover our bills. What would happen to us now?

"I'm sorry, miss," Millie whispered, sitting down beside me.

I wiped my eyes and shook my head, but I could not force out the words.

"She'll be leaving soon," Millie whispered.

I nodded and rose to my feet, starting down the hall. At least I could walk with her to the door.

But something caught my eye—not movement, but stillness, perhaps, or a hint of shadow. Something in the crack of the second door.

I stopped, and peered through the crack once more. The old lady was still there, stolidly writing her letters, and I smiled, feeling the tears start again. Why, if writing letters was all there was to being a companion, it was the perfect occupation for Cassia— and just as well, since she might be forced into it after all!

Then something clicked in my brain, and I stopped, and stared. Sensible black slippers, just like my aunt wore—some sort of white costume, like the togas I'd sewn—all wrapped in a huge old woolen shawl . . .

I knew the embroidery on the shawl. I'd worn that same shawl long ago, when I followed my father all the way to the War Office—

I was in the room before I could finish the thought, crossing to the table, staring down at the lady wearing my aunt's shawl. I had never seen this woman before in my life, I was certain. Her hands were wrinkled with age, though she held the pen with Cassia's ease.

But I was just as certain that I knew that shawl. And I knew that appearances were not to be trusted.

I reached out, grabbed her shawl, and yanked.

The lady gasped, took hold, and yanked back. We struggled for a moment, until Millie's hand reached over my shoulder and grabbed the shawl as well—and the old lady let go.

As the shawl was pulled from her shoulders, I saw her transform into Cassia: her face smoothed, her hands grew strong, and her costume was revealed to be an Ionic chiton (or as near as I'd been able to manage, anyway).

I stared at the shawl in my hands. No wonder my father had not recognized me when I'd followed him to the War Office. I'd been wearing a glamour, and never known it.

"Well?" she snapped as I stood there and gaped.

And, much to my confusion, I burst into tears and threw my arms around her.

Cassia unhooked me at once and crossed to the door, closing it without a sound. She pressed her ear to the door for a moment, then nodded. "We must speak quickly. Millicent hasn't got much time."

I looked at the empty glass on the sewing table, then at the wall. "You heard us?"

She crossed her arms and glared at us. "Of course."

"I want to hear the truth too, madam," Millie said quietly. "Maybe Miss Smith will wait for me."

Cassia considered this, then nodded. "She can't afford not to, not with your talent."

I stared at her, blinking, for a moment, feeling like something deep inside me had cracked. I had turned down Miss Smith for Cassia—but I didn't know Cassia at all. Cassia listened at walls. Cassia had a glamoured disguise.

My eyes widened, and I jumped back, away from her, as she reached for me. "You're a spy."

For the tiniest of moments, Cassia looked as though I had flipped her over my shoulder without a pillow underneath. Then she sank back into her chair and closed her eyes. "When your mother fell ill, your father asked me to come to London to care for you. It was all so new to me—the parties, handsome young men, all the wide world open at my doorstep. . . ." She shook her head. "But I was no fool; I guessed your father's secret within a week." She opened her eyes and looked at me. "Do you imagine it's easy to live a normal life once you know your brother is a spy?"

I stared at her, trying to see the girl she had been, trying to guess why she looked so sad. I was no fool either; I knew the answer. "You became a spy yourself." I frowned. "But you never go anywhere, or do anything!"

Cassia laughed, rather bitterly. "I could hardly take you behind enemy lines, could I? Do you know how many years I've spent breaking ciphers when the servants weren't looking? Asking ladies abroad how many soldiers were in town, what the roads were like, whether food was hard to come by? Not all spy craft is knives and glamours, Annis."

I raised my chin. "I've known for years how my father served his country. Now I know your secret too. Why shouldn't I be a spy as well?"

Cassia looked back at me. "You have no idea how difficult it can be. You don't understand—and you don't have to. You could stay with Lady Dustingham, enter society again, live your London life once more, even marry. . . ."

Marry whom? I could barely remember my London life; I couldn't imagine living it, not after this. "How can I live that life when our money is gone?"

"Oh, my investments are doing quite well," Cassia said calmly. "Not to mention my salary from the War Office. But you would hardly have believed that I'd leave you with a stranger for anything less than absolute destitution and genteel employment, would you?"

I stared at her. I'd chosen to stay with her, to spare her feelings, instead of becoming a spy. But she hadn't chosen me. "What did it matter if I believed you, if you were going to leave me anyway?"

"Don't be such a goose," she said irritably. "I certainly wasn't going to leave you forever—perhaps a year or two, at most. Only while I looked into what had happened to your father, and to his money. The War Office has been trying to learn more, but they've had no luck, and I will not sit still in Flittingsworth a moment longer!"

Relief poured through me. I nodded. "Neither will I! I will go with you. Come now, Aunt Cassia—you will most likely need my help."

Cassia glared at me. "I want you safely out of the way—not trying to track down a murderer! You have no idea what we face, whereas I've been filing tactical reports with the War Office since I was fifteen years old. I know all about how quickly things can go wrong." She folded her arms and closed her eyes. "My friend Mrs. Tarleton wrote that the road from Calais to Paris was muddy but no more so than usual on February twelfth, 1818. The moon was dark, and the sky was cloudy, so she and her husband stopped once night fell. She saw few carriages, and many of the inns were closed."

"My father died that night," I whispered.

"Her husband, who was once Wellington's attaché, was surprised at something in the harbor—she thought perhaps he recognized one of the ships—but when she asked him about it, he changed the subject, suggesting she tell him what hats she would buy in Paris."

I narrowed my eyes. I certainly understood the importance of suddenly introduced hats. "Is he in the habit of suggesting she purchase more hats?"

"Mrs. Tarleton reports that he is not."

I swallowed. "You're not just a spy. You're a spymaster."

Cassia opened her eyes. "Well, I would be if they knew they were spies—but it's a technicality, really. It's quite amazing what's ignored when intelligent women write to each other—and how much one can learn from hundreds of tiny questions. How many ships are in a harbor, when all the officers will be leaving town, where all the metal magicians in France are said to have gone . . ." She hesitated, then went on. "Miss Wilkins sent me a sketch of the bank in Cairo—it's quite lovely, really. When I expressed my distress that such a building had burned down, she replied that she'd just visited it that morning; she had no idea what I was talking about."

"But—my father's account . . ."

Cassia continued. "Lady Schofield conveyed her sympathies, expressing surprise to hear that Mr. Whitworth had left Paris that day, as he had promised to attend her soirée the next evening."

I felt the gooseflesh prickle on my arms. "He had not intended to leave when he did. Or, he gave no indication he would."

She nodded, watching my face.

I shivered. "It really wasn't an accident."

Cassia squeezed my hand. "Of course not. You saw the messages in the handkerchiefs he sent me. I'll admit it was clever of you to find them." She raised an eyebrow at the look on my face. "I let you keep your father's handkerchiefs, but you'd better believe Mr. Smith gave me your reports. This is national intelligence work, not some game."

But if they knew just how useful a sensible lady could be, why hadn't the War Office hired me the first time I visited? Because Mr. Smith was reporting to Cassia, and so Cassia would have found out. "You told them not to hire me," I said. "And that first day, when I said I was Miss Whitworth—that young man thought I was you. Everyone thought I was you, except for Mr. Smith."

"Mr. Smith reports to me," she said grimly. "Of course I told him not to hire you. Do you have any idea how many of the spies I've worked with have been killed during my years with the War Office? Any notion of how hard it is to lie to everyone you know? I've done everything I could to keep you from this life." She folded her arms and met my glare. "You cannot come with me. I am out of options, so I will have you assigned to Miss Smith—though you must first convince her you've decided you want this after all, despite refusing her offer moments ago."

I blinked. "You trust Miss Smith? Do you even know who she really is?"

"Of course I trust her. She saved your father's life on more than one occasion. And no, I have no idea who she really is, and I'd like to keep it that way." Cassia raised an eyebrow. "Trusting someone is not the same as enjoying their company, you know. Anyway, this trip is far too dangerous for an untrained girl; better you stay with Miss Smith than come with me."

I was still turning over the pieces of the puzzle in my mind, slotting them together. "Actually," I said at last, "I believe it might be too dangerous for me to remain here."

"What could happen to you in Flittingsworth?" she asked, folding up the letter she'd been writing and tucking it in her reticule.

"Someone has been looking for the messages my father sent," I said slowly. "Someone who doesn't hesitate to attack me if it means he can steal those handkerchiefs."

Cassia's eyes widened. "Fog. I can think of no one else who would bother to steal those—but he's remained a spy because no one ever has any proof against him. He's here?"

"How can I know for certain it's him? How many glamour artists does the War Office employ?" I asked anxiously.

Cassia looked away. "None, until we formalize your arrangements." Reaching out, she took my hand. "Your father was the last."

I stared at her. "It runs in families." Then at her shawl, then back at her. "But not my mother's family."

She nodded. "Nor in me. He sewed quite a lot before he died, though, and the War Office has sent everyone in its employ some such disguise."

"My father slashed his own clothes to ribbons so that no one else could wear his glamours." And I would never have the chance to see what they did. But I blinked away the thought for later.

"More specifically, so that Fog could not wear them." Cassia bit her lip. "I do wish I knew which of the glamours that your father sewed were sent to him. But the War Office would not tell me."

"Who is Fog?" I asked.

"Your father never learned his name, nor have I—the War Office hides field agents' identities even from its own spies, in case one is captured. Your father was convinced Fog was a traitor, but the War Office didn't believe him. He had no solid proof. They thought your father had a grudge against Fog, from something that happened long ago, and never believed him."

"He thought Fog betrayed my mother, and risked her life," I said slowly.

She blinked. "You've been busy indeed. Now, tell me everything you can about Fog."

So I told her how a man in naval boots had stolen my handkerchief, how five men had attacked us near the countess's townhouse, and how he had stolen a package out of the innkeeper's hands, right in front of Millie.

She chewed her lip for a moment, looking from me to Millie and back. "What did he look like? Could you identify him, if you saw him again?"

I shook my head. "His hat always shaded his face—I think it must be glamoured. He wore naval boots, but that is hardly unusual."

"He was taller than Mr. Harrington, but shorter than Mr. Hustlesmith. He smelled like the sea," Millie said. "And I— I mean, we—stabbed him in the upper right arm, outside the countess's house."

"We don't know it was him we stabbed," I argued. "It could have been one of his men."

Millie shook her head stubbornly. "He smelled of the sea."

Cassia sighed. "Very well. Since I cannot have the War Office arrest everyone in Flittingsworth who smells of the sea—even if I knew exactly whom to trust and who his allies are, which I do not—and if you are truly determined to live this life, you must pull yourselves together at once. Both of you will come with me to London. Tonight. After our arrangements are made, we will go abroad."

I might not be an expert with knives, but I'd gotten away from Mr. Hustlesmith. I might not know much about spying, but my glamours had fooled Miss Smith. And I would still be with Cassia and Millie. I squeezed Cassia's hand. "I am determined," I said.

Millie stared at her. "But I'm to go in the coach with Miss Smith. . . ."

Cassia smiled grimly. "I wrote to my commanding officer four days ago requesting permission to recruit you, Millicent, and I'm not letting that Miss Smith have you without a fight! You will come with us, and we shall sort it out before we leave for Paris."

She looked at me, and hesitated. "This was hardly the plan, but I suppose I've no choice now. Come along—Countess Lieven told me she had space in her carriage for me to travel with her to London tonight, if I had business there. We'll go down to the ballroom and let her know I'll join her after all, with two more passengers."

I froze. "But the countess is not here. She told me she couldn't come."

Cassia shrugged. "She often changes her mind. She told me the secret phrase the War Office assigned to her."

But I shook my head, and explained just what was in the package that had been stolen. "So, if the countess is not really the countess, whoever is wearing that shawl must be Fog," I explained. "Which narrows things down considerably . . . We can catch him right here, tonight!"

Cassia took a deep breath. "Annis, speaking as your commanding officer, you are not to sew one more such glamour without my express permission. When we have time, I will explain to you in very great detail—since you seem to have absolutely no concept of the situation—why it is not in the War Office's best interest to have magic loose that allows treasonous criminals who know our secrets to impersonate foreign dignitaries." She took another deep breath as I nodded. "But, since your blunder could allow us to catch Fog and prove his treachery, we shall have to unmask Fog ourselves."

"Who could he be, underneath that shawl?" I whispered.

"Let us find out." Cassia looked sternly from Millie to me. "You will observe, and wait for my command. We must steal back the shawl; we must catch Fog. And if either of you dares risk an injury, I will kill you myself."

Flexing her fingers, Millie pulled a knife from Madame's boot, shoving it up Madame's sleeve, where it fit quite neatly. She nodded.

Not to be outdone, I took three of my largest needles from my reticule, threaded each one, and stuck them in my waistband for immediate access.

Then I nodded and threw open the door.

Chapter Thirty-Four

ON THE IMPORTANCE OF GILDED TOENAILS:
FOG REVEALED, AND LAST WORDS

War to the knife!
—General José de Palafox y Melci,
refusing to surrender to the French

*T*here was no sign of the countess, nor of the Honorable Miss Smith, as we made for the stairs, and no one at all around as we reached the bottom—until Mr. Harrington stepped out of the shadows, causing me to jump and nearly stick him with a needle.

"Miss Annis—are you quite all right . . . ," he said anxiously, coming forward to catch my hand, then suddenly dropping it as he caught Cassia's eye. "Did that man—"

"Quite," I said. I glanced at his brown Hessian boots in relief, but still sniffed him cautiously as Cassia's eyes narrowed. Of course; she had been out of the ballroom, most likely meeting with Miss Smith. I allowed myself a small smile at knowing something she did not. "It was only Mr. Hustlesmith, Aunt Cassia; I shall tell you everything later." Mr. Harrington smelled of books, ink, and boot oil, with not a trace of the sea. I nodded at her and Millie.

"Mr. Harrington, time is of the essence, and I shall count upon your discretion," Cassia said immediately. "Find Lady Dustingham's coachman. Order her carriage to be readied at once, and impress upon him that no other carriage may leave the courtyard, no matter who is inside or what they say."

He paled, and stepped back.

Cassia snorted. "I assume you are aware the bluebells are blooming in the woods, Mr. Harrington?"

"Yes, madam," he said, bowing to Cassia. "Right away, madam."

I couldn't help but smile. If Cassia could trust Mr. Harrington, so could I.

And, much to my surprise, as soon as Cassia's back was turned, he grinned at me, just for a second, before he hurried away.

Millie poked me unobtrusively with her elbow, wiping the silly smile from my face and returning my thoughts to the task at hand.

Now then: to unmask Fog.

⊸◯)(◯⊶

Before Cassia had taken three steps into the gallery, she was hailed by Miss Spencer.

"We really must go to London, you know, to make certain that horrid Mr. Hustlesmith is properly punished," Miss Spencer told Cassia. "I still cannot believe that he attacked Miss Annis!"

Cassia nodded. "Indeed we must," she said, glaring at me. "But first, do tell me: have you seen Countess Lieven?"

Miss Spencer nodded. "Oh, yes, she is talking with Lady Dustingham; they are old friends, you know." She frowned. "Though she claimed not to know who Miss Moser of the Royal

Academy was, when Lady Dustingham asked after her. You don't suppose she could be intoxicated, do you?"

"I fear that is not truly the countess at all. Miss Spencer, do you by any chance know how to stumble and snatch a shawl off a lady's shoulders?"

"Oh, certainly," Miss Spencer said, looking pleased. "I await your signal."

Honestly! Did the entirety of Flittingsworth work for the War Office, except for me? "Is she . . . ," I demanded.

But Cassia shook her head. "Not yet," she said. "Annis and Millicent, you will circle around first from the side; position yourselves between the countess and the front hall. Miss Spencer, with me."

Following Cassia into the ballroom, I saw that Miss Spencer was correct: the countess was chatting with Lady Dustingham, the shawl I'd sewn just as perfect as I'd known it would be. I ground my teeth in frustration; the countess would be furious, and I could not blame her. But we would make it right.

Without looking at each other, we split apart and set out in formation, Cassia and Miss Spencer chatting their way through the crowd, gaining ground on their hostess without ever seeming to, while Madame moved through a stream of compliments from her customers toward a point between Lady Dustingham and the entrance to the front hallway, with me trailing behind, invisible as a maid. (Though an elderly lady dressed as a pirate, with a wicked-looking cutlass, gave me a very knowing glance as I passed.)

As we threaded our way through the crowded ballroom, I searched for the Highlander or the burly man in the puce ball gown, just in case, but they were nowhere to be seen.

Madame stopped, her position achieved. I glanced around;

Miss Spencer was closing in on the countess while Cassia chatted with Miss Fielde nearby. We were close enough to hear the countess reply to Lady Dustingham, "Why, I could not say what the Russian sentiment regarding the Corn Laws might be, my lady; I should have to ask my husband."

I snorted. This was the spy who had fooled the War Office for more than a decade? Why, no one could possibly believe that was the countess!

Then I grabbed Millie's sleeve. "I pictured the countess with ice-blue slippers, not gilded toenails. So why are her toenails gilded now?"

Millie stared at me. "Your boots didn't change, in the museum. That's how I knew you."

"Neither did Cassia's slippers, tonight. And the naval boots, they're always the same—but the countess isn't wearing naval boots." I whirled about. The only person headed toward the front entrance was Mr. Harrington. He glared at me and turned abruptly.

But—he had grinned at me before, as though we could be friendly once again. . . .

Then I saw the boots he wore: not his own brown Hessians, but naval boots. That wasn't Mr. Harrington. That was Fog.

There was no time to alert Cassia. The man who had killed my father was almost through the doorway.

I ran toward him, with Millie close behind.

"How dare you? My husband gave me that shawl, I'll have you know!" Lady Prippingforth's voice rang out behind us, with Miss Spencer's shocked apologies and Cassia's soothing tones following.

How I wished for the countess's mechanical gate, or at least a less slippery floor to run on! Millie grabbed my arm as I slid, and we ran on.

He was through the entrance, in the hallway—he opened the front door. He turned and smiled. Fog's smile twisted Mr. Harrington's face in a most unpleasant manner.

But he still wore naval boots, and I did not stop, not even when he ducked out through the door and into the night.

Whipping my largest needle from my waistband, I ran down the steps, amongst the carriages in the courtyard, following the crunch of his boots on gravel as he ran.

There he was, his hand on the door of Lady Dustingham's carriage, which had been readied all too quickly.

"You will not escape this time!" I shouted.

And the carriage door swung open from within, knocking Fog to the ground. Another Mr. Harrington looked down at me from over the top of the door. "Did you say something, Miss Annis?"

The Mr. Harrington on the ground wore naval boots. "Capture him!" I shrieked.

The real Mr. Harrington looked down at his imposter and gasped.

Scrambling to his feet, Fog yanked the true Mr. Harrington down and sent him sprawling. "As though that were possible!" he snarled, and set his boot on the carriage step.

But before he could enter, Millie stepped out from behind the carriage and hit Fog over the head with a potted fern.

I ran to her side and grabbed the hems of Fog's trousers in one hand, stitching them together. This Mr. Harrington smelled not of books, but of the sea; a glamour, for sure.

But before I could tie the knot, the true Mr. Harrington pulled me back. "Careful, Miss Annis—that man is dangerous!"

"Of course he is! Find Cassia at once, and let me secure him!" I cried.

The real Mr. Harrington stared at me for a second, his eyes wide, and then he left at a dead run.

Fog stirred as I stepped forward again, then yelled in fury, his voice changing from Mr. Harrington's pleasant one to another.

Quickly Millie reached down, yanked a thread from his cravat, and jumped back.

Mr. Harrington's face disappeared. It was the man in the greatcoat, growling as he got to his feet before I could act, a thin blade already in his hand as he lunged for me. I still could not see his face, though dozens of lanterns shone from the carriages all around us.

Then something whizzed through the air, and he yelled in pain, the blade falling from his hand as we leapt back.

Millie leapt forward and grabbed the blade he'd dropped. "I didn't do it, miss!"

I saw the man's hand was pinned to the side of the carriage, impaled by a knife.

"No, I did!" Cassia said as a very large footman stepped forward to take control of the man's other arm. Then I was being crushed in Cassia's hug, yelled at, and crushed once more.

"Never you mind, Millie; I'm sure you would have, if you'd had the chance," I said consolingly, as soon as I could breathe again. "Perhaps next time."

"Perhaps," Millie agreed. Carefully she pulled the last glamour from Fog's sleeve.

He did not loom faceless any longer. His graying hair was quite ordinary, his coat was rather shabby, and I recognized him at once: it was Lord Prippingforth. He scowled at me, and that, at least, was fierce.

Quickly Cassia searched his coat pockets. Her mouth was a thin, grim line as she handed the contents over to me.

Trembling, I opened the snuffbox to find my own face inside, painted in miniature. Then I clicked open the case of my father's silver pocket watch, blinking back tears when I saw the enameled portrait of my mother, still safe.

"My lord?" Lady Prippingforth tottered forward on her gilded toenails, shawl-less, clutching her jeweled asp. She took in the scene and crumpled to the ground, and I am sorry to say that no one quite managed to catch her.

I turned from the pitiful sight. "You would have left her, to be questioned in your place?" I asked him, my voice full of anger. "She didn't even know what she looked like, or why you gave her that shawl tonight, did she?"

"Just like your father, and his sister, I see—always interfering," he snarled. "Tripping all over my plans, ruining my transaction—do you know how long it took to place Kent with the *Corbeau*, you silly girl? Have you any idea how much money I've lost? Enough to pay all my debts and return to my proper place in the world; enough to give my nephew a fair start in life—in France, if not in England! But no—Bonaparte remains imprisoned, and the Bonapartists refuse to pay me a cent. I should have killed you when I had the chance, like I killed your father. You're just like your mother, a slippery little two-faced traitor who managed to escape even when I told the duc exactly what she was. . . ."

I turned to Cassia. "May I sew his lips shut?"

Cassia shook her head. "I shall be most interested to learn what else he has done while disguised as your father's man of business," she said grimly, watching as Miss Spencer waved Lady Prippingforth's smelling salts under her nose and helped her to her feet.

I turned back to Lord Prippingforth, frowning. "Did you propose to me?"

"Did he *what*?" Lady Prippingforth shrieked. Seizing Lady Dustingham's remaining potted fern, she hit her husband over the head with it, screaming at him all the while.

Eyes rolling back in his head, he slumped, unconscious once more.

Lady Prippingforth picked up her asp, gave a harsh sob, and fainted to the ground beside his feet.

I sighed. Well, I'd sort that out with the true Mr. Harrington soon enough.

Cassia glanced at the guests trickling down Lady Dustingham's front steps. "Annis, please have Lady Dustingham's footman unpin him and tie him up." She turned to Lady Dustingham as I moved to obey. "So sorry about the disturbance, my lady," she said. "And your poor potted ferns."

Lady Dustingham snorted. "Not at all. If someone hadn't rescued me from that woman's inane conversation soon, I'm quite sure I should have stabbed someone myself." Holding up a hand, she said, "Don't bother to pretend to explain. My men tell me the carriage is ready. Do tell me you'll at least take her too?" She eyed Lady Prippingforth, still unconscious on the ground, with great dislike.

Cassia gave an elegant curtsy. "My thanks, my lady; I can assure you that we will, though it does seem she was merely intended as a distraction. We shall leave at once, in fact. Will you please assist Miss Fielde with her society's accounts in my absence, and let her know we've been called away? We'll be gone quite some time. You will let me know when everyone has forgotten about the Misses Whitworth?"

Lady Dustingham nodded, turning to her butler. "Reynolds, if you would add another few bottles of brandy to the punch, that should help to erase most memories in very short order. . . . I shall, of course, be very disapproving of anyone who thinks such goings-on could possibly occur in my ballroom." She turned to the elderly pirate, who had come to join her, cutlass still at the ready. "You will assist me, Lady Badgery?"

"With pleasure," Lady Badgery replied, her bearing every inch a dowager's despite her rakish purple pantaloons. She nodded at Cassia as they turned to go back inside. "Your aim has greatly improved, my dear."

Cassia smiled and thanked her.

Mr. Harrington and several large footmen arrived at a run, gasping as though unused to such exertions. "Your reinforcements, as requested, madam."

Cassia beamed at him. "Mr. Harrington—well done! At least—Annis and Millicent, would you just confirm this is the correct Mr. Harrington?"

I examined his boots and sniffed him, while Millie gave his clothes a critical examination. She nodded as Mr. Harrington stared at us. "Yes, that's the real one," I told Cassia.

"Very good. Now, Mr. Harrington, I'll need you to convey these prisoners to Mr. Smith at the War Office at once—have you handled dangerous prisoners before for Mr. Whitworth, or will you require assistance? I could send Millicent along, if you aren't certain you can handle them. . . . If they regain consciousness before you reach London, please write down everything that either of them says. I'll need your notes immediately upon your arrival."

Mr. Harrington stared from Cassia to Millie and back, his mouth agape. "I must report to Mr. Smith. . . ."

"Do that," Cassia said, nodding. "Pack your things for a week's stay in Calais and Paris, Mr. Harrington, and who knows what to follow. I shall alert Mr. Smith that you are to assist me when I inform him of his duties."

So we would still travel to Paris—we'd spend at least a week in Mr. Harrington's company, with no more foolish proposals, no more lies. . . . I realized that for the first time since I had met him, there was no trace of pity in his gaze, only wonder. I could not help but grin.

Chapter Thirty-Five

OF STARS, AND MESSAGES,
AND WHAT TO WEAR IN PARIS

Every man is surrounded
by a neighborhood of voluntary spies.
—*NORTHANGER ABBEY*, by Jane Austen

$\mathcal{I}$t wasn't long before Cassia had packed the bound, unconscious Lord and Lady Prippingforth into Lady Dustingham's carriage along with Mr. Harrington, who'd declined Millie's assistance and taken several of Lady Dustingham's footmen instead.

Once they were on their way, Cassia stole Miss Smith's hired carriage, and we climbed inside.

"Not *stole*, Annis—it isn't as though I intend to keep it! I am merely commandeering it, as I'd be happy to explain to Miss Smith, were she around."

Millie frowned. "I looked for her when we came out—I thought she could help. But I couldn't find her."

Cassia settled her chiton around herself and patted her hair. "No doubt something came up. Plans often change, when one is a spy." She raised an eyebrow at me. "I suppose it's too late to convince you to make other arrangements now?"

"Will we still go to France?" I asked. Of course I wanted to be a spy—in fact, I was starting to believe I might be rather good at such work after all. But I didn't want to sit around writing letters, like Cassia.

She nodded. "You know I've always wanted to travel. Someone must see what that man left behind him, before our enemies hear of his capture. We may need to find new agents to replace Fog, and anyone he corrupted." She scowled. "And there's still your father's money to track down. I will not leave it in that man's possession."

"Of course not. And I can attend the balls while you visit the banks, and overhear all kinds of useful information—"

"We'll see about that," Cassia said dryly. "Now, dear Miss Spencer, I know you often go abroad to visit your sister, and to seek out new pastries. . . . You've proven yourself quite useful, and I don't imagine I'll escape your questions this time. Tell me: should you like to come with us to Paris?"

"If that's what it takes to finally learn the truth about you, then I wouldn't miss it," Miss Spencer said. "I'll just need to leave a note for my staff; they're quite capable of carrying on without me for a week or more."

"Of course," Cassia said. "We'll need to pack a few things as well—I refuse to take my first trip to France in a toga."

I stared out at the sleepy lanes of Flittingsworth, where I'd gone from being orphaned Miss Annis to the glamour artist Madame Martine. The stars twinkled up above, reminding me of how this all began, and I felt a lump swell in my throat.

I'd take my father's trunk, I decided. I wanted to see if Millie could find anything left of his magic, and if I could sew it back together once more. It had never been done, not that I'd heard, but then, there was no other team like us to attempt it.

I turned my eyes away from the stars and smiled at Millie, sitting so quietly that even I had almost forgotten her. She grinned back at me. Could I have dreamed of a friend like her, back when I was only Miss Annis of London? I reached out and squeezed her hand, so grateful to have her here with us. I tried to imagine how I'd have felt, watching a carriage take her off with Miss Smith, knowing I'd never see her again, and had to look away.

Leaning back, I let myself breathe with the carriage's rhythms, deep and slow, calming my heart. We had caught my father's killer, though nothing would bring him back. But I had a future now—one I was eager to meet. I'd have a chance to truly learn what I could do.

"What's to become of this?" Miss Spencer asked, holding up the countess's shawl.

I sighed. It was so beautiful—but so dangerous too. "Millicent, if you'd please . . ." I handed her the shawl.

Millie whipped out a knife and snicked the knot from the thread of my glamour, pulling it free. The shawl transformed back into my father's two cravats, separate now once more.

Then she frowned, and tugged at another thread.

The first cravat changed under her fingers, revealing line after line of white embroidery, hidden before by a glamour. She handed it to me, and I held it up to the lamplight and began to read as she examined the other.

My dear little sister,

How you'll read this, I do not know—but if anyone can find a way, you will. And I must warn you somehow: Fog has discovered that I've learned of his treachery, and his plans. The War Office may still claim he had no part in Lisette's betrayal, but there will be no such excuses for arranging to free Napoléon.

I have sent my trunk to Hamburg, in hopes he'll follow it there. But I travel instead to London tonight, whence I shall flee with you and my dearest A. to the territories. We can be safe there while his mischief is brought to light. How glad I'll be to spend time with my daughter, even under these circumstances! To have finally found proof of the danger in our midst—proof enough to stop him at last! You cannot imagine the relief I feel, knowing that you and our colleagues will finally be safe, that I can stop my searching. I only hope I have discovered all his allies in this city, and that none will see me leave. . . .

Silently Millie passed me a clean handkerchief, thoughtfully looking away as I dabbed at my eyes.

"They're for you, from my father," I said as I handed the cravats to Cassia.

Millie watched as Cassia bent her head to read the embroidery. "I do look forward to seeing Mr. Smith salute Miss Whitworth, don't you?" she said.

I let out a half sob, half laugh, trying to smile. "As much as I look forward to watching you learn to throw knives!"

As the stars shone above us, I let my heart fill up with love for my father, who'd hoped to spend time with me at last, and I let it fill with sorrow as well, for what would never be. And then I let it all dribble out as the wheels carried us away from Lady Dustingham's masquerade. I let myself dream of what life in Paris could be like, and of all the things I'd ask Cassia, now that she would finally answer. Where would I go? Who would I meet? And, of course, what would future-Annis be wearing, in this new Paris life?

I leaned forward, making sure I had everyone's attention.

"I suppose I'd better make some modifications to our clothes along the way, since we haven't much time," I told them. "Knife-proof fabrics, and I think perhaps something to keep the travel dust from showing. . . . Millicent, do you think we could invent some sort of ribbon that could provide anonymity when it's tied in a bow, but leave our appearances untouched when untied? And who'd like a knife sheath sewn into her gown? Miss Spencer, do you have a weapon of choice?"

I raised my hand to quell the sudden clamor. "One suggestion at a time, please, ladies . . ."

After all, who knew what we might face in our next adventure?

Acknowledgments

To the many, many people who helped with this book's long journey: thank you. Without your cheering, sympathy, feedback, advice, and, most of all, your belief that someday it would all turn into a real story, this could never have happened. With special thanks to Brenna Shanks, Jen Adam, Taryn Adam, Edith Hope Bishop, Aarene Storms, Alene Moroni, Caroline Stevermer, Theodora Goss, Ellen Kushner, Delia Sherman, Liz Wong, and Jane Rosen.

To all who've shared their knowledge, research, and resources with me and found answers to my oddest questions: thank you. Any errors are, of course, my own.

To all of those at Penguin Random House who have become part of my world of stories: thank you. With special thanks to Jenny Brown, Marisa DiNovis, Artie Bennett, Alison Kolani, Iris Broudy, Angela Carlino, Trish Parcell, Adrienne Waintraub, Laura Antonacci, Lisa Nadel, and Kristin Schulz.

To the authors who allowed me to mention their characters: thank you. What an honor, to become a tiny part of the worlds you created—and to give others a glimpse inside!

To my family, who always believe I can do anything, and especially to Eric, who listened to me whine through each and every draft, year after year: thank you. I promise, it's really done now.

And, of course, to my agent, Mandy Hubbard, and my editor, Nancy Siscoe: thank you for believing in me and in this book. I hope it's become everything you dreamed it could be.

Author's Note

I've loved Regency novels since I was a teenager, and have enjoyed how historical figures often pop in and out of scenes, giving a glimpse of the broader world. So I wondered: what if I could include not only historical people, but characters from other Regency novels, giving readers a chance to connect to those stories too?

Holding my breath, I reached out to the authors of young adult and middle-grade Regency novels I admired—and was touched, honored, and so very grateful at the responses I received.

If you've enjoyed this novel, perhaps you might enjoy following these characters into their own books:

This Monstrous Thing by Mackenzi Lee: Mr. Finch

Prada and Prejudice by Mandy Hubbard: the dowager Duchess of Harksbury

The Kat Stephenson books by Stephanie Burgis: Lady Ravenscroft, Mrs. Stephenson and her granddaughters, Mrs. Carlyle

The Season by Sarah MacLean: Lady Alexandra Stafford and her mother

The Lovegrove Legacy books by Alyxandra Harvey: Lady Bethany Chadwick

The Sorcery & Cecelia books by Patricia C. Wrede and Caroline Stevermer: Lady Sylvia Schofield, Mrs. Tarleton and her husband, Lady Schofield

The Mairelon books by Patricia C. Wrede: Mrs. Lowe, Lady Wendall

The Bloody Jack books by L. A. Meyer (permission granted by Annetje Meyer): Jacky of Faber Shipping Worldwide

Secrets of the Dragon Tomb by Patrick Samphire: Mr. Winchester

Keeping the Castle and *A School for Brides* by Patrice Kindl: Mr. Godalming, Miss Crawley

The Dark Days Club by Alison Goodman: Lady Pennworth

La Petite Four by Regina Scott: Lady St. Gregory of the Royal Society for the Beaux Arts and a young lady dressed as William the Conqueror

The Privilege of the Sword by Ellen Kushner: the Duchess Tremontaine

Wrapped by Jennifer Bradbury: Miss Wilkins

Newt's Emerald by Garth Nix: Lady Badgery

The following appear courtesy of history, myth, and legend:

William Shakespeare

Misses Baillie (Miss Joanna Baillie and Miss Agnes Baillie)

Lady Jersey (Lady Sally Jersey)

Napoléon Bonaparte

Arthur Wellesley, First Duke of Wellington

Mary Wollstonecraft

Jane Austen

Dorothea, Countess Lieven

Charles Perrault

Lady Mary Wortley Montagu

General Toussaint-Louverture

Hypatia

Admiral Horatio Lord Nelson

Sir Walter Scott

General Aleksandr Suvorov

Charles Vaughan (Sir Charles Richard Vaughan)

Agustina of Aragón

Russian emperor Alexander (Alexander I of Russia)

Dowager empress Maria Feodorovna (formerly Sophie Dorothea of Württemberg)

Count Morkov (Count Arkadiy Ivanovich Morkov)

Duc de Cadore (Jean-Baptiste de Nompère de Champagny, First Duc de Cadore)

Ann Radcliffe

David Arnold Conradus

Lady Scovell (wife of Sir George Scovell)

Cleopatra

Helen of Troy

Eleanor of Aquitaine

Queen Elizabeth I

Empress Josephine (Joséphine de Beauharnais)

Émilie du Châtelet

Sir Isaac Newton

Lord Byron (George Gordon Byron)

General José de Palafox y Melci

Miss Moser (Miss Mary Moser)

Cinder girl

Titania

Minerva

Melusine

The remaining characters are my own invention.

About the Author

KELLY JONES has worked as a librarian and a bookseller, and now turns her talents to fiction. Her first book, *Unusual Chickens for the Exceptional Poultry Farmer*, was an Indies Introduce Title, an ALA Notable Book, an *SLJ* Best Book, and a *Kirkus Reviews* Best Book. You can find her at her website, curiosityjones.net, or on Twitter at @curiosityjones.

TEEN
Jones, Kelly
Murder, magic, and what we wore /

Dec 2017